The Genizah at the House of Shepher

Tamar Yellin

The GENIZAH *at the* HOUSE *of* SHEPHER

The Toby Press

First Edition 2005

The Toby Press LLC, 2004
POB 8531, New Milford, CT. 06676-8531, USA
& POB 2455, London W1A 5WY, England
www.tobypress.com

ISBN 1 59264 115 6 *hardcover*

A CIP catalogue record for this title is available from the British Library

Typeset in Garamond by Jerusalem Typesetting

Printed and bound in the United States by Thomson-Shore Inc., Michigan

To the memory of my parents

Arie Leib Yellin
1913–1977

Edna Yellin
1920–1981

קל וחומר

Extrapolate.

—The Rabbis

Thou shalt not steal.

—Deuteronomy 5:19

Part One:

Shalom Shepher and the Ten Lost Tribes

Chapter one

The week following his bar mitzvah, in the spring of 1853, my great-grandfather, Shalom Shepher of Skidel, got married. He took up residence with his father-in-law, the Rabbi of Bielsk.

In those days he studied a lot and ate a lot. Eighteen hours were spent with the holy books, one hour was for walking and four hours were for sleeping. That left a whole hour in which to eat, and a great deal of food can be consumed in that time.

The marriage room contained a chest, a chair and a bed. Shalom Shepher instructed his wife in the rites of marriage. She crept out at night to sleep with her sisters.

Shalom Shepher told the Rabbi of Bielsk: "If you have married me to a child who neglects her husband and prefers to sleep with her sisters, I will divorce her and marry a woman instead."

From that time the Rabbi forbade his daughter to sleep with her sisters any longer.

Shalom Shepher ate a lot and studied a lot. He read the commentaries and the commentaries on the commentaries. He read Talmud, both Mishnah and Gemara, and above all he read Torah, until, were you to commit the sacrilege of sticking a pin through the pages of that holy book, our hero could have told you every word through which the pin had passed.

Two maxims from the sages were carved upon his soul. One was:

It is not your duty to complete the work;
Neither are you free to desist from it.

He loved this paradoxical epigram, with its eternal invitation to feelings of guilt and inadequacy.

The other was:

Do not say: When I have leisure I will study.
Perhaps you will have no leisure.

In Bielsk he perfected the skills he had begun to develop in Skidel. He learnt to split hairs and chop logic. He learnt to filibuster and digress, to draw out the sweetness of an argument. He developed the art of pilpul, that scholarly tug-of-war beloved of the rabbis, and fostered the ability to take every side at once in order to prevent a debate from reaching any conclusions.

As he spoke he had a habit of twisting one sidelock round his finger, which reminded the others of his extreme youth and also irritated his opponents beyond expression. He became known for his learning and his good looks. The latter were a little exaggerated in legend. He was short in the leg and broad in the chest, and like many members of my family had a tendency to flatulence and high blood pressure in later life. But he had large quantities of red-gold hair, which were taken to denote kinship to King David and also generosity.

He made life hard for the Rabbi of Bielsk. At the age of sixteen, Shepher was the greater scholar. He also had a superior sense of humour, which is essential if one is to understand the writings of the sages. The Rabbi would declare something kosher, and Shepher would contradict him; the Rabbi, unnerved by his brilliant protégé, conceded; whereupon Shepher would dig up another precedent and once more pronounce it kosher. One might say that he ran rings round the Rabbi of Bielsk.

Before he reached his eighteenth year he had established himself as a corrector of scrolls. From that time, because of his great diligence, there was an increase in the number of parchments consigned to the genizah of the local synagogue, where because of their errors they could not be used, and because they bore the name of God they could not be destroyed; and where they would remain until they were buried, or crumbled into dust, or, as sometimes happened, were lost in a fire.

It was his particular pleasure to sit in the attic genizah of the synagogue at Bielsk. There, with a five-rung ladder between himself and the world, he studied the texts and documents which had been placed there when they became too dilapidated for further use. Although he was only eighteen, the beadle of the synagogue referred to him as Reb Shalom. My great-grandfather accepted the title of respect. He was the greatest corrector of scrolls in Lithuania.

Chapter two

When he was eighteen years old Reb Shalom became ill. Despite the consumption of a whole chicken cooked daily for him by his wife, he grew thinner and thinner. Eventually, for the first time, he lost his appetite.

After a while, seeing that he did not get any better, he decided to visit a great doctor in Vilna, the Jerusalem of Lithuania.

The great doctor examined him and noticed that he was spitting blood. He said to him: "I can't do anything for you, but if you can manage to go to Italy you might get better."

Reb Shalom pondered for a few moments. At last he said: "How would it be if I went to the Land of Israel?"

The doctor did not know what he was talking about. "Do you mean Palestine?" he said.

Reb Shalom did not know what the doctor was talking about.

"What is the name of the city you have in mind?" the doctor asked.

Reb Shalom replied: "Jerusalem."

"Oh, yes," said the great doctor. "Jerusalem will do just as well as Italy."

Shalom Shepher returned to Bielsk and told his wife that he was going to live in Jerusalem. Immediately she burst into tears.

"How can I leave Mummy and Daddy?" she sobbed.

He said: "If that's how you feel about it, we can get a divorce. We haven't any children so it will be an easy break for us."

He went to his father-in-law and told him: "I am going to live in Jerusalem and my wife doesn't want to come with me. Since that's how she feels, I shall give her a divorce. We haven't any children so it should be easy on her. I will send her some money every month until she finds another husband."

And he divorced her.

Then he made a small bundle of his prayer-shawl, phylacteries and psalter, and set off on foot for the Black Sea.

It took him two years to reach the Black Sea. He was ill on the journey and wherever there were Jews they took him in to convalesce. He never recovered his appetite and his appearance was that of a dying man, but he knew it was not death, but great spiritual yearning that possessed his body.

Wherever there were Jews and they discovered who he was, they brought him their scrolls to correct. He lingered in many communities examining the holy parchments. For this reason it took him a long time to reach his destination.

And when my great-grandfather reached the Black Sea he boarded a small Greek ship for the coast of Palestine; and it was another six months before his ship came within sight of the port of Jaffa.

Chapter three

In November 1938 my father boarded the vessel 'Methuselah' at the port of Jaffa and sailed for Southampton. He was possessed by a great spiritual yearning to leave Palestine and go to England.

Like his forbear he was short and stocky, with the same tendency to heartburn and painful wind which plagued him all his life. Indeed, I wonder whether there is not some connection between great spiritual yearning and the inability to digest food. Some people never yearn spiritually their whole lives and always enjoy excellent digestion. I, on the other hand, feel my yearning as a hard obstructive lump somewhere under the sternum, and to eat means to suffer. In that respect I am my great-grandfather's spiritual heir.

"My heart is in the East and I am in the farthest West," sang the poet Judah Halevy. "How can I taste what I eat, how can I have appetite?" My great-grandfather stepped on a boat to the East, and my father stepped on a boat to the West, and I am in England with chronic indigestion.

The act of climbing on a boat is in fact no cure for this type of malady. Nor is taking a ship or an aeroplane. When my father reaches Southampton he will yearn for Palestine; when Shalom Shepher enters the gates of Jerusalem he will be possessed by other dreams. Such men father anxious children.

This much I know about that fateful departure of 1938. He wore a white shirt and no tie. He smoked a cigarette. Across his forehead was one long, angry eyebrow. On his lip was a scar where the lip split open every winter. He was twenty-three years old and he felt as though he had lived for centuries and was sick of life as only a twenty-three-year-old can be. On the quayside below, the woman he loved was waving him goodbye.

No photograph was taken of the occasion. No-one described it to me. Yet the image stands in my mind of this decisive moment.

There are certain choices from which all things flow. My great-grandfather travelled east and begot my grandfather. My father travelled west and met my mother. The line of tension between choice and chance is the thread by which the miracle of existence hangs.

Chapter four

I came to Jerusalem at night, in darkness, after a long absence, rain streaking the windows of the taxi as we rode from the plain to the hills. Outside, at first, there were bright signs, a golden egg, a drive-thru takeaway, a giant smile surrounded by flashing lights. We might have been in America. We might have been anywhere. Then we were on the highway. We were nowhere. Darkness, hunched trees. A change in the air. A whiff of petrol and bitumen, a hint of the sea or the desert. Strangeness. Rain.

Then as we began to climb I closed my eyes and thought I recognised the old route, its rises and turns inscribed on my memory. But the road had changed. It had flattened, uncoiled and stretched itself into something unfamiliar. And when I opened my eyes, instead of the darkness of the hills there were masses of lights, strings and clusters of lights as far as the eye could see.

"What's that?" I asked.

The driver answered: "That's Jerusalem."

The engine strained and the windscreen was flooded with rain. And then we were on the road I recognised: a steep curve, a petrol station, ruins, and, hanging from the edge of the deep valley, a shanty which had clung there, perhaps, for more than a hundred years and still not fallen off. Of all the cities of the world Jerusalem has one of the shabbiest gates of arrival, and coming or going one is greeted by graves.

My driver had the address: Kiriat Shoshan; and sliding from lane to lane he rushed the lights, pulled up at the next red, crackled his radio. Did I know this stretch? I was already lost again, in a labyrinth of traffic and asphalt and hotels and shopping malls, at sea in a changed city. Yet this road I did remember, as we turned into a quiet boulevard lined with apartment blocks, a long straight road with a regiment of trees, opening at its far end into a small square containing a children's playground, a sandpit and a synagogue. And there on the corner of the square was the house itself, older than ever, more worn and weather-beaten, with one of its shutters hanging half off and, darker and denser than I recalled, the line of five cypresses my father planted.

Thin clouds blew over; a toenail of moon hung in a ragged sky. I stood with my suitcase on a well-known patch of ground, as if on a small disc in the middle of a strange universe.

And sitting in the window was my uncle Saul, just as I had imagined him, hunched at the kitchen table in my grandfather's caftan, huddled over the paraffin heater, listening to the radio. He rose to his feet and peered at me through his round glasses.

"Hello Saul," I said. "It's me, Shulamit."

Twenty years had not made much difference to him. He was old before and he was older now. His hair was silver then and it was silver still. He walked as he always had, with a shuffling stoop, hampered now by the folds of my grandfather's caftan, which hung on him limply, tattered by moth and wear, and gave off a morbid, rotten odour. God knows where he had dug it up. From the bottom drawer of the pot-bellied walnut dresser, maybe, or the camphor-smelling wardrobe in the back bedroom. He wore it, I suppose, because it was warm, and possibly also for another reason: imagining, perhaps, that by some act of transubstantiation he had become my grandfather.

He was as I remembered him, a man of few phrases and a few very pungent gestures, able to express with one eyebrow the whole significance of twenty years' silence and absence punctuated only by a cheap New Year card. "Shulamit," he said. And he welcomed me into the house with a reverent motion, like the curator of a museum which was soon to close.

I dropped my bag and stepped forward, to take in the full squalor of that house which had once been the living heart of the family and was now a slum. Furniture stood piled in obscure corners. There were towers of boxes and stacks of bedlinen, fragile pyramids of kitchenware; domestic rubble swept into untidy heaps. Torn strings of tatting decorated the windows. The walls were bare, but a dusty mobile of blue-green Hebron glass still hung from the doorframe where I remembered it.

I turned to my uncle, who gazed across the sea of memory with the same inward stare, magnified by the lenses of his ancient spectacles; and who looked up at me now as though I were nothing more than a ghost, come back to haunt his already haunted solitude. I managed a smile.

"I've come for a visit," I said.

Chapter five

When I think of the longing which filled my father and great-grandfather I remember that they were Jerusalemites: my father by birth and my great-grandfather by adoption. Jerusalem is a place which engenders longing.

I cannot help regarding the city as a strange accident. It is not positioned on any trade route. Nor is it really in the ideal position for a political capital. The region is hostile to both industry and agriculture. For centuries the nations have dreamed of it returning to some state of glory which supposedly it once possessed, but Jerusalem remains obstinately provincial, gripped by that spirit of desolation so often associated with the presence of God.

The road from the coast to Jerusalem winds from the plains to the hills. It passes through the territory of Abu Ghosh, past the monastery of Latrun and through the dark ravine of Bab el Wad, the Gate of the Vale. If the nations ever stream towards Zion, they must pass through this sinister gorge. It has always been a place of ambush.

The Jews captured Jerusalem from the Jebusites, the Babylonians from the Jews and the Persians from the Babylonians. The

Greeks snatched it from the Persians, the Maccabees from the Greeks and the Romans from the Maccabees. The Temple of Solomon was thrown down and rebuilt, was dedicated, desecrated and resanctified, and at last destroyed under the Emperor Titus, for which act he was punished in the following manner: a gnat, entering his head, knocked against his brain for seven years, and when he died they opened his brain and found there something like a sparrow.

As for the Temple treasures, they have been sighted all over the world: two pillars in San Giovanni in Porta Latina, Rome; a bronze candelabrum in the cathedral at Prague; another in Constantinople. The golden plate of the High Priest was taken to Rome; other gold and silver items were hidden in a tower at Barsippa and under the great willow tree in Tel Beruk. The throne of Solomon itself was taken from Babylon to Persia, from there to Greece and Rome, "and," writes Rabbi Eliezer son of Rabbi Yossi, "I saw its fragments in Rome."

The Byzantines took the city from the Romans, the Arabs from the Byzantines, the Crusaders from the Arabs. The Jews returned, were exiled, returned; were tolerated, banned and readmitted. The Crusaders gave way to the Mamelukes and the Mamelukes to the Ottoman Turks.

The Sephardi Jews fled there from the Inquisition, from southern Europe and the Arab lands. The Ashkenazi Jews came from Poland, dressed in white robes, with their leader, Rabbi Judah the Pious.

When they reached Jerusalem Rabbi Judah the Pious founded a synagogue, and died. His followers mortgaged the synagogue and living quarters at a high rate of interest and could not pay. They were driven out and the synagogue burned. That was the end of the first settlement.

A hundred years later, seventy students of the Gaon of Vilna made the journey to Jerusalem: from Shakluv by raft along the rivers, and from Odessa by fishing-boat to Jaffa. Disguised in eastern dress they gained admittance to the city, and settled around the ruined synagogue of Rabbi Judah the Pious.

When my great-grandfather arrived Jerusalem was still contained within its walls. The gates were locked at night and reopened in the morning, and all around lay wilderness, wild animals and robbers.

Perhaps the wilderness has been exaggerated. There were also villages: Et Tur, Lifta, Deir Yassin. Vegetables were grown in the village of Silwan, roses were brought from Kolonya. The roses were sold by weight, and in season the fellaheen women could be seen soaking them in the aqueduct on their way up to the Jaffa Gate.

There was the city of streets and there was the city of roofs. It was possible to cross Jerusalem without setting foot on the ground. Every cat knew this and so did every robber. On cool evenings the citizens of Jerusalem went up onto the roofs and enjoyed the breeze. Women sat behind perforated walls where they could observe without being observed. Neighbours could be visited by stepping from one roof to the next.

The city was crowded and the houses small. Nevertheless whole rooms went to waste, as it was the custom to throw rubbish into the bottom chamber of the house, where it festered until the local boys carried it away on a donkey through the Dung Gate and flung it onto the spoil heaps which adorned the edges of the city.

And the Dung Gate, when questioned on the matter, said, Rather the rubbish of Jerusalem than the jewels of the whole world....

At the end of the summer the cisterns were low and the people were obliged to buy their water from the villagers of Silwan. The village youths brought the water on their backs, in bloated goatskins, from the spring of Ein Rogel. When the cisterns were low the scum would come to the surface and sometimes the dry cisterns cracked and sewage seeped in from the nearby water-closets. Even if the cisterns were clean, they were fed by rainwater, which was not always clean. The rain ran down gutters choked with dust and debris blown from the streets, and down the streets ran open sewers clogged with the outer leaves of vegetables and the dung of dogs and camels.

In Jerusalem there was a proliferation of dogs which multiplied without check. The Muslims hated them like the devil, unlike cats, which they loved. The dogs ran after every lantern carrier in the night and filled the alleyways with night-time howls and strange noises. They foraged in the debris left by the vegetable market on David Street and they hung round the tannery next to the Church of the Holy Sepulchre. They fought for entrails outside the slaughterhouse in the Jewish Quarter, and devoured the bodies of donkeys and camels which were left rotting in the street where they had fallen. At last the Pasha thought he would do the citizens of Jerusalem a favour and ordered his soldiers to shoot all the dogs, which brought an increase in fever to the city because there were no longer any dogs to consume the rotting offal.

In October the siege of the cisterns ended and the rains fell, which were called the shooting rains because the drops fell like lead shot. All over Jerusalem the rain performed its dance: bouncing off the domed roofs, trickling down the gutters and gullies and channels into the wells and cisterns of Jerusalem, disappearing down ancient drains and swallow holes into the vast reservoirs beneath the Temple Mount, Jerusalem's hollow watery heart.

Jerusalem was a city of small trades in which the Jews found their niche. There were Jewish grocers, tinsmiths, sugar-sellers and many, many shoemakers. There were thirty-four Jewish tailors; none Muslim. Conversely, all sixty-six coffin-makers were Muslim (Jews were buried in shrouds).

No Jew worked on the land, or cut stone, or built houses, or owned property. Their businesses were concentrated on the Street of the Jews, a stinking lane lined with torn and filthy awnings, miserable wine shops and displays of bric-à-brac. Here it was possible to purchase ancient volumes of Talmud, Yiddish chapbooks describing the miracles of the Baal Shem Tov, and leather amulets to ward off sickness. Here the Jewish woman could, if she so wished, obtain a second-hand copy of Caro's *The Laid Table* which would define for her the laws and limits of her entire married life.

Close by, Reb Jacob the seller of old clothes draped his stall with the cast-off wardrobes of the dead. He never looked a customer in the eye. Transactions were made across the psalter, and bargaining was peppered with sacred verses. Often it was impossible to tell whether he was addressing God or man, as he poured out his wrath upon the heathen, lifted his eyes unto the hills and sang the praises of a silk waistcoat all in the same breath.

Here the children gathered as Reb Israel the Righteous bent

to draw water for the institutions. He never smiled. He never spoke. Each week he fasted two out of the seven days. But the children loved to watch him raise the bucket from the darkness of the well, and to speculate on what might ride up in the sparkling water.

Here, on a slab of Roman masonry outside the synagogue, sat the old loafers who had come to Jerusalem to die. In their youth they had been groomed as talmudists and never taught a trade, but since they were also bad students they had been idle their whole lives. Now their sole means of subsistence lay in reciting prayers for those already dead. In summer they sat outside with their prayer books, murmured portions of the liturgy and spat reflectively at the feet of the passers-by. In winter they made the rounds of the synagogues and study houses, always taking the spot closest to the stove. They wandered in and out of the services, gossiped during the reading and sang lustily during the prayers. A few carried grubby pocket-books in which they gathered and recorded the takings of various charities: the Dowries for Poor Brides, for example, or the deposit needed for the publication of scholarly works written in their youth and long since eaten by mice.

Sometimes they gathered in the nearby bath house, where Reb David of Vilna, author of the famous almanac, led daily sessions of numerological jousting. Reb David, who under different circumstances might have been a great mathematician, was a numerologist of exceptional ability. It had been a passion with him in his youth and in his maturity it had become an obsession. Gradually it took over his life, until in old age he devoted himself entirely to his calculations. He was rarely seen without a slip of paper and a pencil, and had the permanent skyward gaze of a man totting up numbers in his head.

Each autumn he published a diary of sacred quotations whose numerical total was equivalent to the Jewish year. They might be regarded as either prophecies or curiosities. Meanwhile he was secretly working on a project of far greater significance: the date of the end of the world. Since there were enough relevant verses with enough suggestive totals to place the apocalypse anywhere within the next several thousand millennia, he only succeeded in endorsing what the world knew already; though it is always good to have some confirmation.

At dawn, after a night of sleepless calculation, he would join Reb Zalman the watchman on his rounds of the quarter as he cried: "Rise up, holy people, and serve the Creator, Blessed be His Name!" Reb Zalman was a pious scholar and a man of many wives. For the wife of his youth, his first, who had died in childbirth, he retained the greatest affection. Since then he had never been a bachelor for long. To marry was not difficult: it required only a blank contract bought at the local stationer's. Divorce was more complicated: that required a dispensation from the rabbis. The rabbis did not like Reb Zalman's frequent divorces, but since he was old and his wives were old, they continued to humour him.

Reb Zalman had strange habits of excessive piety, though perhaps in Jerusalem they did not seem so strange. He would drink his tea boiling as he stood outside the gates of the study house at midnight, muttering quick blessings as it burned his mouth. If he saw a funeral procession he would join it. Sometimes he stood by the steep alley which led from Habad Street to the Armenian Quarter and which was reputed to be the toughest hill in Jerusalem because the martyred bodies of Hannah and her seven sons lay below. He stopped the passers-by and insisted on carrying their bundles up the hill, to the gratitude of some and the profound embarrassment of others.

Jerusalem lay sleeping on the ashes of her seventeen destructions. Houses were built upon houses; ruins tottered on a foundation of ruins. Sometimes there were earth-tremors and the ruins collapsed down into each other like an ancient honeycomb. There were strange events: shooting stars, a rain of yellow mud. Each year on the anniversary of the Temple's destruction, the lights on the Temple Mount would be extinguished. Tears would spring from the stones of the Western Wall.

Jerusalem was a city of many wells. At one time the wells of Jerusalem were left uncovered, which could be very dangerous where the mouth of the well was flush with the ground. In the Hurvah Square at the heart of the Jewish Quarter there were several such wells.

It happened once that a boy from the Tree of Life Yeshivah

went missing. They searched and after three days they had not found him.

Then the elders of the yeshivah gathered and decided to draw lots to discover the whereabouts of the boy.

They asked the lots: Is he alive or dead? The answer came back: Dead. They asked: Where is he? Answer: In the well. Which well? Answer: In the Hurvah.

Then the people searched the wells in the Hurvah and they found him in the third well, head downwards, with his lunch in his pocket.

After that the wells in the Hurvah Square were covered, and only Reb Israel the Righteous was permitted to uncover them each day, to draw water for the Tree of Life Yeshivah.

Chapter six

Someone appeared to have been mixing concrete in the bath. In the middle of the bathroom floor a zinc bucket stood like an abandoned child: it seemed to contain underpants, and a scientific bloom of grey-blue water mould.

I splashed myself quickly under the rusted cold water tap—armpits, face and neck—and dried myself with a towel which smelt all too sweetly of home. Emerging, I bumped clumsily into Saul.

"Oh—Ouf—!"

This was our morning's greeting.

In the semi-abandoned kitchen an ancient kettle stood on the primus stove and a disembowelled loaf of bread lay on the table in a pool of crumbs, where my uncle, listening to his radio, had sat pulling fistfuls of it for his supper without bothering to wield a knife. Among the crumbs lay a number of dead matches he had used to light the fire and, later, to pick his ears.

The refrigerator was empty, and streaked with yellow dirt.

Thirty years ago this had been the living heart of the house: a pulsing centre of nourishment and talk, boiling, beating, baking and conversation. Here my aunt, Batsheva, had walked back and forth, pounding matzo meal in a brass mortar; here at the kitchen table my grandmother had rolled and cut noodles for the Sabbath soup. Here we hungry children had come to raid the fridge, whose shelves had groaned under the weight of apples and grapes, plums and peaches from the Machane Yehuda market, blocks of white salt cheese, trays of honey cake and halva and stuffed monkey.

Now it had reverted to a primitive state: cramped, minimalist, resembling an army mess with its rusted taps and primus stove. The brown tile, added sometime in the fifties, and the rough-and-ready units knocked up by an enthusiastic cousin, were coming away from the walls; behind them lay bare stone, cobwebs—the lurking evidence of a more basic past.

But the house had always been primitive, cavelike, wearing its stones naturally, its walls bare; it had always had the air of a temporary dwelling. Even as children we had known its days were numbered, that every visit we made drew on a finite store: like an old and sick relative one visits and takes leave of, never knowing if this time might be the last.

"And where is your brother, Reuben?" Saul had demanded last night, as though he expected us to arrive in tandem as we always did, one trailing at the other's heels, the long and the short of it, the redhead and the dark, even though we had been young adults when he last saw us: still children after twenty years.

"Mike, now," I had corrected him. "He calls himself Mike."

I could not tell him that Reuben was not interested, that Reuben had tried to forget; that Reuben did not want to come.

It was Uncle Cobby's letter which had brought me here; a fragile scrawl in trembling schoolboy script which was an event in itself, for only a landmark moment in the family history could have inspired him sufficiently to write to me. Aunt Batsheva was dead; the house had reverted to its proper owners; time had run out for its hallowed walls. By summer it would be gone: a five-storey apartment block would take its place. If I wanted to see it again I must come immediately.

I could hardly say, even now, what maelstrom of feelings rushed in and took hold of me: what vortex of nostalgia, grief, regret

I was suddenly sucked into when I read his letter. For years now I had existed in a state of numbness, the kind of deep calm which succeeds a violent storm. I hadn't believed myself capable of strong feeling any more. I lived an orderly life; I lived alone; the past and my heart were buried and forgotten. And now this sudden resurgence, this impulsive rush into everything I had escaped from, subdued and shrouded in forgetfulness.

I called up my brother and asked if he wanted to come.

"You must be joking!" he snapped. "Why the hell would I ever want to go back there?" And he added: "You shouldn't go either. You'll only upset yourself."

But I wanted to go; I wanted to be upset. I wanted to feel something after all this barrenness. So at the first opportunity I booked my lone ticket and packed my single bag. I returned on the wings of eagles in a jumbo jet, and rising high above the busy glittering world, I looked down on the tiny distant pinprick which was my former life.

I pushed open the stiff back door with its nine panes of variegated glass and stepped outside. The morning was warm and soft; no longer damp, but with a blue sky of indefinite depth and a whiff of spring in the air, though at this time of year the squally latter rains could fall at any moment. The square was as it had always been, bordered with pepper trees and ringed by apartment blocks: greyer now, and scarred with leprous patches, but hidden in rising skirts of cypress and oleander. The house had changed however: its shutters broken, its garden awash with litter, decorated with a smashed perambulator which sat atop the rubbish like a strange cherry on a very ugly cake. The wall at the corner of the plot had fallen, and the cactus plants stood shrivelled, half-dead, their black limbs strewn like snakes across the broken path.

I rounded the path and climbed the few steps to the verandah, where in a tide of dead leaves two broken chairs sat turned towards each other, like a long abandoned conversation. The square was quiet: a young mother wheeled a pushchair past the synagogue and a religious Jew in caftan and sidelocks lingered opposite, under a pepper tree.

I remembered how once the house had been filled with people, how I, a visiting child, pale and alien in my English skin, had touched the spines of the unfamiliar plants and felt a fear of scorpions. Or sitting in the shade of the cypresses, how I had watched the patient ants, hour after hour, pursuing their labouring trails in an ecstasy of idleness. The house was empty now but here I was again, still English and pale, still afraid of scorpions, despite the fact that in all those years I had never laid eyes on a single one; though one evening, returning from an excursion, I had seen my father, with a practised hand, remove a black snake from the heart of the oleander.

But that sort of thing was to be expected: my father retreating to his earliest self, instinctive and at ease, like a captured animal released into the wild; climbing trees to collect carob pods, brushing a three-inch cockroach indifferently from his shoulder. He was a native restored to the tribe, comfortable as we had never known him; while we the outsiders, Reuben, my mother and I, struggled with sunburn and mosquito bites, strange customs, stomach upsets and a foreign language. Summer after summer my mother would spend her days lying in the darkened guest room lined with family photographs, a cologne-soaked handkerchief covering her eyes; fearing perhaps not scorpions but something more feral and terrifying: my father's absence, her own abandonment.

"You won't recognise the Plotsky house."

I started. Saul's face had popped up at the French windows like a pale marionette's. The next moment the window itself sprang open. The wood had swollen, and the frame scraped across the tiled floor with a wrenching splitting sound.

"The Plotsky house is gone. And the Plotsky garden. All apartment blocks. They sold it for three million."

"And Avram?"

"Avram went to America. Avinoam Plotsky killed himself." Saul shuffled across the verandah, his slippers nosing their way through leaves and dust, his eyes blinking like some burrowing creature's unaccustomed to the sunlight. "Terrible to kill yourself with three million." He peered across the square as though looking for something.

"Terrible to kill yourself in any case," I said.

I was flooded by sudden guilt: guilt at the years of painful procrastination, guilt at having stayed away too long. As if by returning more often I could have slowed the pace of change, arrested progress; saved poor Plotsky even, in whose tropical garden I had played games of jungle exploration as a nine-year-old. All those years in which I had kept away I had never once thought of him, and now he was dead.

Now Saul began absentmindedly to explore his right ear with his little finger, waggling it back and forth, examining the excavated contents, meanwhile staring out across the square. His gaze seemed to meet the gaze of the caftanned stranger, though what they were to each other I couldn't begin to imagine. Perhaps he was merely remembering. He used to like to stand here when I was a little girl and watch me playing on the leapfrog tyres; when I returned indoors he would pat my head and call me the Queen of England.

He smacked his lips—I could hear the false teeth clacking—and breathed deeply. "So tell me, Shula. Are you still teaching?"

"Lecturing," I corrected. "In biblical studies."

"And singing?"

"Oh, no. I gave up singing long ago."

"A pity. You were such a lovely singer."

Saul himself had missed his own vocation. He was ten years retired now, from his teaching post, living in an apartment of legendary squalor beside the Sea of Galilee, whose calm waters had held him mesmerised for more than half a century. And yet of all the family it was he, perhaps, who had loved this house the most. Now he had ridden down like a white knight from the north, to stand guard over its benighted walls.

"We all become teachers," he remarked cryptically. "None of us do the thing we're meant to do. Anyway," he added, with a sharp turn of voice which startled me, "I know why you've come."

"Oh—and why is that?"

"It's because of the Codex," he said, and turning away, began shuffling back indoors. I made after him; he seemed to have abdicated from some kind of standoff, and when I glanced across the square again, the sidelocked stranger was no longer there.

Chapter seven

The year following his arrival in Jerusalem, in the winter of 1862, my great-grandfather got married a second time. He took up residence with his new father-in-law, Isaac Raphaelovitch of Kovno.

Isaac Raphaelovitch had almost despaired of finding a husband for his daughter. She was twenty-three, four or five years beyond marriageable age. She was tall and swarthy, she was not beautiful. For years they had travelled, selling books and trinkets from a suitcase. The girl was considered hard and, worst of all, had a reputation for being learned.

Isaac Raphaelovitch wanted a scholar for his daughter. He fancied himself a scholar and he knew she was no simpleton. He went to Shalom Shepher and said: "You are a young man and you're still not married. My daughter is just the right age for you. Why don't you come round and have a look at her? She isn't beautiful but she's clever and she makes a good kugel."

Shalom Shepher replied casually: "I don't mind whether she's clever but if she can cook a chicken she might do for me."

Isaac Raphaelovitch became enthusiastic and exclaimed:

"And what a chicken she cooks! You should only taste it. Tomorrow, then."

At this time my great-grandfather was living in a dark cellar where the rain dripped through a grating into a lead bucket and the constant beat of footsteps came from above. His only furniture was a mattress, a stove and a lamp, and his only luxury a murky coffee-pot which he wrapped in swaddling rags to keep it warm during his long absences from the cell.

In Jerusalem he maintained the routine he had begun in Bielsk. He spent his days at the Tree of Life Yeshivah, and his nights in discussion at the Zion's Comforter Study House until the second watch. Before dawn he rose to pray with the Vatikin, whose custom it was to utter the prayer 'He redeems Zion' as the first rays of sun peeped over the domes of the city.

In those days he was very thin, because he lived on a diet of dried figs which he kept in a cloth bag on a string around his neck. He stalked about in a caftan which had once belonged to a shoemaker, and which still smelt of leather and polish. His streimel he had bought from Reb Jacob the seller of old clothes, who assured him it was the former property of a great rabbi.

He soon established himself as a corrector of scrolls. They nicknamed him 'Eagle Eyes' because, it was rumoured, he could pick out an error in a scroll at ten paces; also '*shayner Yid*' or Beautiful Jew because of his aristocratic looks. He kept himself in figs by writing prayers for amulets and parchments to go inside phylacteries, and Torah scrolls for use in synagogues.

His work as a scribe he performed in the following manner: from a certain dealer on the Street of the Jews he obtained parchment which had been sliced from the underpart of the animal's skin, soaked in limewater for nine days, dried and rubbed with gallnuts. When he had pricked out the margins and columns with his stylus according to the standard format, he began to write with a mixture of gallnuts, gum arabic, copper sulphate crystals and vinegar: an ink which dried to a hard, glassy finish, but which could be scraped away with a blade to allow corrections.

His quill he tested in the traditional way: he wrote the word

'Amalek' and crossed it out three times, to fulfil the prophecy: "I shall blot out their name from under the heavens." Before he wrote each verse he spoke it aloud. In this way he tried to avoid the common errors: the dittographic, the haplographic and the homoioteleutonic. Before writing the name of God he said: "I intend to write the name of God." This concentrated his mind and helped prevent errors when writing the Name. These could not be corrected. It would have been blasphemous to erase God's name with a blade.

He took great care, through the counting of letters and measuring of lines, that each column should begin with a 'v,' according to long custom, and that the six key words of the Pentateuch should head their columns. He decorated the appropriate characters with daggers and crowns, and embellished them with love, because he loved the letters of the Hebrew alphabet like twenty-two children.

Every half-column he rested for ten minutes, stretched his aching neck and flexed his fingers. In this way he completed four and a half pages if he worked a full day. At the end of the week he assembled his parchments and checked for errors. If a scroll contained eighty-five consecutive letters without a mistake, it was still kosher; but errors must be corrected within thirty days, otherwise it would become invalid. He took his work down to the dealer on the Street of the Jews, who examined it in turn, grunted and criticised a letter here and there. He did not believe in encouraging slipshod work by flattery. He fished out a few coins from under his caftan—three or four francs—and issued my great-grandfather with fresh parchments for the week to come.

Having spent all his money on figs and on remittances to his former wife, there were occasions when Reb Shalom did not have enough to pay the beadle for his entrance to the Zion's Comforter Study House. This did not trouble him, as it gave him an opportunity to emulate the great Rabbi Hillel, who had worked as a day labourer and then studied through the night by pressing his face to the skylight of the study house and listening to the debate. One wintry night a scholar, glancing up, was startled to see the face of Shalom Shepher glued to the skylight above his head. When they went up onto the roof they found him spread-eagled, covered in snow. They brought him down and thawed him out with brandy, after which he joined in the discussion with even greater zest.

Marriage promised a vast improvement in his standard of living. Though hardly rich, Raphaelovitch had the privilege of renting a two-roomed house on Habad Street. The front half of this palace contained the kitchen, store place and charcoal stove, and its white walls were hung with copper and tin utensils of every description. The inner half was salon, dining room, study and bedroom and was furnished with cushions in the Eastern style. The floor was paved in the smooth pinkish-gold stone of Jerusalem. A brass oil lamp hung on a chain from the ceiling and the low table was covered with a square of Damascus silk. A curtain drawn across one corner of the room protected the young woman's privacy.

Raphaelovitch said to his daughter: "When the young man comes, I want you to cook a chicken for him and keep quiet. He isn't looking for a clever wife, so you don't need to say anything. Let the food do the talking."

He had his books spread ostentatiously on the table when his guest arrived, to create the impression of a great scholar, though in fact he was nothing of the kind. Raphaelovitch had read a great many books in his time, but was hampered by his inability to remember any of them. All he could recall were the titles, of which he kept a careful list tucked inside his sleeve for emergencies. He read at speed, believing that the mind could retain more that way. Apart from the standard texts he never went over a book twice, since anything of importance must have been stored in his brain the way sedimentary rocks are laid down by time. On the other hand, any book, once read, became his possession, and he could not bear to part with it. For this reason he had eventually packed up his business and settled in Jerusalem with the remainder of his stock.

Among the volumes now spread on the table were a well-used copy of the Zohar, Maimonides' Code and a sixteenth-century handwritten religious treatise picked up in a job lot from the house of a dead rabbi. This was among those books which, in a fit of sentimentality, he would present to his son-in-law on his wedding day, and which would fetch up in a London auction house a hundred years later for a large sum of money. But by then it had long since passed out of the hands of the family Shepher.

Shalom Shepher had made no special effort towards this important meeting. He came just as he was, even down to the bag of figs, which he had forgotten to remove despite the chicken dinner awaiting him. But he did just happen to have washed his hair, and his sidelocks were glossy and smooth, several hours' twining having been the only evidence he gave of nervousness.

His attention was drawn immediately to the books on the table, and Raphaelovitch, seeing that his books were likely to be a greater temptation than his daughter, tantalised the young man by clearing them away. One by one the volumes were closed, kissed and returned to the chest. Finally nothing remained but the square of Damascus silk. "A devoted scholar is the wealthiest man in the world," Raphaelovitch said. "Not that I don't see the importance of money, but knowledge is worth its weight in gold. Why is money important? Because it buys books and keeps the stomach quiet while the brain is at work. Of course, it isn't money but food which keeps the stomach quiet, but it is the money which buys the food and not the other way round. Speaking of which, my daughter has prepared us a chicken. Come, wash, sit, and let's see if we can do it justice." Shalom Shepher washed his hands in a tin bowl, made the blessing and sat.

At that moment, Batsheva Raphaelovitch entered from the courtyard, carrying a jar of water in the crook of her arm, and the almost-betrothed accidentally met. Actually it was not accidental, but planned. Isaac Raphaelovitch had instructed his daughter beforehand: "When you hear him knock, go out back and fetch some water from the yard. Then if he sees you coming in by accident, I can say my line about the servant of Jacob meeting Rebecca at the well." Raphaelovitch did not add that there is always something beautiful about a woman bearing water from the well, and that he hoped this romantic first impression would distract the potential suitor from his daughter's shortcomings.

My great-grandmother did look rather beautiful as she entered the salon, with her shawl draped around her head and neck, the smooth earthenware jar on her arm and her full skirts embroidered with flowers. This was remarkable, because she was in fact an ill-favoured young woman, with long face and narrow body. It was she who introduced the dark, lanky element to our family gene pool, and thereafter it was a battle between the stocky but golden-haired and beautiful physique of Shalom Shepher (inherited by my father) and the sallow, stringy appearance of his wife (my aunt Shoshanah, with her horsey face and round, hunched, defeated shoulders, was said by everyone to be the image of my great-grandmother).

Soup was served, clear and oily, and Shalom Shepher as the honoured guest was given the little yolky eggs from inside the chicken. The chicken itself appeared in a burst of steam from the kitchen, adorned with vegetables and thick noodles. It was so thoroughly boiled that the carcase collapsed when Raphaelovitch began to carve it, and the meat literally melted in the mouth. The host observed his guest and saw that he was pleased, heaped his plate with food and attentively watched him eat. Shalom Shepher, his stomach shrunken from a diet of figs, could not eat as much as he had hoped. Nor was the taste of chicken quite as he remembered it. A delicate, fig-like savour, like a memory, seasoned everything he ate.

At last the meal was over and Raphaelovitch fetched from the cupboard a murky bottle and a couple of tumblers which he polished with the end of his sleeve. He set them down on the table and poured a small amount of liquid which looked and smelt like brandy but, as Shalom Shepher was about to discover, tasted like nothing on earth.

"Now pick up your glass in your hand, my boy. That's right. What shall we drink to? Not to the beauty of the bride, that might bring bad luck. Though, God knows, in that respect, what can happen? My wife the girl's mother, may she rest in peace, was not known for her good looks either, so I can honestly say I'm not disappointed in my daughter. She is an excellent girl in every way except her age, and that gets a little worse each year. So, what shall we drink to? Not to the health of the groom, and you'll know why when you taste this brandy. I brought it from Kovno to poison my enemies, but that is a joke, you know. All the same it doesn't make sense to drink a man's health with something that tastes like poison. Better to make a toast to life, since worst luck, that is something you can hold on to even when your health is shattered. To life, my boy, to life!"

The marriage contract was duly drawn up: the dowry to be placed with a trustee thirty days before the wedding; the bride's father to meet the cost of the canopy and reception, and supply his daughter with gold rings for her ears and fingers and necklaces of Turkish coins; also to provide the bridegroom with a new streimel, phylacteries and prayer shawl.

My great-grandfather married my great-grandmother because she could cook a chicken. If she had not known how to cook a chicken he would not have married her. If Batsheva Raphaelovitch had not known how to cook a chicken I would not exist, nor would I be here now, recording this mythical history of the house of Shepher.

Chapter eight

"I've no idea what you're talking about."

Saul hovered next to me as I scrubbed the inside of the fridge. While approving my woman's work, he was understandably perplexed by it. He picked up the tubs of houmous and soured cream I had brought from the Supersol and examined them with a suspicion verging on disgust. Here I was, trying to bring order and comfort to a house which would be rubble in a few weeks. Why and for what? My motivation was a mystery, even to myself.

"This Codex," I repeated. "I don't know anything about it. But I would like to."

"Humph!" Saul set down the tubs. "Bad for the stomach," he said. After a moment's thought he added: "Bad for the heart."

"Good for the heart," I said decisively. "Our family never suffered from heart problems in any case."

"Your Uncle Ben Zion, he died of heart. Your Aunt Shoshanah. She also. Heart."

"I thought it was cancer."

"No, with Shoshanah it was heart. She would have survived the cancer. Everyone else it was cancer. Your father—cancer. Your mother." He pointed in my direction with a withered finger. "You want to look out for yourself. Eat plenty of fresh vegetables."

"Like you, eh, Saul?"

"Me, there's no need to worry. I only need to watch the stomach."

I caught a dribble of brown water with my sponge. "Well, Saul, this is a jolly conversation." I looked him straight in the eye. "This is the first I've heard of any Codex."

A shudder of pure scepticism seemed to pass through Saul's body. If he hadn't been in his father's house he would have spat, perhaps. "You're all here. The whole lot of you. Gathering like vultures. You can smell the money."

"What money?"

"You think a thing like that isn't worth money? Of course it is. A document like that."

"What sort of document? Is it a bible, then?"

"Worth thousands, probably. To all those *schnorrerim*."

"What *schnorrerim*?"

"Vultures. Robbers. Our esteemed relatives. And all the rest of them." He examined me in silence for a few seconds, then peered shiftily out of the window. "I think your problem is heart."

I scrubbed harder. "There's nothing wrong with my heart."

But there was something wrong with my heart, I couldn't deny it. My heart had been killed long ago; I could feel nothing. And if it was true now perhaps it had always been so. I had been restless for years, to be sure, and increasingly dissatisfied, though that remained a secret I kept to myself; and I did not answer, when questioned about my life, with the genuine replies which circled in my head: that I was a *luftmensch*, a floating person, living on air, existing day to day and hand to mouth; a *matmid*, a perpetual student, studying and studying and learning nothing, ignorant even of my own desires. I was a tree without roots, a building without foundations, ready to blow away in the first wind. Though this may have been only an illusion I cherished. I nurtured the dream that in the near or distant future, I would grow true to myself: would tire of my grey days poring over textual variants in the Pentateuch and take wing, at last, for the horizon. But the future is always ahead of us, and procrastination is the family sin.

It might have been otherwise. I couldn't deny I'd had my opportunity. I could have sung solo for the city once; and there had been a young saxophonist, a dark-eyed Daniel, an atheistical-rationalist-anarchist-activist with the face of a mediaeval mystic, an idealist full of pure visions of the future who wanted to go and work for the utopian secular state of Palael. Its creation, he told me, was our moral mandate as Jews.

"If it meant anything, that was what the Bible meant."

He had wanted me to come with him, but when at last time had run out and Daniel was standing with his saxophone packed, I was still toying with my intentions; I couldn't persuade myself to make the move. So he packed his bags and presented me with an ultimatum: either I came with him or we were at an end.

"I can't decide," I told him.

"Don't try to decide. You can't decide between ketchup and brown sauce. Just come."

"I'll think about it," I said.

Fifteen years later I still thought about it as I drifted from one brief encounter to the next, shrugging my shoulders, going with the flow, harking back always to that first innocent love. I told myself that now, perhaps, I would be capable of loving Daniel, I even imagined Daniel still capable of loving me. But it was too late. Life has its own way of sealing off our choices, and the decision I could never make had made itself at last.

I lived by myself, in a bubble of self-sufficiency that some would have called reclusive, following the routine I firmly believed kept me sane: teaching my few students, pursuing my own private preoccupations, holed up night after night in dusty libraries or chilled in the lone light of my anglepoise. I did so knowing that my existence had something of the ridiculous about it. What use, after all, did the world have for yet another study on the orthographic relationship between that which is written and that which is read, or the comparative philology of Ugaritic and Akkadian? Though these were details which held genuine fascination for me, they were as weird as the dodo in an academic environment ever more conscious of utility and finance, and whose future grew more precarious with each passing year. Nor was I ever likely to find the true grail of my researches: the original, the Ur-text of the Hebrew Scriptures.

Saul was the one to know all about heart, I thought bitterly, wiping my hand from the stickiness of the fridge. As I did so a shudder of the past blew through me, piercing some chink in the present and cutting it like a knife. I remembered the summer of my father's funeral, that funeral of absolute horror which nothing had prepared me for, when in a dazzling wilderness of tombs and dust we had followed my father's body on a stretcher to the grave, his body wrapped in a shroud which bore a patch of blood, and watched them rain down earth and stones onto my father's unprotected face. Afterwards, in the darkness of the guest bedroom, a quorum of black-hatted men droning their prayers outside, I had watched Reuben as he fiddled with his radio. I said to my brother: "They buried him like a pauper." And Reuben, his face hidden behind his dark donkey fringe, answered casually: "Well, the dead are poor." Saul sat at the corner of the kitchen table, fixed me in his spectacles and said: "You know your father never really loved your mother." Twenty-five years later I was still aching for the opportunity to prove him wrong.

The moment passed, I finished my cleaning and stocked up the fridge. The few items looked scant and lonely inside its vast whiteness. Later that afternoon Saul would sit with me in the cold salon, farting gently from the rich diet I had fed him with; together we would turn the black pages of a family album adorned with a copper panel of the Western Wall: tense studio gatherings replete with starched collars and buttoned waistcoats; sepia portraits of our lost and nameless Lithuanian branch. Wedding pictures, regiments of cousins. My Uncle Cobby and his wife Fania, my Aunt Miriam and her husband Dov. Our own arrival on the dock at Haifa: my mother in a dazzling white sundress, my father attired formally in a Homburg hat.

Tucked in amongst them would be the photograph of a girl, dark-eyed and dark-haired, dressed in the tweed and buttons of the nineteen-thirties. A photograph which had been slipped in, which didn't belong. Not an aunt or a cousin, nor one of the fiancées who appeared later, in an austere war-wedding, next to a grim-faced groom. Anomalous and appealing: I would wonder who she was.

"Who is that?" I would ask my uncle.

And he would answer, casually: "Oh, that's Hannah. Didn't you know? She was your father's girl."

Chapter nine

The couple slept behind the curtain in the house on Habad Street. All night Raphaelovitch lay with his ears pricked to hear the sounds of procreation.

I have said that my great-grandmother had a reputation for being hard, and she was: as cold and hard as a brass candlestick. There was no love at the beginning of their marriage and there was no miraculous love at the end. Every day Batsheva cooked a chicken for her husband and father. She gave Raphaelovitch the white meat, rightly assuming that Shepher would prefer the dark. When her husband passed through the kitchen in the morning she was plucking the feathers; when he came back at night she was boiling the bones. They did not exchange a word of endearment on either occasion.

Soon after her marriage she sold off her wedding jewellery and went into business making vinegar. Hence her local nickname, Batsheva the Sour. When not cooking chickens she was busy boiling and straining, mixing and reducing, fermenting and straining again, before pouring the vinegar clear and golden into shining bottles which she sold from the house on Habad Street. With the profit she began to experiment, for my great-grandmother was a born scientist.

She attempted fermentation from the juice of oranges and figs and prickly pears which she collected by hand outside the Dung Gate. She made orange vinegar, fig vinegar and pear vinegar. She even made vinegar from honey. She went down to the spice market and bought seasonings of rosemary and thyme and laurel leaves, garlic and cinnamon and hot red peppers. All the wonderful varieties of sour and spicy, pungent and fiery, blossomed under her skill. To the women of Jerusalem, who were profoundly superstitious, she explained the properties of every bottle: how this one cured headaches, and that one soothed ague; this one acted as a tonic, and that one encouraged restful sleep. She used the knowledge she had picked up from the fellaheen women in the market, and what little she had read, and for the rest invented, though she never displayed imagination in any other area except the making and using of vinegar.

With the bottles left over from each batch she began to make pickles, and the making of pickles became a new voyage of discovery and a new obsession. She pickled lemons with hot peppers, figs with cinnamon and cloves, and cabbage with coriander seed. She experimented by curing vegetables in brine and softening olives in lye. From the ink-maker on the Street of the Jews she obtained copper sulphate crystals and vitriol, cited in the ancient recipes, and alum and lime for crispness and colouring. Her hands became scarred from the abrasive mixtures, and wherever she moved her clothes left an acetic tang in the air. She developed a genius for converting the natural sweetness of fruit into acidity. Nothing satisfied her in her quest for new combinations: almonds and walnuts, tomatoes and melons, even rose petals and mint, all underwent the process with greater or lesser success. "If you can eat it, pickle it," she said.

The cool places of the house on Habad Street became filled with sealed mysterious crocks and heavy jars in which pickles bloomed like strange flowers. To Batsheva they were things of beauty, alterations of nature and therefore a kind of art. Purple cabbages in cross-section, magnified lemons and medleys of distorted fruit were ranged like specimens around the courtyard.

Instead of sweetmeats she served up pickled onions, sauerkraut and spiced pickled cucumbers which gave Shalom Shepher acute indigestion and brought bitter acids to his throat. The cucumbers, which were to form the bulwark of Batsheva's reputation, were made to a secret recipe and may or may not have had hallucinogenic properties. They were especially popular with students of the Kabbalah.

Isaac Raphaelovitch kept a crock of cucumbers on the table, and no meal was complete unless he finished off with one, much as other men would finish off with a cigar. He encouraged his son-in-law to eat them too, inventing stories about their nourishing effect on the brain, or their improving action on the eyes. The great sage Shammai, he said, had been practically raised on pickled cucumbers. Shalom Shepher was dubious, but thought it would probably account for Shammai's sour temperament.

"I married the rose of the Sharon," he joked, "and she turned into a field of cucumbers." Meanwhile he bought sticky sweets, left them in his pockets and allowed them to melt, and sometimes he stood outside the confectioners' stalls in the bazaar, gazing at the tiers of forbidden pastry soaked in syrup and sprinkled with nuts, or filled with honey and dusted with cinnamon, reflected in polished mirrors, row upon row. In his hunger for something sweet he chewed the carob pods which lay scattered under inaccessible trees, and nibbled dried figs, and even sucked for hours at a piece of cloth soaked in wine while he studied. He longed for the soothing milky dishes of Pentecost, or the sweet almond bread baked at New Year; and week to week he looked forward to his Sabbath invitation at the house of the rabbi, whose plump wife served slices of apple strudel after the service.

Batsheva extracted the sweets which had stuck to the insides of his pockets and threw them away in disgust, and her heart did not soften for a moment towards her foolish and sweet-toothed husband. She went on serving him with vitriol and spices, and turned all the household fruit to gall, while she and her father, both long-faced, dark and lanky, munched on pickled cucumbers as if it were a conspiracy.

The only tenderness she felt was towards the multitude of cats which leapt the roofs of Jerusalem and came down to her cistern to drink. She put out water for them, fed them scraps and ran her long, acid-reddened hands along their smoky backs. The cats knew where to come, and congregated in her courtyard among the pickle jars. And it is often the case that those who have no affection for their fellow humans feel an affinity with cats.

Isaac Raphaelovitch, raising an admonitory finger, warned his son-in-law against the dangers of allowing her too much freedom. "Take charge of your wife's earnings and make yourself master in your own house," he said. "After all, you don't want her to be building herself a nest egg." My great-grandfather ignored this piece of advice, though in later years he would have cause to regret it.

Nor did Batsheva pay much attention to her husband's doings. She was not impressed by his debating in the study house, since she never witnessed it. He made less money selling parchments than she did from her vinegar and pickles. Once she had enjoyed reading, but the requirements of business and family now demanded that she abandon books. She followed the religion of the kitchen. The Sabbath meant meat and candles; New Year, honey cake and tailors' bills; Passover, spring cleaning and fresh utensils. And everything had somehow to be paid for.

She maintained a sceptical attitude towards her husband's reputation. So far as piety was concerned, she had seen far too many madmen on the road already. As for his exceptional eyesight, she snorted: "He can't see in the dark." Reb Jacob Itchka the wagoner suggested once that Shalom Shepher might be one of the thirty-six righteous men who appear in each generation. Batsheva retorted: "Reb Itchka is one of the forty million fools."

But Isaac Raphaelovitch was delighted with his son-in-law. Here was his opportunity to study with a true scholar, and he never stopped pestering him for an hour's reading. Shalom Shepher was obliged to humour him. Naturally, Raphaelovitch was eager to display his learning and to impress the young man with his list of books. His reading, on the whole, was spiced with pure nonsense. Often Batsheva would put her head round the door and observe how they sat, her father bent over the page, her husband leaning back with his eyes shut; her husband apparently asleep, her father unashamedly picking his nose.

Some time passed before speculation ended and the marriage was blessed with children. In due course Batsheva gave birth to a daughter, and then to another daughter. Before long there were three, a daughter a daughter and a daughter, all of them initiated from an early age into the mysteries of vinegar production. With their long solemn faces and their dark lank hair, wielding their miniature funnels and saucepans in the kitchen of the house on Habad Street, there could be little doubt that they were the offspring of Batsheva Raphaelovitch.

In all there would be thirteen children, of whom seven survived. Six daughters grew up and married impecunious scholars. One married an adventurer who left for America, got off the boat in Ireland and disappeared. Another was widowed young, turned to good works and neglected her relatives. A third, Hannah Raisl, took up with a watchmender so bad at his trade that for thirty years she ran the business herself.

The only son was my grandfather, Joseph Shepher. He had my great-grandfather's build and my great-grandmother's colouring. He had Reb Shalom's stomach and Batsheva's bile. In short, he inherited the worst characteristics of both his parents, though, much to his credit, he made the best of them.

From an early age he suffered bouts of acute indigestion. This might have been hereditary or it might not. It might have been the result of hidden longings, or it might have been caused merely by excess acid. Batsheva the Sour did not spare any of her children. It is said that even the milk they sucked at her breast contained its own measure of gall.

Chapter ten

Saul said: "I've seen him around here before. Staring up at the house with his moon-eyes."

"What does he want?"

He shrugged. "How should I know? Do I care to make conversation with these people?"

I was watering the dead plants on the verandah. It was my second day of residence at Kiriat Shoshan, and so far I had cleaned and stocked the fridge, made up the beds with fresh linen and restored the bathroom. Already the past felt much more like home.

From my vantage-point on the verandah I could see the man with his black sidecurls and striped caftan lurking under a pepper tree by the children's sandpit. He had an oriental appearance, his face was olive and pale; his clear eyes flickered every so often in the direction of the shuttered windows. Did he really believe we couldn't see him? Or was it his desire to draw our attention without taking the trouble of accosting us? I glanced at him furtively over my watering-can; our eyes met. His were oddly familiar: they brushed me up and down with an appraising, complacent look, as though he knew and acknowledged exactly who I was.

This disturbed me more than a little, firstly because I had some vague notion that it was forbidden for a religious man to gaze into the eyes of a strange woman (hair and arms uncovered, head full of sinful thoughts, stomach awash with a mix of milk and meat), but also because the nature of his gaze suggested some fixed purpose, sinister or otherwise, and by returning it I feared I had opened up the gates of his intention. I expected him at any moment to start across the square.

The water was running over the brim of the dry plant-pot and onto the floor. When I looked up again the man had vanished.

There was no sign of him in the square, on the street, between the beaten-up cars along the pavement. I hurried to the other side of the house. There was no-one there: only a stray cat sunning itself under the cypress trees; it bounded off nervously at my approach.

Later, plucking at a bowl of black olives in the kitchen, Saul shrugged again. "What do you think? He's probably after the Codex."

"After it? What do you mean?"

He raised his eyes mischievously, and laughed. Never a big laugher, Saul: this was a small, sour, sardonic chuckle, lodged in the back of his throat, and he glanced at me sidelong in a way which reminded me oddly of our caftanned stranger, as though he knew something he was not about to share.

The night before, in the dimness of the abandoned salon, with the click of dead leaves and the mewing of cats outside, he had told me as much as he was prepared to about the object of everybody's fevered interest. He had found it himself, of course; not that it was his by right. But something should accrue, shouldn't it, to the discoverer? All the more galling, then, to have it snatched out of his hands, taken into protective custody by his officious brother. "That Cobby! Always doing things by the book!" Saul spat in annoyance. It languished now in the archive at the Ben Or Institute, where it could only be visited by express permission, until the family decided what best to do with it; but not before Cobby, in his innocent and mild and thoughtless way, had offered it free and gratis to the nation, and thereby succeeded in rousing the dead and nearly dead, the somnolent, the sulking and the dispossessed, that is, the whole ancient leviathan of the clan of Shepher.

"But what is it, exactly—the Codex? What is it like?"

"What do you want? It's a bible—a *keter Torah.* You know what is a *keter Torah*? A crown of the Torah. A handwritten copy."

"Yes," I said. "Of course I know what is a *keter Torah.* But where did it come from—what is its provenance?"

Saul grimaced. "Who knows? It must have been up there for years. Your grandfather never knew about it, that's for certain." He gestured broadly to the surrounding clutter, as though the provenance of the Codex were somehow written there, the same way fossils materialise out of vast layers of sedimentary clay and rock; and he drew up his shoulders in that closed, defensive, characteristic family manner.

There were secrets enough, I thought, as I wandered the cold rooms of the house, stumbling over hidden boxes here, bumping into piles of linen there; observing the pale ghosts of the furniture standing sheeted under the livid glow of forty-watt bulbs. One might find anything: a whole history lay in these chaotic remnants. And history was fragile, no-one knew better than I the truth of that. A moment's whim might turn it into ashes.

Twenty years ago, just after my mother's funeral, I had returned to the big house we shared for the last five years of her life and sorted all her possessions. I cleared the shelves and emptied all the cupboards. I scoured wardrobes and disembowelled drawers. Nothing remained: not a thread was spared.

I called up my brother and asked him if he minded. His reply was unequivocal: "What the hell would I want with all that junk?"

So I set to work and got rid of everything. Clothes and shoes went to the charity shop; furniture and ornaments to the auction house. Piece by piece I discarded our childhood. The past was nothing but a heap of bric-à-brac.

Then I built a huge bonfire at the bottom of the garden. I threw onto it everything that would burn.

Postcards and photographs were consumed in moments. Mementoes and souvenirs vanished in a flash. A letter, written in my grandfather's tiny curlicued script, danced like a blue butterfly on the smoke and disappeared.

I had not intended at first to burn these things. Then as the flames rose higher I was seized by a kind of madness. Why, after all, did one keep anything? The past was nothing but anguish: I was well rid of it. It was a purge, a great purification. I felt my heart growing as light as ash.

Then I sold up and moved to a distant city. I lived in a high building with a tall staircase, a flat with white walls and not much furniture, and a window from which, on clear days and in the right light, you could see a line of silver-blue which was the sea.

There I lived alone, if semi-attached to a series of unsuitable and evanescent lovers, while the books I loved most grew in piles around me and threatened to topple down onto my head. I lived a life without roots and devoid of rituals, and joined the ranks of the scientists who tame Scripture by analysis and, while lovingly dissecting it, need not consider its content. I had kept the festivals once, but now they caused me pain, reviving memories of childhood which were a source of grief. The sight of the Sabbath candles only made me cry. As for the laws and customs, they now seemed meaningless; and my progress mirrored that of the philosopher Rosenzweig, who returned step by step to the traditions of his ancestors: when asked whether I had given up a particular observance I tended to reply: "Not yet."

Many years later I regretted my youthful act of madness. I took those few items which had escaped the flames—my mother's brooch, a stray photograph, my father's watch—and displayed them with reverence on the mantelpiece. But the image of a blue butterfly of paper rose sometimes like a sad ghost in my imagination, tormenting me with its lost-forever words.

Now I had come back to the source, to the family itself, which I had long grown indifferent to and stopped thinking of, just as I had rejected my own past and all my religion. I had returned in the nick of time, to snatch the tail end of my history as it slithered away into oblivion. Walking the rooms of the house, so dreamlike and yet familiar, solid as ever yet trembling on the edge of dissolution, it was as though I had woken from a long sleep.

That evening we sat facing each other in the desolate salon, Saul in my aunt's rocking chair, I on the dusty divan; I with my book and he with his radio. My uncle said: "Your mother was always reading. Just the same. Always with a book."

Always with a novel. We were alike in that. Yet I wondered whether she felt, as I did just now, this great irrelevance, the impossibility of reading here, under this family roof. Words unravelled; descriptions of the English countryside seemed immeasurably distant and unreal. I turned aside with a sigh and let the book half-fall. I wanted to know things, I wanted to make Saul talk. I wanted the truth, I wanted to see the Codex. Was the Codex the truth or was it merely another version? Here in front of me my living uncle sat. How to draw out the history he held, the past he represented, all the memories which would die with him?

I leaned forward with all the eagerness I could muster; caught the flash of his glasses, his evasive glance. "Talk to me, Saul." I imagined myself saying it. "Tell me where I come from. Tell me about the past."

Chapter eleven

The weather was wet and the cisterns filled. On the surface of the water lay a translucent scum, perhaps the last evidence of drowned rats.

October was cholera month. The disease came from Egypt, via Jaffa and Hebron, despite a quarantine of thirty days on ships from Alexandria. In Alexandria there was a crush of panic at the port, where people were desperate to escape. Every fishing boat was filled; large sums of money were changing hands to obtain passage. At Jaffa the fugitives were held in quarantine on the large rocks at the harbour mouth and brought food by rowboat to prevent them coming into contact with the townspeople. By the time they reached Jerusalem the epidemic was already raging.

In the Ashkenazi community, Shabbatai Shimshon was the first to die; in the Sephardi, David Salomon. The cholera dissolved itself in cisterns and standing pools and trickling effluvia, it ran through the gutters and drains and twisted its way among the alleys of Jerusalem. It crouched at the bottom of Hezekiah's Pool and it waited in the Pool of Siloam. They drew it up in buckets from the Well of the Leaf and the Well of the Souls, and caught it bubbling from the spring of Ein Rogel.

When it rose from the water it took the form of Ketteb Merriri, the mythological demon dressed in eyes and scales and hair, with one large eye across its heart. It passed in vapour between the lips of the women as they talked, and from hand to hand among the children as they played. A man could go out into the street and meet it, take it home like a friend and introduce it to his family. A man would go out into the noonday sun and return with the sickness inside him and say: "I have met Ketteb Merriri."

In the house on Habad Street Shalom Shepher sat and wrote prayers to ward off sickness and enclosed them in leather amulets, which he gave away because he would not take a profit from the cholera; Batsheva force-fed her family with cucumbers until the pickle juices ran out of their eyes and down their cheeks. She put down food in the yard for the hungry cats which swarmed and multiplied now that their Arab benefactors had the sickness, and held the cats' tails as a talisman against disease, which she thought she had heard of somewhere but was probably a ritual of her own invention. One evening she took a brush and whitewash and painted an enormous hand across the face of the house to ward off the evil eye. Long after the paint had faded the house was still known as the House of the Hand on Habad Street, and whenever people looked at it they were reminded of the cholera.

Shalom Shepher performed the duties of a pious Jew. He visited the sick and brought them pickles, and made up the quorum in the house of mourning. If there was a funeral procession he would follow it. Night after night the graveyard on the Mount of Olives was illuminated with wandering points of light as Reb Shmuel Zvil, chief gravedigger, with his donkey and lantern, led the way for the members of the burial society: the body lying covered on a white bier, a trail of mourners following behind. A bride was buried on her wedding day; whole families were interred together. Returning, the mourners would adjourn to the bath house, and by next day a number of them would sicken.

Cholera was the product of malicious spirits which lay in wait for the miserable and sniffed out fear. The only way to cheat it was to laugh in its face. So the brotherhood of scrubbers made the rounds of the city with their weird orchestra of flute, harp, drums and cymbals, to raise the spirits of the people with cracked music and bad jokes; since it was also their task to rub the limbs of the convulsed victims with oil and mustard and to lay out the dead bodies, they had greater need of cheer than anyone. Their mirth held more than a touch of madness, and the sound of their frenzied music, weaving the streets at midnight or at the dangerous hour of noon, inspired terror in all who heard it, since a visit from the scrubbers could only mean one thing: that the demon cholera had struck again.

Shalom Shepher, sitting in the House of the Hand on Habad Street, wrote prayers inscribed with the name of the healing angel Raphael and incantations to drive out dybbuks. He folded them tightly and sealed them in amulets on lengths of twine. These proved so popular that he soon found himself short of parchment, and fresh sheets were now hard to come by on the Street of the Jews. One night Reb Jacob the seller of old clothes came to his door. He had just returned from a funeral and lost his amulet at the bath house. Reb Shalom was sorry, but he couldn't help him. There wasn't a scrap of parchment to be had. First thing in the morning he would go out and buy some, write an incantation and deliver it himself. Reb Jacob, with a cry of despair, disappeared into the night. The next morning, amulet in hand, my great-grandfather hurried to his house, where he found the old man's funeral procession on the point of leaving.

Shalom Shepher fell into a depression because of his failure to save his friend. That was when the cholera took its chance. As a rule the illness progressed through three stages, sickness, diarrhoea and convulsions; once the convulsions began there was no hope of recovery. My great-grandfather had the sickness, had the diarrhoea, but did not reach the convulsions and recovered. It was his second resurrection from dangerous disease.

Tradition has it that his life was saved by vinegar, that it was his wife, Batsheva, and not the ministrations of the scrubbers or the attentions of the German doctor which pulled him through. His own stubborn constitution must have played its part. But by all accounts,

Batsheva stood sentinel. She wouldn't let the pestilential scrubbers come anywhere near him. No poisoning doctor ever entered the house. She took on the case and cured him, not out of devotion, of course, but from a sheer determination not to be beaten, and to prove what her home-made remedies could do.

For three days he lay in quarantine behind the vinegar-soaked curtain. No-one except Batsheva was allowed to pass. "Not that you aren't the best qualified to nurse him," Isaac Raphaelovitch prevaricated, "and not that you aren't actually his wife. But perhaps it would be best if he were taken to the Rothschild Hospital." Batsheva treated this suggestion as she treated everything her father said: with perfectly poised contempt. "Perhaps it would be better for me to kill him immediately," she said, "since if he didn't have the cholera before he went there, he would be sure to have it by the time he left." And she swept behind the curtain, leaving the old man in some genuine doubt as to her intentions.

That night he slept on the floor in the kitchen while Batsheva tended to the sick man. Not for one moment did she fear she would lose her patient. Not for one moment did my great-grandfather believe that he would die. "Unless," he joked later, "from the smell of vinegar." He did not trouble to say how far he had travelled in those three days of struggle and suffering, when the face of his wife bending above the bed merged sometimes, improbably, with a vision of angels. Batsheva had her own poultices and medicines, her own secret tricks and incantations. But Reb Shalom was determined to live, and besides, he knew it was not cholera, but great spiritual yearning that possessed his body.

Meanwhile Isaac Raphaelovitch lay awake, painting versions of catastrophe for himself. His son-in-law would die, his daughter would catch the cholera and perish also. He alone would be left to care for the children. "Lord of the universe," he prayed, "make me a grave and a shroud! Better for me to die now than to see these little ones without a guardian."

At dawn on the third day Batsheva came into the kitchen and woke her father. "The crisis is past," she said. "He will recover." From the grimness of her expression you might have thought her husband had passed away.

News soon spread of Shalom Shepher's miraculous recovery. Before long there was a brisk market in rubbing vinegar and embrocations from the House of the Hand, and Batsheva, who felt no compunction about taking a profit from the cholera, saw her business thrive.

For two months the cholera held sway in Jerusalem. Then, as inexplicably as it had sprung up, it sank down, dwindled, and disappeared. The demon was sucked back into the reservoirs from which it had arisen. The evil spirits returned to the wells and pools and cisterns from which they had come.

In the Sephardi community, Isaac Adani was the last to die; in the Ashkenazi, Reb Israel the Righteous. And it is said that the last to die in any epidemic is always a great man.

After this the city breached its walls and stretched like a grey tentacle up the Jaffa Road. The Muslims moved out to the east, the Jews to the west, and new Jerusalem began. Many Christians had taken refuge in the hillside convents and monasteries when the sickness started, and credited their survival to their superior spiritual state.

Chapter twelve

Saul said: "She was your father's girl."

I sat and looked at the photograph I held between my thumb and forefinger: mounted on thick card, like an identity pass, with the name of a Tel Aviv photographer printed on the back, an address on Ben Yehuda street; scuffed at the corners, as though it had been carried in a wallet or a pocket, and faded, as though it had seen too much sun. The face was pale and serious, the eyes large, the hair curled formally around the neck and temples. A studio portrait: a presentation piece.

"Who was she? What was she like? Why did it end?"

"What can I tell you? Who knows what she was like? Her name was Hannah. She was your father's girl."

Later, as if conceding, he added: "She was a *Yekke*, a German. I think she was a teacher at the music school."

It was too rich, I thought, that Saul, with his riffs of authority, his "You know your father never loved your mother," should prove so oysterlike when it came to this. His reluctance only increased my curiosity. I threw him my own sidelong look, concealed the photograph in my pocket and bided my time.

Wherever he wandered, through the rooms of the house, I could hear my uncle by the faint drone of the radio which dangled from his arm: in the bathroom, in the kitchen, in the high bedroom at the end of the corridor where he slept fully clothed in a rat's nest of filthy sheets, the murmur of news reports heralded his gloomy presence. He donned his caftan only in the evening, when the temperature dropped sharply and he was forced, grimacing and reluctant, to light the paraffin stove which was our sole source of heat. Now he was obliged to share its meagre output he was more reluctant than ever, and put off lighting it until after night had fallen. He sat clutching his radio, enjoying the feeble warmth it generated as a by-product of the six-o'clock news.

All his life he had practised extreme thrift. As a young man he had lived on bagels and watermelon; once he experimented by boiling an onion in water, and the experience was so momentous he never repeated it. Now, in his old age, he lived like a monk on his pension and always remembered the poverty of his youth. To Saul there was no such thing as spending money wisely. The act of spending money was itself unwise.

As a boy he had wanted to become a great writer. For years he filled notebooks with poems and stories which he hid under the mattress of his bed. Since he was a sloven and my father obsessively neat, it was my father who made up the bed and discovered the notebooks. He kept his discovery secret for a while; then he could contain himself no longer and one evening, when the family was seated at dinner, he produced a poem and began to read aloud. The result was both hilarious and tragic. It was a mortification for which his brother never forgave him.

The puzzle, as Saul would later tell me, was simply this: the poems, which were meant to be serious, had the family in fits of laughter, whereas the stories, which were meant to be funny, hardly raised a smile. It was this paradox my uncle never came to terms with, and which may be said to reflect most of his difficulties in life.

His politics were like his temper, fiery and right. He had been a member of the nationalist militia, and was possibly in the unit which was implicated in the massacre of two hundred Arab villagers at Deir Yassin. He was imprisoned briefly by the British in the compound at Latrun; but this was perhaps the climax of his seditious involvement.

He became a teacher in Tiberias, where he taught at the same school for thirty-seven years. Here he cultivated the aura of the reclusive intellectual. He washed irregularly, and suffered from an inability to tuck his shirt properly into his trousers. He also had a habit of leaving his top button undone behind his tie, which gave people the impression he was untrustworthy. Though he continued to write, his sole publication would be the obituary of his own father, and he waited in vain for the revelatory experience which, he felt, would one day be the making of him. This sense of expectation buoyed him up for a number of years. Then, when he saw that he was unlikely to achieve anything astonishing or permanent, he settled into a petrified and embittered state. The realisation came to him in a night, and by the next morning he had aged so noticeably that colleagues commented to each other on his changed appearance.

Now he was leading me wordlessly down the dim corridor behind the salon, his slippers shuffling on the tiled floor, his breath a thin wheeze in the silent stillness. Here behind the closed door he slept in the tall, funereal room which had once been my grandmother's and which, the only time in childhood I had ever entered it, had been filled with pot-bellied wardrobes and heavy dressers and smelt of starch and the camomile liniment they spread on my grandmother's eczema every night; and where there were three beds, one for my grandmother, one for Shoshanah and one for Aunt Batsheva, pushed against each wall. I had always thought it strange that they should sleep all three squeezed up together. Once, as a reward for helping fold the washing ("A proper duty for a girl to learn") I had been led down the long corridor to this fearsome and forbidden room, which I had only known previously as a line of light under a closed door but where I had guiltily glimpsed, once, my grandmother half-undressed in a pair of thick beige stockings. The shutters were closed; there was no natural light, only the glow of a bulb under a very dusty and cobweb-covered shade. Both the light and the smell of the room were unbearably oppressive. Aunt Shoshanah pulled open a deep drawer of the Viennese dresser, and from under a thick pile of bedsheets and pillow cases and embroidered linen tablecloths used for Sabbaths and festivals she brought forth an ancient tin of Neapolitans, and gave me one.

Saul, however, had no thought of leading me there. Halfway between the bathroom and the salon he stopped; behind a maroon curtain, in a small area still smelling of rags and carbolic soap where the household tools were stored, and which had always frightened me a little as a child with its dim redolence, its lurking brooms, a ladder stood. An old painting ladder, splashed with emulsion and bitumen from the rare occasions when they had carried out repairs. Its rungs were chipped, but it was still serviceable. Gathering the flaps of his caftan, Saul began to climb. There was something astonishing and preposterous in the swift way he left the floor.

Only a few rungs separated us when he lifted the flimsy hatch and pulled himself, with surprising agility, into the room above. A puff of dust, a wave of baked warmth descended to me, and my uncle's face, like a gargoyle, peered down from aloft. "*Nu*, then. Are you coming up already?"

I climbed and followed. A thin, mothy darkness greeted me; I lifted my head into the upper space.

The attic was still and warm, full of the leftover air of the long day. There was a dry, resinous scent, at once exciting and familiar: the smell of old books and paper, of time and decay.

By the few grains of sunlight the roof allowed I saw a broad, barnlike expanse, covering nearly the entire area of the house: a neat network of joists, the building's ribs; an interior scalework of overlapping tiles. I saw a vast floor like a battlefield, strewn with boxes and trunks, packing-cases and old laundry-sacks, clothes, suitcases and furniture. A tumbled, wild, chaotic glory-hole. And everywhere paper: hanks and heaps of it, half-disintegrating sheets of it, toppling piles of files and documents. An archive it was in only the loosest sense of the term, or if it had been, one struck by a hurricane. It was as though a ghostly regiment of Cossacks had galloped through a lawyer's office, leaving a cloud of affidavits in its wake.

Unhesitating now, I pulled myself up without difficulty through the attic's mouth, and stood fully upright beneath its generous roof.

Saul indicated the zinc water tank in the middle of the floor.

"That's where we got down and hid," he said, "when they came up shooting from Deir Yassin. You know, in '29."

"Why there?"

"Somebody told my mother bullets can't pass through water."

He moved on, bending and searching, breathing heavily as he poked through the mess, groaning softly with the effort and the heat; giving off an odour of sweat and unhealth which increased perceptibly as he exerted himself. I thought then that he was of a piece with this dust, that he too might dissolve and become part of it.

"This is where I found it," he announced. And without a word more he dived in again, plunging his hand into a packing case, his profile taut and beaked like an eager bird's.

Lightly and gingerly I trod across the chaos. The boards were sound, though creaky, and getting down on my haunches I turned over a sheaf of ornamented pamphlets in black and scarlet ink. *The Society for the Promotion of the Hebrew Language,* I read. *Rules and Principles.* The brittle paper crumbled in my hand.

This was the secret the house had been keeping from me: here was the treasure which had called me back. And yet it was a poor sort of treasure. It was nothing but history, raw and unadorned: the minutes of the Committee for the Preservation of Jerusalem; the monthly accounts for the Sick Teachers' Fund; back copies of the newspaper my grandfather had cranked out on an old linotype before the First World War. Correspondence in triplicate, and faded ledgers, and records of wheat distribution for the city's poor.

It had lain here for decades, a slowly growing mountain: a mere mound at first, perhaps, but eventually an Everest, increased by the matter added to it year by year. Ignored and forgotten for decades, only imminent destruction had forced its discovery. No wonder the Codex had lain concealed here for so long. I slowly rotated my gaze. A heavy curtain of dust obscured the far reaches of the attic, where under the lowest rafters I could just make out the orderly ranks of boxes whose contents were still undisturbed.

How could one piece together the story that lay buried here, the stories that surely lay buried, hidden in the dregs of some packing-case, tucked away in some rusted lever-arch file, waiting in vain for a hand to uncover them? How trivial seemed these broken bits and pieces. Was there really nothing left of the past but these dry bones, these bare skeletons of fact; these worn questionable heirlooms? A ram's horn, a fragment of Torah scroll, a list of train times out of Jaffa station. An old exercise book in English copperplate: *A noun is a word used for naming some person or thing*, the pages disintegrating even as I turned them. And yet like Saul I was unable to stop, drawn into a vortex I could not resist. The name on the book was my father's

Amnon
Amnon Shepher
Amnon

repeated with flourishes, childish and unformed: his first English. I couldn't ignore the call of that lost name, or the sight of the handwriting, still alive after almost seventy years.

I pulled the whole heap toward me. At the far side of the attic, my uncle's gleaning movements mirrored mine.

An interjection is a word used to express some sudden feeling

I hoped for nothing. My lungs full of dust, I reached into the box.

Chapter thirteen

After his miraculous recovery my great-grandfather was filled with a strange restlessness. When he sat in the study house he wanted to be out walking. When he was out walking he wanted to be at home. When he tried to write a scroll his mind wandered, and he was obliged to put it aside in case, God forbid, he made an error in copying the holy Name.

He attempted to read, but he couldn't concentrate. His thoughts flew and scattered like a flock of birds. He was nagged by the urgency of a revelation. He was filled with the restlessness which wants the end of the world.

Shalom Shepher went to see the rabbi. "Here I am in Jerusalem," he said, "and yet I am still not satisfied. I am full of longing to travel further east."

The rabbi had a glass of tea before him. He stirred it thoughtfully and said: "That is very strange."

"Perhaps," my great-grandfather murmured, "I am the victim of my evil impulse. Perhaps there is no end to a man's desire to travel east."

Shalom of Skidel returned to the study house and began to

read. He read of the hereafter and the world to come. He read of the Messiah and the End of Days. He read how, in the last years before the Apocalypse, the suffering of the people would increase; how Jerusalem would mourn and be brought low, and her beautiful places be laid waste. There would be war and pestilence, and the pious would perish. Sons would insult their fathers and daughters rebel against their mothers. The face of that generation would be like the face of a dog, the hand of the scribe would falter and learning wither away.

He read on, and learned how the earth would writhe in the time of Armageddon: how famine and flood, fire and drought would sweep the world. In one place there would be plenty without contentment; in another there would be poverty without peace. The mountains would shake and the solid ground tremble; the rocks would cry out and heavenly voices be heard.

Then my great-grandfather read of the days of the Messiah: of how the land would be healed and the earth renewed. How loaves would grow in the fields and flagons of wine in the vineyards. Trees would produce fruit daily and garments spring ready woven from the backs of sheep. The sun's light would cure sickness, and miraculous waters would flow from beneath the Temple. The dead would rise from their graves and the lost tribes of Israel return from the four corners of the world.

Shalom Shepher went back to see the rabbi. The rabbi was eating slatko with sugar biscuits. "I think I have found the cause of my restlessness," he said. "I believe we are living in the final days. The Holy One, blessed be He, has called me into His service. He wants me to travel to the ten lost tribes."

The rabbi dipped his biscuit and considered it. "That is an interesting proposition," he said. "If you want, I can send you to Europe. We need a representative to collect charity for Jerusalem's poor."

"Oh, no," Reb Shalom replied. "I have been looking into it, and it's to Babylon that I must go."

He went home and continued his investigations. He searched through histories and travelogues and folktales, legends and diaries and anecdotes. He read of how the tribes were carried away beyond the River Sambatyon, a torrent of sand and stones which roared six days a week and rested on the Sabbath; of how their king was six yards tall and rode a leopard, and lived in a palace of precious stones. He read of Aaron Halevi, who travelled to the tribes in a boat without nails, through a sea which spouted columns of fire and smoke, and who reported the existence of twenty-four kings ruling over twenty-four kingdoms, under one supreme king who possessed a retinue of a hundred and fifty thousand armed men. These rode vicious horses fed on mutton and wine, which had to be bound and muzzled before they could be mounted; the riders' feet had to be tied to the stirrups to prevent them being thrown.

He examined the account of Eldad the Danite, who left his home beyond the rivers of Cush, was shipwrecked and sold into slavery; bought by a Jewish merchant for thirty-two pieces of gold, he was taken to the kingdom of the tribe of Issachar in the mountains of Paran. He read further of Montezinus, who believed the American Indians to be descended from the missing Israelites, and of the Amazonian clans who grew their beards long, practised levirate marriage and spoke a fragmentary Hebrew. The Kareens of Burmah had "a Jewish appearance" and the Hindus of Kashmir "a Jewish cast of face." The Basques, the Spanish, the Franks and the Huns, the Creoles, the Mexicans, the Afghans and the Japanese, all had been identified with the ten lost tribes.

In old chapbooks he discovered the spurious fancies of Micah ben Moses, who claimed to have been given safe passage across the rocky concourse of the Sambatyon. On the other side was a kingdom of green fields and vineyards, mountains and vast wildernesses. The chief city was dominated by a huge synagogue with a dome of multicoloured glass, in which the holy ark and its eternal light faced west towards Zion. In a cedar box he had seen the brown half-perished cloak of the prophet Jeremiah, and in a palace adorned with gold he had held audience with the king himself, seated at the head of a dais reached by invisible steps: only those with sufficient faith could mount the steps to meet him. And the king was a man learned in the Torah, a warrior-scholar with whom he spent many hours discussing the Law.

From the Sephardi community he got permission to examine

ancient manuscripts, title deeds and genealogies from old Baghdad, and travel journals from Mesopotamia. He consulted mythological maps adorned with sea monsters and faded astrological charts. By numerological interpretation of certain biblical verses he sought clues to the location of the tribes, and laid his travel plans accordingly.

He didn't expect he would need a great deal of money, since wherever one went there were Jews, and wherever there were Jews there would be hospitality. But he made the rounds of the community all the same. The pious were impressed, and gave what they could. He also helped himself to funds from Batsheva's hoard, which she kept hidden in a jar behind the salt pot. The theft outraged her when she discovered it, and she stored her money thereafter in a safer place.

He received support, too, from a rich native of Baghdad, who, though Sephardi by custom, had taken a liking to the dawn ritual of the Vatikin. This gentleman had the distinction of possessing two wives, living in separate houses; the elder, whom he preferred, raised the children of the younger. "I have a brother in Baghdad," he told Reb Shalom. "He will give you all the help you need, though I'm sure he doesn't know the whereabouts of our lost brethren." He also handed him a pouch containing three golden napoleons.

My great-grandfather went down to the Street of the Chain, where the Sephardi muker sat on the steps of his courtyard in slippers and turban, smoking a nargileh. The man confessed he had never been to Babylon, but for thirty piastres he would take him as far as Damascus. Shalom Shepher promised him fifteen piastres on the day of departure and fifteen when they reached their destination.

Then he went home and made a bundle of his prayer shawl, phylacteries and psalter. Batsheva saw and asked what he was doing.

"I am going to Babylon to look for the ten lost tribes," he answered. Batsheva immediately flew into a rage.

"At a time like this, you up and leave! And what am I supposed to do, please tell me, while you're gone?"

Reb Shalom paused a moment in his packing. "That is an interesting question," he said. "But you have children, and you also run a profitable business. I'm sure you can keep yourself occupied until my return."

"And what if, God forbid, you don't come back? Am I to sit here, while you lie dead in a ditch somewhere, and live as a grass widow the rest of my days?"

Reb Shalom did not choose to answer this, but fastened his bundle with a furious knot.

Shalom Shepher went to see the rabbi for a third time. The rabbi was eating lokshen kugel with raisins.

"Soon I will leave on my journey to the ten lost tribes," he told him. "But it seems to me I will need letters of recommendation."

The rabbi picked at a raisin which had lodged in his teeth. "That's very true," he said. "I will write you a letter of safe passage." He wiped his fingers, took up his pen and paused. "To whom do you think I should address it?" he asked.

"Perhaps it would be best if you wrote two letters," Shepher said. "One an open letter, and one addressed to the leader of the tribes."

The rabbi agreed that this would be more prudent, and he wrote the two letters, one of which read as follows:

With God's Help, The Holy City, Kislev 5, 5626

> Honoured and beloved brethren, since it became clear to us that the days of dissolution are upon us, and that the days of the Messiah are at hand, we were filled with longing for our scattered brethren, whom the Lord has scattered to the farthest corners of the earth, and we desired much to see the face of our brethren, in whatever place the Lord had scattered them, until such time as He should bring them back, like streams in the Negev and upon the wings of eagles, to the Holy City of Jerusalem. And so did he take it upon himself, our beloved brother, REB SHALOM OF SKIDEL, to undertake this perilous journey, to seek out our lost ones, to lament with them over the glory of Zion which is past, and to rejoice with them over the King Messiah who is coming. And he is a Jew of good character, one learned in Torah and assiduous in the commandments, pursuing peace and loving peace, a man of wisdom and great in knowledge. May he find favour

> in your eyes, that you should welcome him to your kingdom, offer him shelter in your houses, and show lovingkindness to your brother in all manner befitting a fellow Jew. And may the Redeemer come unto Zion, and may Jerusalem be rebuilt speedily in our days. Amen.

Reb Shalom tucked the two letters inside his caftan.

On the seventh day of the month of Kislev he and the muker set off before dawn from the Damascus Gate and took the caravan route to Nablus. In his bundle my great-grandfather carried a bag of dried figs, a jar of cucumbers and a twist of poor quality Syrian tobacco kept moist with a strip of carrot. A straggle of old men and children followed them out; the rabbi blessed the journey with the quotation: "I bore you on eagles' wings, and brought you unto Myself." Then they watched the two mules make their way slowly up the Kidron valley.

From the summit of Mount Scopus Shalom Shepher turned and took his last view of the holy city. Then he set his face towards the east. And it was another two years before he re-entered Jerusalem through St. Stephen's Gate.

Chapter fourteen

Silence in the attic. Only the brief rustle of turning paper, the slow creak of splintered wood. We sat there unspeaking, Uncle Saul and I. Breathing the dust of our ancestors. The warmth of countless summers trapped against our skin. The soul of the house hovered under this roof. When I looked down my hands were black with it.

Only three days ago I had been in England, living a life which seemed simple and uncomplicated but which, I saw now with sudden clarity, was nothing more than a thin ice sheet over a deep abyss. I had closed up my life within a rigid cage; the rituals of youth had been replaced by obsessive routine. From my clean little house I stepped out each day into my spotless car; I carried my papers in a neat briefcase. I was brisk, spinsterly Dr. Shepher to the students who smiled behind their hands when she waxed lyrical about variants; whose face reddened with emotion when she translated:

> How shall we sing the Lord's song
> In a strange land?

who broke down unaccountably, once, at the singing of 'Jerusalem.'

Tidy Dr. Shepher who was aging into dull midlife, who lived alone and marked essays until midnight, who was probably earmarked for redeployment. Who had no past and no secrets, who skated smoothly, primly on the surface.

Now the ice had cracked and I had fallen through, down down to the wreck of the past that languished there: where the death of my childhood and the bodies of my parents lay, lost letters, a prayer-book, a half-buried Sabbath candlestick; scorched family photographs and the ghost of Daniel. Always the ghost of Daniel with his curls floating like seaweed and his sad eyes. And his eternal question: Why didn't you follow me, Shula? Why did you stay behind?

The air in the attic was warm, like underwater, and I could hardly breathe for the history it held. And the questions flooded me, filling up my lungs, quivering vividly before my gaze: Hannah's photograph, my father's face, my mother lying silent in a darkened bedroom; a stranger with sidelocks and familiar eyes; a mysterious Codex. Inhaling deeply I took my last leave of the surface, as with firm fingers I turned the next brittle page.

Chapter fifteen

At first Batsheva hardly recognised him, because he had fallen victim to the disease known as habb-es-sene, which was then prevalent in Syria, and which left large white blotches on the face of the sufferer. Immediately she began to question him, but instead of answering he unrolled from his bundle a golden shawl of Damascus silk. Wrapped inside this was a book of learned sayings for Isaac Raphaelovitch, and a bunch of liquorice for the children; and then my great-grandfather lay down on the bed behind the curtain and fell asleep.

He was exhausted, and thinner than ever. His face, which had changed beyond recognition, was lined and worn. He had the look of one who has crossed deserts and climbed mountains, and returned at last, footsore and unsatisfied, to the point from which he began.

He slept for sixteen hours, and when he awoke he sat in the kitchen and ate a bowl of soup. Little by little the children, timid at first because of his appearance, gathered round him; they soon forgot their shyness, and he began to talk to them about the ten lost tribes.

Had he seen the tribes? Oh, yes, he had seen them. And where were they? Beyond the River Sambatyon. Where was the Sambatyon? Beyond Babylon. And where was Babylon? Naturally, in the east.

Then the children pressed closer, and asked him what he had seen in the land of the tribes. First of all, he said, he had been met by miraculous riders on the banks of the River Sambatyon. These rode flying horses: he was taken up into the air and given safe passage to the other side. On the other side was a vast plain as big as the sea, covered with fields of roses and melons and cucumbers: golden roses and cucumbers the size of trees. They rode for three days through vineyards hung with giant grapes. The dust on the ground was made of powdered silver, and precious jewels lay scattered about like stones.

On the third day they had reached a city of spires and domes and gardens, in the middle of which was a huge palace. Here his hosts welcomed him and washed his feet; he had been given an audience with the king, who spoke perfect Hebrew, was wise and learned, and a descendant of the tribe of Dan. He wore robes of purple silk, and a crown set with sapphires and diamonds. His advisers were all great scholars, and a royal yeshivah lay in the palace grounds. The students were young men of intelligence and great physical prowess, who raced horses named after famous rabbis.

The children begged to know more, and Reb Shalom told them how the tribes lived in peace with one another: how Reuben was brother to Asher and Gad to Naphtali. Their houses were open, without locks or bars, since theft was unheard of and there was no crime. On Sabbaths and holy days a soft light shone from the topmost tower of the palace: the whole city glowed, and no-one had difficulty finding their way to and from the house of prayer. There was nothing ugly there: the privies themselves were like palaces, even the tannery was sweet-smelling, and fear and danger were unknown.

Through the heart of the city there wound a river of pure water, filled with magical speaking fish which could repeat verses from the psalms. It was forbidden to eat these fish, although to do so would bring special knowledge. Living in a far part of the city was an old man who had eaten one. Because of his crime he had been ostracised, but people still went to him in search of truth.

"What did you ask him?" the children wanted to know.

"I asked him when the tribes would return to Zion."

"And what did he answer?"

"He said it would be soon, but not yet."

He had remained in the city for a whole year, studying the customs of the tribes, which were, of course, different from the customs of the rest of the Jews, because for more than two thousand years they had been hidden from the world. And he could have stayed a lot longer, a lifetime even, arguing the differences between them. But his place was not there, and all too soon it was time for him to leave. Once more he must make the perilous crossing of the Sambatyon. Any who crossed it once would be cured of their afflictions, but to cross it twice was to take back all the diseases it had washed away. This explained his disfigurement; and for this very reason his muker had chosen to remain behind.

Before his departure he had picked up a handful of precious jewels and thrust them into his pocket, but on crossing the river these, too, had been turned back into mere stones. And he brought from his pocket a handful of pebbles to show the amazed children, which he had been using on the last part of the journey to tease the vultures by the road.

Then the children begged for more stories, so he told them of the journey he had made into the mountains, where he had crossed a river of silver and one of gold; of the strange delicious fruits which grew wild in the valleys, and the birds of all colours which flew among the trees. The air was so pure it could make the old young again. He had danced beneath waterfalls and bathed in tranquil pools.

Batsheva, who was listening, observed that the land of the tribes sounded so much like paradise it was no wonder they didn't come back to Jerusalem. Perhaps, she remarked, it would be better for us to go to them. Shalom Shepher ignored her and went on talking to the children. In fact, it was only to children that he would talk about the ten lost tribes. His tales grew ever more wondrous and fantastical, ever more magical and elaborate. The tribes became giants, their territory infinite; their king a second Solomon with supernatural powers. Their rabbis rode upon cohorts of winged horses, and their Sabbath worship was led by Elijah himself.

It was a legend in Jerusalem: one of those stories which enters the local folklore and ossifies unquestioned into myth. Even those children who had grown up and learned better would refer to my great-grandfather, long afterwards, as Shalom-Shepher-who-travelled-to-the-ten-lost-tribes.

But sitting on the steps of a courtyard on the Street of the Chain was a certain Sephardi muker, roadworn and travel weary, who smoked a nargileh and told a different tale. Sometimes he claimed that they had journeyed as far as Syria, where my great-grandfather had fallen ill and been taken in by friendly Jews. Sometimes he confessed to having reached Damascus, where Reb Shalom had paid him the balance of his fee and they had gone their separate ways. Sometimes he revealed that the whole time had been passed between the genizah and the bath house in Aleppo, and sometimes he declared that, far from travelling to the tribes, the two of them had spent the entire two years in a narcotic haze, smoking a hookah in some roof garden in Baghdad.

As for my great-grandfather, he sat in the study house, or bent over certain parchments in a corner of the salon, absorbed in his work, oblivious to question and demand. Often he was observed turning the pages of a holy text, scribbling down the hieroglyphs of a calculation.

Meanwhile Batsheva carried on the pickle trade which sustained the family, and Isaac Raphaelovitch continued in his struggle to become learned, until one day he ate a pickled cucumber before it was ready, and was poisoned with botulism. The doctor bled him with cups and purged him with salts, and on the third day he died. Then Batsheva cleared out every still and pickle jar in the house, sold all the equipment to a broker and went into the flour trade instead. She never pickled another cucumber in her life, and carried the secret of the recipe to her grave.

Many in Jerusalem mourned when the pickle business ended at the House of the Hand on Habad Street.

My great-grandfather did not leave Jerusalem again after this date. Exhausted from his great adventure, he remained faithful to the holy city. As the years passed his sight deteriorated, though he never lost the nickname 'Eagle Eyes.' He sat in the corner of the study house, where the children who had grown up and become parents would point him out to their children as 'Shalom-Shepher-who-travelled-to-the-ten-lost-tribes.' It was hard to believe, when for forty years he had not left the city. Sometimes he was seen walking very slowly up the Jaffa Road.

And when the young men who had been children asked him, "How long, Reb Shalom?" he always replied, "Not yet." And when the old men who had grown old with him asked, "How long?" he answered, "Not in our generation." His skin acquired the sheen of yellow parchment, his voice was like the vibration of a cobweb; he took on the appearance of a worn out Torah scroll. He sat in his corner and worked on his calculations to establish the true date of the end of the world.

It is said he came very close to his goal. Within days of his death he was on the verge of discovering it. Perhaps he actually did so, and the date lay hidden somewhere among his papers.

We shall never know. After his death, the little scraps of paper went into a box. The box passed to my grandfather, who transferred it to the attic of the house at Kiriat Shoshan. There it remained for seventy years until we went up and opened it. And then, not being educated in the lore of numerologists, and not understanding what the figures meant, we tossed Reb Shalom's calculations onto a pile and they were burnt, along with the house itself.

Part Two:
Kiriat Shoshan

Chapter one

Moses received the Torah on Sinai, and handed it down to Joshua; Joshua to the elders; the elders to the prophets; the prophets to the men of the Great Assembly.

He wrote the Five Books at dictation, sitting on the mountain, in forty days and forty nights. Like Shakespeare, he never blotted a line. He wrote 'In the beginning.' He wrote of the Flood and after. He recorded, in detail, how he sat on the mountain for forty days and nights, and wrote. And when God dictated the story of his own death, he set it down with streaming eyes.

'And he handed it down to Joshua; Joshua to the elders; the elders to the prophets.' So began an elaborate game of Hebrew Chinese whispers. Copies were made, and copies of the copies. Versions written down from memory and versions caught imperfectly by ear. Errors crept in. Discrepancies multiplied. Eventually we must imagine our religious leaders chasing a flock of rogue texts like butterflies over the hills of the Promised Land, each of them claiming to be more or less the word of God.

Perhaps it happened differently. Perhaps it did not happen in this way at all. Instead a chain of stories, like bright beads, danced around the campfires of the ancient Hebrews; they ran from mouth to mouth and camp to camp; were modified, adjusted, plagiarised; ultimately they were written down and from a tangle of traditions one text was shuffled into order: that grand corpus of legends, histories and laws we call the Pentateuch.

How was the word of God to be protected? A master scroll was kept in the Temple precincts, to which all copies were to be compared. But this in itself was the copy of a copy of a copy. There were in fact three books of the Torah in the Temple court, and all three contained conflicting readings: the Codex Meon, the Codex Zaatutay, and the Codex Hi, named after their most glaring inconsistencies. There was also the Severus Codex, taken from the Temple by Vespasian in the year 70 and placed in the Severus Synagogue in Rome. Both codex and synagogue have long since vanished, but a list of thirty-two variants survives in the Paris National Library, including the reading of Genesis 1:31: "And behold, death was a good thing."

Ultimately it was the Masoretes, those scholarly pedantic families of Ben Naphtali and Ben Asher, who, sitting on the shores of the Galilee in the breeze which blew through the date palms, aligned and analysed, annotated and notated, scrutinised and purified the text of the Hebrew Bible. And even they could not produce an authoritative copy, the Ben Asher being considered somewhat superior to the Ben Naphtali.

They did not eliminate the variants. Instead they inserted the majority reading, and noted the alternatives on the side. Where there were obvious errors they did not alter them. The errors too were sacred, dictated from the mouth of God. God Himself, it was said, had specified the nature and number of these seeming errors.

Their work was imbued with an intense pedantry, and necessarily so. For the Torah is not only a verbal but a mathematical text: a giant codebook in which all the secrets of the universe are held. Acrostics and incantations, puzzles and prophecies. My forbears, too, were among those who buried themselves, against the strictures of the more level-headed rabbis, in calculations and numerology, seeking the passages which foretold the date of the Messiah's coming. So that it is not without reason that the sages warn: Change a single letter, and you destroy the world.

The oldest surviving Masoretic text is the St. Petersburg Codex, dated 916, a work of phenomenal scholarship and a labour of love. Yet the most perfect version is said to have been the crowning achievement of the family Ben Asher, completed in the year 900 and kept in Jerusalem, carried from there to Cairo by the Seljuks, and from Cairo to the synagogue at Aleppo, where for centuries it was protected from prying eyes until, in 1947, the synagogue was burnt to the ground and the codex, apart from a few fragments, was lost forever.

No record survives of those other Pentateuchs which bloomed once over the face of the desert like so many spring flowers and then withered away: the underground texts, the unacknowledged ones, the local, heretic and sectarian ones. Those inspired by a God Who spoke differently, perhaps, to a Moses who recorded other words, but still, to those who heard them, divinely given. Like sacred chaff they have long since been winnowed off, to leave only the heavy grain of the official version. The odd one survived, perhaps, hugged under the shirts of Solomon's sailors when they were shipwrecked on the shores of distant lands, or later, clutched in the hands of exiles carried away by the Assyrians: those ten lost tribes of Israel who were swept beyond the Euphrates and then disappeared for ever.

And if there really were such texts, perhaps they too were copied and handed down, dictated from generation to generation, in those isolated communities of the Caucasus and remote regions of Africa where the legendary tribes were scattered. So that one day a traveller from the outside world might come, and discovering a Torah unlike any he had ever seen before, bear it back secretly to Jerusalem....

Meanwhile the process continued and gathered pace. In 1525 the Bomberg Bible was published, the first printed edition of the Hebrew Scriptures, and from that time, by default, the standard one. Scholars made use of it for their investigations and scribes as a reference when they wrote their scrolls. A hundred and thirty years later Baruch Spinoza raised his head from the text and denied the Mosaic authorship of the Torah. There were inconsistencies, he said, and contradictions. In one passage the Flood lasts forty days; in another for a hundred and fifty. In one account Noah sends forth a dove, in another he sends forth a raven. And so it was, said the rabbis, and so it must always be; for none may alter the sacred revelation. They excommunicated him.

Nineteenth century scholars, men of faith themselves, applied the principles of science and made brave forays into the jungle of biblical exegesis and philology, variants, duplications and omissions, filling those dark green volumes—does anybody read them now?—the International Critical Commentary, in which psalms were reduced to a patchwork of stolen phrases and histories to nothing more than formulae, and almost everything was a gloss, an error or an interpolation from a later age. They became adept at picking the biblical verses to pieces, until what had seemed simple became complex and what had been complex became an insoluble tangle, and yet through all this their faith survived, for they regarded the Lord God as a compositor of supreme brilliance Who drew together the mass of texts at His disposal just as He would draw in the threads of chaotic history at the last trumpet. And the rabbis themselves believe that at the End of Days Elijah will return and sort out all the textual difficulties.

The Torah existed for nine hundred and forty-seven generations before the world's creation. And when God created the world (which was not His first: He had already made and discarded seven or more) He used the Torah as His guide and blueprint. For an imperfect and cryptic world, an imperfect and cryptic Torah is a perfect blueprint.

And that in turn recalls another legend: before the Creation, the Torah was nothing more than a heap of letters which could have been arranged in any order. When Adam sinned, they rose and arranged themselves in the order we know today. When the Messiah comes, they will unravel themselves like knitting and create a new Torah, a new heaven and a new earth.

Chapter two

Sometimes it seems to me that my family history is like this: a mass of conflated texts and contradictory traditions. An obscure document full of holes. A ramshackle narrative, stuffed with trivia and repetition, stitched together with hearsay and anecdote and perhaps lies.

Which is why, if I am to call this a history of the house of Shepher, I feel that I should qualify the title: call it not a history simply, but a mythical history.

For generations my family were scribes and correctors of scrolls. They spent their days bent over the desk, examining the letters of holy writ, or writing them carefully with a reed pen. They were close workers, keen-sighted and meticulous. Particular and perfectionist. They had to be. The integrity of the Torah depended on their efforts. If they changed one letter, they destroyed the world.

It is hard to know why they were like that. Whether they were pedants because they were scribes or scribes because they were pedants. Perhaps, after all, it was a little of both. So that even today we have our secular pedants, our own heretic perfectionists.

Where did we first come from? If the Bible is an authority

we are the children of Adam and Eve, whose creative thinking got them cast out of Eden, and who bear an uncanny resemblance to later Shephers in their record of theft, domestic discord, mutual blame-laying and bad luck.

Where did we really come from? According to the archaeologists, we are the descendants of warlike tribes who made life uncomfortable for the Egyptian empire back in the third millennium B.C. A host of roving brigands, rebels, mercenaries, nomads and sometime farmers who stirred up trouble all over the Ancient Near East. It's also said that when the Israelites left Egypt we were only a few thousand, swelled by the numbers of other escaped slaves and destitutes and malcontents, all joining their aspirations to ours.

What role my ancestors played in these great events I can't be sure, though I feel fairly certain it wasn't a prominent one. Most likely they formed part of that chorus of complainers who drove poor Moses to strike the rock instead of speaking to it at the waters of Meribah, a crime for which, we are told, he was refused entry to the Promised Land.

My ancestors, however, entered the Promised Land. And since they were members of the tribe of Judah they settled in that area between Hebron and the plain, in the hills surrounding the future Jerusalem.

We were farmers milking our herds and tying our vines in the Judean hills. And at this time, if not at any other, we should have been content. But there is this one boy, this Hilkiyah or Shivtiyah or Jeroboam son of Zimriyah, who is never happy trailing the goats down the valley of the Kidron or sitting out with the harvesters under the stars. When he looks at the hills he thinks of further horizons and when he looks at the stars he feels his heart expand, as if there must be something more he could do in life, some other possibility than this. He envies his sister, who makes up songs at the well and is clever with words while all he seems to have is this vague, painful, undirected ambition.

What becomes of our young Izriyah? Poor boy, there is little doubt about it: he comes to grief. It isn't his destiny to be one of the prophets, to make his mark in politics or to see the world. He farms in the valley of the Brook Kidron; he lives an exemplary life, he has children; he never entirely quells the nagging sense of having missed his path. His bones are dust, his longings are dust, all that remains of him is dust. He is one of us.

So much for the prehistory of the Shephers. But we do not remain farmers. Long after the Assyrians have swept the ten tribes of the north into oblivion, after the Babylonians have destroyed the Temple and carried us away; after we have sat weeping by the rivers of Babylon; when the Persian king, Cyrus, has allowed us to return: there we are in Jerusalem, serving as court scribes under Ezra, as religious officers under Nehemiah. In the fifth century before Christianity, we proto-Shephers have found out our affinity with the Word. We can pick nits, we can perfect text. We can analyse line after line of the square Hebrew script which is now used in preference to the old Phoenician style. We have subsumed our troublesome ambitions in holy white-collar work, and, though we were fine farmers, we are better bureaucrats.

Then as now we had our rogue characters, those who cared more for business than for books. We had our traders who travelled down into Egypt and as far as Carthage, settling, some of them, in Cyrenaica, where they were massacred by the Romans; and we had an enclave in Alexandria. Since the Babylonian exile we had even prospered on the banks of the Tigris, indeed, that branch of the family never returned, and our descendants live there still; though not, of course, under the name of Shepher.

After the sack of Jerusalem we were taken to Rome and Tarsus, where some of us converted to Christianity and were lost for ever. But those who would one day be Shephers found themselves in Constantinople, and from Constantinople we migrated northwards into the kingdom of the Khazars. There we became traders in fur and slaves, travelling as far east as China, where one of us fell in love and settled; and their offspring practised Judaism for another five hundred years before the rituals were forgotten.

Benjamin of Sarkel married Michla, a Khazarian Jewish convert with the voice of a nightingale. Of all her nine children only one inherited her voice and the rest croaked like frogs. Thereafter, one or two in every generation of Shephers sings like a seraph. The rest of us are tone-deaf, a phenomenon we have never been able to explain.

Upon the destruction of the Khazar kingdom we fled north into Russia, and from there west into Lithuania, and settled around Grodno. Three hundred years later the Jewish scholars of Bavaria were driven east by persecution; in 1357 Rivka, the daughter of a Bamberg rabbi, married Uziel the son of Isaac a cloth merchant, and the scholarly and trading sides of the family were linked for ever.

Thereafter we find in the mythical annals Simeon, a trader in amulets and herbal medicines; Tirzah, author of Devotional Songs for Girls and Women; Arie Leib who ran away after the false messiah, Shabbatei Zvi; and Shlomo of Skidel, also known as the Pedantic, who composed a learned treatise of one hundred and ninety-seven pages on a single verse of the Torah.

Nor must we forget to mention Zvi Hirsch, hanged for horse-rustling in the eighteenth century. It's hard to believe, perhaps, but even a family of talmudists must have its criminals.

Yet the most remarkable was perhaps our forbear, Reb Isaac of Skidel, of whom it is said that the intensity of his thoughts during study caused the birds that flew over him to be instantly consumed by fire.

Wherever we scattered we became numerous, partly through natural fecundity, partly through obedience to the rabbinical dictum which says 'A childless person is accounted dead.' Because of the tendency of Shepher children to survive in large numbers, the parents had to supplement their income by motley means: by taking in washing, for example, or schoolteaching; as flour-dealers and dealers in small wares; as barbers and watchmakers; as sellers of sewing machines and even, in one case, as a digger of graves.

There is nobody rich in our family. A distant cousin, in one of the branches we are not speaking to, was said to have married a millionaire; but this is probably a bitter exaggeration. No Shepher ever thrived in a business venture, or made a scoop on the property market, or sold at a profit, or won a lottery. On the other hand, we have countless tales to tell of missed opportunity, bungled deals and disaster. But for these we should have been richer than the Rothschilds by now.

Most of us agree on our mutual poverty. On the subject of the Shepher family appearance there is fierce debate. Some deny that there is any such thing as a Shepher 'look.' Others claim evidence of a Shepher nose and a Shepher mouth, even a Shepher walk. I myself would be the last to deny the existence of a particular kind of Shepher laughter. Some of us complain of the curse of having Shepher teeth, which grow crookedly and rot; modern dentistry has spared me that inheritance, but no cure has yet been found for the family digestive problems. Since our transplantation to the East we have bloomed with recurrent skin cancers. But on the whole we suffer from chronic minor conditions, and live long lives; and we have a noble tradition in hypochondria. I read once of Charcot's 'Juif Errant' who, poverty-stricken and destitute, nevertheless struggled from Poland to Paris to consult a famous physician about his imaginary ailment. That man's name was indubitably Shepher.

But really, the question of the family characteristics will never be resolved, since for every example there is always an exception; on the other hand when you meet a Shepher you know you have met a Shepher. It's something indefinable, and speaking for myself, it makes my armpits sweat. It also fills me with a terrible happiness. Moreover you wouldn't believe the places where it can happen. My cousin Itai met one by the name of Pedro, backpacking in the Himalayas; he wore a crucifix but his ancestors were Jewish. I attended a lecture once with my heart shaking because the professor was so clearly one of us. A stranger called Shepher rang my brother up a number of years back, but my brother didn't want to know: the voice down the telephone was too much like my father's. Shepher lookalikes have been spotted as far apart as Reykjavik and Delhi, Naples and Shanghai. It's something in the face, they say; it's something in the eyes. It's the laugh or the gestures; it's nonsense. It's something and nothing. I'm no anthropologist, but I think it would be fair to say that there are Shephers everywhere.

Temperamentally we are a race of gentle depressives and

resigned insomniacs, a tribe of early risers who face the world sober and find it grim; one may so understand the peculiarity of the Shepher laugh. We are natural lawyers. We have our share of burnt-out artists and defeated dreamers. But centuries of copying have made us purists, lovers of small print, slaves and masters of the art of repetition.

At any rate, the strength of the family character may be measured thus: we absorb our incomers. The family ingests all foreign matter, transmutes it, and produces from it a new generation of Shephers. Even those who keep their own names become Shephers by default.

As for the name, we only acquired it recently. Until the modern age Jews in the East were referred to by their town of origin, as the child of somebody or according to the work they did. I don't know how we acquired the title Shepher, which means beauty, and whether it refers to the physical or the spiritual I can't say. But it found favour with us, and stuck for good once we had reached Jerusalem, where the use of a surname made postal deliveries less confusing.

We are a family of fights and conflicts. I cannot begin to count the quarrels which have filled our history and which are still going on, the feuds, wrangles, tiffs and rows, the silences and vendettas, the minor snubs and major confrontations which scar our clan gatherings and make the family what it is: terrible, inescapable. Suffice it to say that at any given moment someone is not speaking to someone else; a third is trying to make peace between them and a fourth is waiting for an apology. Even the most pacifist among us is drawn into the vortex of quarrels we did not cause.

There is now, living in the religious quarter of Mea Shearim, a whole branch of the clan of Shepher to whom nobody has spoken for over eighty years. The reason for this is simple and obvious enough. They are extremists, members of the ultra-orthodox sect of the Neturei Karta, who believe there should be no Jewish state until the coming of the Messiah. Eighty years ago, when my grandfather was a young Zionist, they turned their backs on him as an apostate, and the rift has never healed.

My great-grandfather was the only member of his immediate family to reach the Land of Israel. Cousin Hayman, a grand-nephew on his sister's side, arrived in Palestine in 1920 with a pioneering group. Thirty years later, disillusioned with the Jewish state, he returned to the Soviet Union to live the life of a true Communist. A few of us left Lithuania for America at the turn of the century; hence the Shepher chain of garages in, I think, the Midwest, and the shortlived Shepher Language School in Boston. The rest intended to leave but put it off and put it off until it was too late; not even their names are now remembered.

There is nobody famous in my family. We are lawyers and doctors, teachers and opticians. A cousin of mine was recommended for the President's Prize; but, as my Aunt Shoshanah said, no-one ever remembers a runner-up. My grandfather was well-loved, and when he died it was suggested they name a street in Jerusalem after him. In the Land of Israel this is the surest mark of fame. The municipality refused, however. They named the street after a scientist instead. Sliced by a main road, stopped up at one end by a bollard, no nameplate was ever erected, nor does the street in question appear on any map.

That should have been the Shepher luck.

Chapter three

Here I was in the garden where I used to play, back in the family after all these years.

Strange how I felt the characteristics growing, the features re-emerging on my own face. Like rocks revealed by a retreating tide, I saw them again in the mirror: my Shepher eyes, my Shepher nose, my Shepher mouth.

I couldn't speak to Saul without re-hearing, like a tormenting echo, my Shepher voice.

My instinct had struggled against it, this co-option into a type, into a group. Like everyone else I had wanted to be unique. Was that why I so rarely visited my brother Reuben? I knew that it bothered him too, that he didn't like it. Sitting facing each other across his dinner table, we laughed in the same way, caught each other out in the same gestures.

For twenty years I had floated free of moorings, proudly creating myself in my own image. Now here I was back in the family house: I looked in the mirror and I saw a Shepher.

All that morning I had crouched in the airless attic, turning over documents until my hands were black with dust and my head spun. By mid-afternoon I had to get out of the house. I caught the first bus downtown and no sooner had I arrived than the heavens opened. I got off halfway along the Jaffa Road. It was narrow, shabby and colonial as I remembered it, choked with traffic as it had always been, and great sheets of water had collected at the street corners. Jerusalem was as melancholy as ever. The shops had changed but the atmosphere had not. No number of malls could erase it. On my way through Mea Shearim I almost ran head first into a talmudic student hurrying out of the yeshiva, his streimel covered by a plastic bag; he darted off without apology, leaving behind a whiff of starch and sweat. I splashed through the streaming streets, glancing into windows and open doorways, glimpsing brief pictures of religious life: a headscarfed woman, a group of sidelocked children, a study-house ablaze with brilliant lights. I wondered what they would think if they knew the things I knew, if they realised that I too had religious knowledge. Did they feel the same longings, experience the same hunger, did they ever doubt their lives, did they ask questions?

I couldn't find my bus, and walked most of the route back to Kiriat Shoshan, along busy main roads not meant for pedestrians, hooted at by angry and impatient traffic. My clothes were soaked, but even when I got back to the house I was still restless; I went on wandering under the gathering street-lights until dusk thickened and I was prevented by my own tiredness and the falling night. As I slipped indoors I thought I saw someone lingering under cover of the oleander. But when I looked from the window all was still and quiet, nobody was in sight, so I must have been mistaken.

Chapter four

As children we spent the summers at my grandfather's house, in Jerusalem, in Kiriat Shoshan. It was an old bungalow on the corner of a square bordered with pepper trees, in a garden of cacti and succulents beside the path which had once led down to the village of Deir Yassin.

The square was quiet and the air pungent with the scent of the pepper trees, and we played outside in the afternoons. Behind the house was a large patch of waste ground which through some miscalculation or delay had never been put to use. It was the original rough flank of a Judean hill, bristling with huge white rocks and cloaked in brittle thorns as in a kind of natural barbed wire. Walking there in open sandals was perilous, but the place was alive with stick insects, lizards and beetles, strange giant ladybirds and colonies of ants to watch by the hour, milkweed with pendulous green pods which jumped when brushed with a stick, and rare amethyst-coloured passion flowers clinging to the rocks. These plucked, petals removed to reveal the stamen, tasted better than honey.

My grandfather built the house at Kiriat Shoshan in 1927, and it was to stand for nearly seventy years. He helped to lay the foundations and roofed it himself with red French tiles. There was a cistern for rainwater under the kitchen floor, and one room possessed a sliding roof so my grandfather could sleep under the stars during the Feast of Tabernacles: it was the largest tabernacle in Kiriat Shoshan. My father planted a row of cypresses down one side of the house, and later a pepper tree seeded itself in front and threw its web of shadows onto the verandah.

The house was a stone box, cool in summer and cold in winter. There were gloomy high-ceilinged bedrooms and a bathroom with a cold stone floor. There was a black-and-white tiled salon containing the large oak table used on sabbaths and festivals, a rocking chair and cushion-strewn divans, family photographs and various gaudy tropical and Parisian scenes. From here a pair of French windows opened onto the verandah, whose walls an unknown artist had covered with scenes of river and hill, valley and cypress grove.

The district of Kiriat Shoshan was originally a satellite of Jerusalem. Half a mile of rocky ground divided it from the city. My grandfather was one of the founders. It was known at first as Kiriat HaRopheh, or the Doctor's District, in honour of a wealthy benefactor who never succeeded in living there. His half-completed villa surrounded by briars and rotting timbers was referred to for years locally as 'the doctor's house.' The name Kiriat Shoshan means district of lilies, or lilytown or roseland, but as far as I know there were never any roses there. It was an area of bare scrub dotted with a few junipers where the fellaheen grazed their sheep. Perhaps the settlers named it in expectation of gardens.

My grandfather borrowed money to build the house at Kiriat Shoshan. He took out a loan for the land and a loan for the French tiles. Later he purchased on credit to make improvements. He borrowed for his daughters' weddings and to send his sons abroad.

My grandfather was a great worker and a great worrier. Harnessed to his days as days are harnessed to the sun, the burden of the uncompleted task never left his shoulders. Before he knew where he was it seemed to him he had borrowed more money than he could repay in one lifetime, and at night, instead of sleeping, he lay awake turning impossible numbers over in his head.

For more than twenty years he lived like that. Like a man with his teeth gritted. Like a man with a mountain on his back. But then one day my grandfather lost his nerve. He woke up one morning and would have no more of it.

He did not discuss the matter with his family. He never revealed his intentions to his wife. He met with a lawyer by the name of Rosenblatt. Rosenblatt found him a buyer, sold the house and land and paid off all his debts. Not long after, rampant inflation struck the Promised Land: the value of the loans went down, the value of the property shot up, and my grandfather, if he had only waited, would have found himself sitting on half a million.

And yet he received a reasonable price. When he had cleared his debts there was even a sum left over. And this is what he did with the money: against the advice of Rosenblatt he bought half a dozen plots of land, each no bigger than a tennis court. Three were restricted by law to agricultural use. One was appropriated for a government road scheme. Another disappeared beneath a forestry project. Not one of them had any commercial value. They were known in the family as the Territories, and constituted my grandfather's main legacy to his children.

"If only he had bought something down in Beit HaKerem," Uncle Saul lamented, "it would be worth millions by now." Instead my grandfather felt moved to buy fragments of the Land of Israel which he had taken pity on. For twenty years the six symbolic jars of soil sat on the windowsill in the big tabernacle, until they were finally banished to the attic: six handfuls of the soil of the Land of Israel; proof positive of ownership.

The owner was now the tenant of the house at Kiriat Shoshan. My grandparents continued to live there for a peppercorn rent; later this privilege was extended to my aunt Batsheva. The landlord lived at a distance, and had bought the property solely as an investment, which was destined one day to mature well. He was referred to only as the Ballabessel, or in other words: the Master of the House.

Meanwhile, in case he ever visited Jerusalem, he asked that a guest room should be set aside. My grandmother obliged, and earmarked a large room to the right of the salon. It was named for its owner: the ballabessel for the Ballabessel. At first my aunt used to dust there once a week, then once a month; eventually it was abandoned completely. The door remained locked and the shutters closed, and the room waited in darkness for the bridegroom who never came.

It was this door, coated and ridged now with the dust of years, which was a source of fascination to me on my summer visits to Kiriat Shoshan. For it seemed that behind it lay not just one room but many: a whole houseful of undiscovered chambers. I thought that the Ballabessel lived there in permanent darkness, like a kind of troglodyte; and placing my ear to the wall, I imagined I could hear him moving ponderously on the other side. I lay in wait for him but never caught a glimpse. Clambering round the back, I tried in vain to peer between the peeling shutters, but at that side of the house the ground sank into a deep pit filled with mutant rocks and thorns and discarded rusty metal, the traces of earthworks from when the place was built; I could not reach the secret window.

By this time Kiriat Shoshan was part of the municipality of Jerusalem. A six-lane highway sliced between it and the city. Offices had been erected on the site of the doctor's house, and my grandfather's bungalow was the last survivor in a growing forest of apartment blocks.

It was an anomaly, a fragment of history left behind: too ramshackle to be attractive, too recent to be of interest. Those who loved it had neglected it. They refused to spend money on a property which was not theirs. So the walls remained unpainted, the wiring primitive; the black-and-white tiles in the salon cracked and were not replaced. The shutters drooped, the iron gate turned rusty on its hinges. Before long the place was filled with that foreknowledge of its own death which some houses seem to have, and which resists all attempts at renewal.

While I was growing up we visited, on average, every other year. We would arrive in July and languish there through August, trailing back in early September through a Europe sere and exhausted from the long hot summer, returning home on the first cold eddies of autumn. The England we left behind had been green and lush, and we would return to find it packed up and littery like a beach after a bank holiday.

We had missed everything, and the time in between was slow like molasses, over in a moment like some golden unrecoverable dream.

We sat in the house, my brother Reuben and I, through endless afternoons which half-killed us with boredom, while the adults slept in gauzy, darkened rooms and every sound we made was magnified like a crime; when, being seven years older than I, he was far more skilled in the arts of indifference and together we played out our whole repertoire of torment and ignoring, quarrelling in whispers, quashing the cries of pain brought on by Chinese burns, smothering our laughter as we ran outside, heaving, into the violent sunshine. It was here, in the sweaty silence of the afternoon, that my brother, all of a sudden a young man, told me calmly how he longed for the death of my father; here in the shade of the cypresses that childhood ended.

The house was full of the ghost of my grandfather, who died at the time of my birth and whom I had never seen, but whose exhausted wraith travelled from room to room, sucking the life from its weary inhabitants; settling over my mother's motionless form where she lay, breathing sadness, under the tomblike weight of her great headache. He waited, hunched, among the stinking mops and brushes in the back corridor, and shuffled, perhaps, behind the door of the ballabessel, along with snakes and cockroaches and reproaches, death and debt and bad business decisions, all the then nameless fears which lurked in the depths of my awareness. My Aunt Shoshanah sat at the kitchen table, narrowly watched me reading and declared: "We Shephers. We all like books, wear glasses and become teachers."

My father said: "Shula is going to be a singer."

But the years passed and my father died; I continued to like books, acquired glasses and became a teacher. My voice died in my throat and I ceased to sing. The family fate embraced me without my volition.

Now, in these last days, the door of the ballabessel stood wide open. Its shutters were torn off; plain daylight flooded it. Soon its walls would be smashed, its ceiling would be ripped open. Its secrets would fly off to the world's four corners. I stood in its empty shell and realised it had no secrets, that the fears it had held were as insubstantial as ghosts: the figments of a girlish imagination.

Chapter five

"Nu—so tell me, Shula. Are you still singing?"

I regarded the dry cake on the plate before me: two large slabs, chocolate and lemon, and a cup of pale weak tea. Next to that, a thimbleful of dry sherry.

"No. I'm not singing any more."

Next to the sherry, a dish of sliced melon, a heap of strudel, a glass bowl of pistachio nuts. Uncle Cobby peeled a pistachio with shaking fingers. He had aged greatly since I had last seen him. He was an old man. His body was shrunken, stooped; the hair which had once been grey was now silver-white. When I embraced him I felt the bones of his back, his very skeleton.

"A pity." Aunt Fania appeared from the kitchen like a conjuror with a bunch of grapes. "We always thought you would be a famous singer."

I inadvertently gulped the sherry, and winced. Perhaps it was not sherry. Perhaps it was sweet dessert wine which had gone off. "My voice was too soft," I explained. "I didn't have the stamina."

"Nonsense!" Fania and Cobby declared in unison.

Here I was once more in their crumbling flat, in this western suburb of Jerusalem where they had lived for as long as I could remember and where their name had faded next to the button of the intercom. I had mounted the dark, stone-smelling steps with a strange sense of having been flung back through time into my earliest childhood. The rusted iron rail under my hand, the brown half-tiled wall with its red security light on every landing, were so familiar, so long-forgotten, it was as though I had entered a recurring dream. Only the figure which passed me on the stairs, the rustle of his caftan, the swift sweep of his eyes, the redolence of musk and sandalwood he left behind, belonged to a more immediate and puzzling present.

It was our friend from the square at Kiriat Shoshan, our lurking house-watcher: complete with sidelocks and fedora and wearing an expression of disappointed self-absorption. His gaze met mine, we recognised each other; he nodded at me, brushed by and went off, swirling his coat, downstairs. I was left standing in astonishment as Uncle Cobby greeted me.

"Who was that?"

"Oh, him! What did he say his name was? Something Gibreel. Staying somewhere in Mea Shearim." My uncle peered dismissively down the stairwell. "Come to see the Codex, like all the others."

I glanced down too, but had lost sight of him; the next moment I was pulled into my uncle's tight embrace.

Now I sat on the brown couch under the painting of old Jerusalem which had been theirs for as long as I could remember: a romantic image in golds and pinks and blues. The couch, still covered in its original shipping plastic, caused thin rivulets of sweat to run down behind my legs.

"So," Cobby leant over confidentially, "tell me about your love life."

He placed a hand on my knee; I placed my hand on his. The skin was clammy, liver-spotted. "I have no love life. You know there's no room for anybody in my heart but you."

My uncle's arm trembled as he squeezed my knee. He had been a strong man when I last saw him. Now, in his old age, he sat in his high apartment and listened to the radio, ate lunch like a schoolboy at the kitchen table and lay down dutifully in the afternoons. Each morning he worked at the handwritten history of his firm which the managing director had asked him to compose, unaware perhaps that it was only a ruse to keep him happy in a retirement he had never wanted.

"We have cable now," he confided, with the air of a man who has achieved something in life. Though I had returned like the prodigal niece after twenty years, he couldn't miss an instalment of the American soap opera he followed daily, and while Fania prepared dinner we watched together.

"You were always a good girl, Shula." He nudged my shoulder.

"Yes, I suppose I was."

"Your mother and father would be proud to see you. Such a woman! Such hair." He handled my long locks. "It's sad about Reuben. What went wrong with the boy, I wonder?"

"Goody Two Shoes must have a Black Sheep."

He didn't reply. He breathed into my ear: "You know, I still hope to see you have a family."

"Cobby," I reminded him, "I'm not even married."

"All the same. A person should have children."

"Cobby," I told him, "I'm nearly forty years old."

"Forty! You're not forty." He drew back in astonishment and examined my face. "I can hardly believe it. Little Shula. Forty!"

Later, in the chaos of the study, I sat on his cheap office chair amid heaps of lever arch files and legal documents while he tested my blood pressure. The bandage felt strange, wrapped tightly around my arm. I was suddenly afraid of what he might discover.

"This Codex Saul found," I said. "Is it important?"

"Who told you Saul found it? I found it myself." He pumped a few more times and checked the gauge. "It could be quite old. You can't be too careful with your blood pressure. Watch the salt."

"Where did it come from?"

Cobby removed the bandage. "Who can say? My friend Shloime at the Institute is taking a look. You've nothing to worry about. Don't eat too many bananas. They're bad for the constipation."

"I don't even like bananas."

He folded up the gauge and stowed it away. "Already my cousin, Sara Malkah, is phoning me up. Where there's money there's trouble. What can you do?"

"That man you were saying goodbye to when I arrived—"

"That *frummer*—that religious?"

I nodded. "He's been hanging around the house."

Cobby shrugged. "So what? He wants to see it. They all want to see it. Every day they come here—all the *frummers.* Sometimes I let them see it. Sometimes not."

"Do you suppose I could see it?"

"What for? You're really interested in such things?"

I smiled at him in amazement. "Cobby. I'm a senior lecturer in biblical studies. What do you mean? Of course I'm interested."

He grimaced. "Well then, I don't see why not. But it isn't here," he added. "My friend Shloime has it at the Institute. I'll have to ask him for you. We're being selective, you know, as to who we'll allow."

He winked and departed; and solitary I sighed, resigned to the knowledge of my lamentable lack of lustre in the academic universe. Once more I examined the items on the crowded shelves: pharmaceutical freebies, framed photographs of grandchildren already faded; a silver bonbon dish embossed with the emblems of the twelve tribes of Israel, a wedding present to my uncle Ben Zion and returned upon his death. There were books, too, that I remembered from childhood: *The Life of Madame Curie*, *Inorganic Chemistry*, the old grey-backed copy of *Leninism* by Stalin, whose opening sentences Reuben and I once memorised to impress our friends:

> Leninism is the Marxism of the
> epoch of Imperialism and the
> Proletarian Revolution in general.
> Is this definition correct?
> I think so.

Strange, I thought to myself, how a book sleeps, and then springs to life out of the slumber of its great irrelevance. Like those pieces of evidence I had been carrying down, fragment by fragment, out of the attic archive these past two days: lost letters, old copybooks, my grandfather's war diary; the whole history of my family, suddenly alive and seizing me, after all these years of ignorance and indifference.

Fania entered with a pile of bedding. We opened out the divan; she spread the sheets with the agility of a much younger woman.

Though nearly ninety, she still wore her hair red, plucked her eyebrows and received weekly visits from her manicurist. She wore her best shoes to the Supersol. An inveterate Viennese, she had lived her entire adult life on a thin veneer, a linden tree transplanted to the poor soil of the desert, pretending to itself that its roots are in the Herrengasse.

"You look like your mother," she told me. "Your mother when she first came here looked like a film star in that white dress."

"She put on weight later."

"Later, later. Later everybody puts on weight."

Left with this knowledge I changed into my night things; cleaned my teeth in the tiny damp bathroom with its standard issue medicine cabinet carrying a red Star of David. There was a smell of mildew and washing powder, white tiles and a bath with support handles. Laundry hung from a small balcony with screen windows. I looked down. It was a long fall for a pair of pantyhose.

Brushing my hair, I examined my face in the mirror. They said I looked like my mother, but I couldn't see it. Or perhaps I didn't want to see it, preferring to think, if I must, that in most ways I took after him.

I had his colouring and his eyes. I was not dark. My hair was light gold, like his, my eyes blue; I had dry pale lips which split open in winter.

The line of my jaw was hers. I had to acknowledge that. I disliked the line of my jaw, which was too heavy.

I didn't want to believe I resembled either of them. It was my opinion that I looked English.

Uncle Cobby had said: "Of course you look English. You've lived your whole life in England. If you had been born here," Uncle Cobby said with authority, "you would look like us."

I gazed at myself in the mirror and wondered how it could be, that by a mere accident of geography I could look so different. I wanted to ask Cobby, What is it then? Is it the weather? The milk? The military service?

I folded my arms and leant out over the city. It was a mild night; far lights twinkled, white and blue and yellow. From the flat opposite came music; in the distance I could hear a siren wail. The air smelt of pavement dust and petrol and something else familiar and indefinable: the pure breath of the desert.

The past rose up like something tastable. I was filled with the deep strangeness of being here.

Chapter six

My great-grandfather, as we have heard, was a corrector of scrolls and later a great fanatic. My grandfather was a Zionist. What sort of a Zionist? "A real Zionist," according to his obituary. What this means exactly I am not sure. The author of the obituary does not explain it. Let's leave definitions aside, and state merely that my grandfather was a Zionist.

He was a modest man. Too modest, perhaps, for he is now almost completely forgotten, except by some few scholars digging through the archives at the Ben Or Institute, or by those who attend the small synagogue in Jerusalem which still bears his name. He was a passionate grammarian, and left at his death some eight hundred pages of linguistic analysis in manuscript, as well as thousands of other papers and letters which no-one has so far bothered to collate. During his lifetime he published three books of Hebrew grammar for use in schools; at the time of his death he was working on a detailed study of the Hebrew verb 'to be.'

My grandmother was a woman of cast iron opinions, rather to the right in her politics, and formidable in debate. They had seven children, none of whom found satisfaction in their lives. Four of them married and had children. One of them went to America and never came back, but that is hardly a remarkable thing for a Jew to do. Another went to England and married there and had children and never came back, although he intended to year after year and put it off and put it off until it was too late and he died, an exile and a stateless person, and was shipped back home to be buried.

My grandfather was a moderate and a mild-mannered man. He was a follower of Rav Kook, who said a very beautiful thing: he said that the Temple had been destroyed because of groundless hatred, and that it would only be rebuilt on a foundation of groundless love.

As a boy he slept with a picture of Theodor Herzl beneath his pillow and a newspaper cutting about the first Zionist conference in Basle. He caught a glimpse of the great leader once, with full beard and the face of a visionary, posing for a photograph outside his lodgings on the Mamillah Road.

Much later he would read how, on that visit, Herzl had taken care not to ride a donkey through the gates of the city lest zealous locals mistake him for the Messiah. He realised then that the man who had written *The Jewish State* while inspired by nightly performances of *Tannhauser* also had his flaws of secret pride.

He was a child of many afflictions, forever covered in allergies and complications: his nose always running, his eyes inflamed, something always in the process of breaking out or clearing up. For three years his skin was invaded by a travelling pruritis. A permanent cold sore bloomed at the corner of his mouth.

His earliest memories were of sitting under the table to which his mother had tethered his ankle with a length of twine, and of being lifted up by his father, on the roof of the house in Habad Street, to see the midnight lights of Ramadan glittering across the Muslim Quarter.

When he was five years old his father presented him with a page of holy writing smeared with honey, wrapped him in a shawl and carried him off to the rebbe to learn his first letters. For seven years he sat at the feet of the rebbe, who carried a long stick with which he rapped the fingers of any boy whose gaze wandered during the reciting of the liturgy, and by the time he was fourteen he already knew a good portion of the holy book by heart.

He was a careful student and a quiet boy. In the household of six quarrelling sisters and a brace of brothers-in-law he was the chief mender of fences, the near-saintly arbiter of domestic disputes; but he was to derive nothing but heartache from his role as diplomat.

It was probably this which gave him his lifelong air of settled melancholy, and drew the deep groove of anxiety, slightly to the left of his right eyebrow, which appears so prominently in his earliest photograph. It is a study in tension, a generic image: the first hard evidence of inhesion in the family Shepher.

When my grandfather was seventeen years old the broker arranged him a match with the long-necked daughter of an Odessan beadle, but on handing him a plate of pastries the eyes of the younger daughter met his over the cinnamon cake and they fell instantly in love. Since the beadle possessed funds only for his elder daughter's marriage (beadles ever being notoriously poor), my great-grandmother then did what she had long intended: she went to the secret hoard which she kept hidden in an old Sabbath scarf, and counted out the money for her son's canopy.

From that time, Reb Shalom refused to address his wife.

Since he had not been a particularly conversational husband to begin with, this made little difference to Batsheva. She had long got used to having a silent spouse. The fact that the beadle, Batsheva, the beadle's family and, ultimately, Shalom Shepher himself were all delighted by the match did not prevent him maintaining a quarantine whose origins were soon forgotten and whose continuance, like that of so many ancient traditions, was purely a matter of principle. His refusal to speak to her except through the offices of an intermediary was at first ridiculous, then irritating, and finally nothing more than an eccentric habit, in a household where eccentric habits were commonplace.

Among the wedding presents was a brass samovar, a really expensive item, more valuable than anything else my grandparents possessed. My grandmother hated this samovar, which sat in the corner of the room like a carbuncle, demanding to be polished. It was covered in fluting and scrollwork and grinning festoons of flowers where the dirt settled and the duster couldn't reach, and as soon as it had been polished it started to tarnish again, so that she was never free of the task it represented.

She never used the samovar except on special occasions, for example during the visits of her sisters-in-law. Then she made tea and set it on the table to flatter them. She had no idea that they resented the samovar almost as much as she did. They thought she was trying to impress them and draw attention to her wealthy connections. So they made a point of never enjoying the tea which came out of it, but drank it in little sips, like poison; and after they had gone she would find half-full glasses of cold tea scattered all over the room. Secretly each one coveted the samovar, but they would never have given their sister-in-law the satisfaction of admiring it. Once they were out of the house they would criticise everything about it: the furniture, the utensils, the dirt in the crevices of the samovar, my grandmother's clothes and her opinions which she couldn't help expressing; and when, a few years later, the break occurred which was to sever my grandfather from his sisters permanently, it was the samovar which bore the brunt of their malevolence.

At this time my grandparents were living in a two-roomed tenement along the Jaffa Road. This was because Zweiger the fat brother-in-law, Hannah Raisl and their six children now occupied all the available space at the House of the Hand. It was a twenty minute walk from the tenement to the Western Wall, for which Shalom Shepher rebuked his only son, misquoting the passage from Scripture: "If the Temple is far away, it is your own fault."

Three months after the marriage Leah declared herself pregnant, and Joseph, whose work as assistant teacher at the religious school earned barely more than a pittance, went to his brother-in-law in search of extra employment. Zweiger claimed to be a watchmaker, though he was actually only able to repair watches, and this he did purely on a casual basis, leaving his wife to earn money through her mother's flour business. Nevertheless, Joseph begged him to take him on in some capacity.

Zweiger shrugged his shoulders.

"Do you have any skill in watches?" he inquired.

"You know I don't," the young man replied. "But I'm sure I could learn fast."

Zweiger raised one eyebrow as though insulted. "On the contrary! It takes a great many years to acquire the watchmaker's skill. And that is only if you have a talent for it."

"I'm sure I'd be well suited."

"That's debatable, but in any case, I already have an apprentice," he indicated his seven-year-old son, "and I can't afford to take on another one."

"But you don't pay him anything!"

"No, he earns his own keep, and I'm afraid there just isn't enough business around for you to do the same. You should stick to teaching. It can't be harder for a Jew to make a living in that racket than it is in this."

My grandfather gave up the idea of watchmaking and stayed with his vocation, using the holy tongue to teach the holy tongue; an act of sacrilege for which he had, once, a pisspot emptied on his head, and for which he was later awarded a medal by the Ministry of Education.

He and my grandmother were a modern couple: he clipped his sidelocks short, and changed his caftan for a European jacket; she wore her own hair under a flowered scarf. As the sisters-in-law used to say, "They look like a couple of Cook's tourists." They spoke Hebrew together and once, to the scandal of some, were even seen attending the opera.

On the wall of the salon they kept a framed photograph of Theodor Herzl which they took care to turn round or take down whenever Reb Shalom came to visit, such an icon being both heretical and idolatrous. Years later, in his maturity, my grandfather would struggle to the same conclusion and consign the unholy image to the attic at Kiriat Shoshan, where strange veins and patches bloomed on the face of the Father of Zionism.

One by one his children entered the world, and with each one he grew a little poorer. In the margins of his days he checked Torah scrolls and parchments for phylacteries and sold them to dealers and middlemen who carried them to Europe and America. He copied documents at a *grush* per page. He peered at the accounts of the Society for Wheat Distribution and the Joint Relief Committee, and sat up late recording the arguments of *machers* and worthies and all the tin-pot big shots of Jerusalem.

In his pocket he carried the battered first pages of the novel he planned to write, which would be the first great Hebrew novel of the holy city; sometimes in a spare moment he scribbled a line or two. The groove to the left of his right eyebrow deepened; a troubled and sad look came into his eyes.

Sometimes of an evening he would find himself in the company of his father, who sat hunched over his studies in a corner of the room; he would attempt conversation, but either Reb Shalom was deaf or was pretending to be: he had little to say to the son who, failing to do better than himself, could never be anything other to him than a disappointment. All day long the old man wandered the streets, clutching under his arm the same box he took with him from one daughter's house to the next and which he never parted with under any circumstances. No-one was certain what was in the box: an ancient copy of the Zohar, perhaps, or an annotated volume of the tractate on Shabbat. Numerous small scraps of paper on which he scribbled messages to himself, or calculations, pushed up his sleeves or into his pockets or deposited in the box, fell in trails from the folds of his caftan as he shuffled up the Jaffa Road. He took to wandering through graveyards and among ruins, and to hanging around the caravanserai. He sat in corners muttering one-sided conversations. He came home with tales of meeting Elijah, of conversations with Ezekiel.

On one occasion he called unexpectedly at the tenement. It was wash-day, and in the flurry of his unforeseen arrival my grandmother forgot to turn the photograph. Reb Shalom, catching sight of it, drew near, examined it long and closely and announced, without fanfare and in a quiet voice: "Moses our teacher."

My grandmother was relieved: she took the declaration as a mark of approval. At least, Reb Shalom never eyed it again; and she no longer turned the picture after this occasion.

Chapter seven

My uncle said: "My first idea was right. According to Shloime, the Codex is at least thirteenth century."

I pricked up my ears.

"Three columns, rather than two. That shows it is old. And written on vellum. And with full *masorah*—you know what is *masorah*?—annotations."

"Yes," I said, patiently, "I know what is *masorah.*"

"The part which puzzles him is the colophon. The piece which describes the origin of the book."

We sat on the balcony above the boulevard. A spring breeze blew gently, rustling the fronds of Aunt Fania's potted palms. The hoot and fury of intense traffic rose from far below.

"That, he is inclined to think, must be a forgery."

Aunt Fania entered, bearing a tray of iced coffee: the one delicacy in which she did excel. I looked at my uncle, sitting back now in his open shirt, revealing the grey scrubland of his withered chest: an ancient European in the Middle Eastern sun. There was a large dark coin of skin below his left nipple, which, if he had time left to worry about such things, he might one day choose to regard as sinister.

"You put too much sugar again," he complained. "I always tell you not to put too much sugar."

"Go on with you. I made it just the way you like it," Fania said.

Hard to believe, I thought, that he was Saul's brother, though there were resemblances, now, which had grown more obvious with age. In most respects, however, they were chalk and cheese. Their whole lives had been lived at opposites, from the day Cobby joined the Socialist Youth Party and Saul came home a member of the nationalist militia, and from that day to this they had rarely spoken; though once, according to legend, Cobby had punched Saul in an argument about politics, outside on the verandah at Kiriat Shoshan.

He was regarded by many as the stupidest member of the family, but if this was the case, he was also the happiest. He preferred arm wrestling to wrestling over politics. If asked to speak about his scientific work he was always pleased to do so, at great length and with many pauses, with much digression and obscure verbiage, punctuated by the whorls of his aged stutter; the more carefully one listened, the less one understood. He never tired of repeating his well-worn views, which he conceived to be radical; mainly because Aunt Fania never tired of repeating hers, which were conservative. He liked to sing but had no ear for music, and he read only scientific journals, considering fiction to be frivolous. Twenty years ago he had read an American self-help book by a quack psychiatrist, and twenty years later he was still picking its arguments to pieces. He drove an ancient Peugeot with sticky plastic seats, never faster than thirty miles an hour, but he had a great deal of difficulty with maps. They never portrayed the route as he knew it with all certainty to be.

"And another thing," he smacked his lips distastefully. "He also thinks the text is a corrupt version."

"Corrupt!" Whenever I heard this word, I envisioned a text of the Bible through which veins of subversive mould streaked colourfully, staining the white pages of divine truth. It was a very popular word with academics. "No wonder," I noted cautiously, "so many people are interested in it."

It was true: since the day of my arrival the phone had hardly stopped ringing; intrigue and altercation abounded, and my own request to see the Codex had so far gone ignored. The hydra forces of the family were roused: distant forgotten relatives had recalled their kinship to the ancient clan, the warring factions were assembling, and Sara Malkah herself, queen of them all, now threatened arrival on the quaking scene.

That afternoon I accompanied Aunt Fania to the Supersol and stood next to her while she chose live carp from a tank, teetering on her high heels, her eyebrows drawn in with a russet pencil. She laced her arm around mine as we made a slow tour of the aisles, observing plenty, purchasing very little, and I realised that she came here nearly every day, not to shop so much as to stay true to pattern. Pinioned by her arm I could smell her French perfume: *L'Air du Temps.*

"There's going to be big trouble," she said. "You want to know why? I know this family. You think after seventy years I don't know this family? Then think again."

I deferred to her greater knowledge, and let her select biscuits. There was a foreign smell of cinnamon and vanilla; the Supersol was quiet, almost deserted on this weekday afternoon. "It's the acid stomach. Your uncle will be eating himself up from the inside. So," she persisted, "there really is no boyfriend?"

"No boyfriend," I confirmed.

"It's a shame. You really should have someone. A woman your age should have a proper home."

"I do have a proper home."

"Of course. But I mean children." She squeezed a loaf of bread with cerise fingernails. "Ugh! Already stale."

"Not everybody wants children."

"Nonsense! You just haven't found the right person. You should hurry up."

I held my peace, wondering briefly if she were really right, reminded all the more poignantly, now that I was here, that the right person had come along, once, and that I had let him go. I was suddenly tugged by an urge to see Daniel again, to resolve matters finally and lay his ghost to rest: to say the things I had rehearsed a hundred times in my head and never had the opportunity to speak aloud.

Aunt Fania selected olives; she hardly seemed to notice my growing silence. Deep inside I felt a plethora of small memories break open like bright coals, burning me from within: Daniel cross-legged on my student bed, carving his arguments with vigorous gestures; Daniel onstage, immeasurably distant, breaking my heart with the notes of his saxophone; his narrow, unsteady fingers tracing a long shiver down my spine; his brown eye, full of sadness and reproach, as I had last seen it.

All these painful remembrances burst open, noiselessly, like plumes of lava deep under the sea; cooling instantly in the chill of my calm demeanour, which fooled everyone, apparently: even me.

"Do you like pickled cucumbers?" Aunt Fania looked at me strangely. "What are you thinking about?"

I smiled. "They give me heartburn. The Codex," I replied.

Chapter eight

My great-grandmother passed away with the century, and when she died Shalom Shepher took up a wandering existence and threw himself on the charity of his children, as it is said: "Honour thy father and thy mother, provide them with food, drink and clothing, bring them home and take them out, and supply them with all their needs cheerfully."

From Sukkot to Chanukah he stayed with his eldest daughter in the House of the Hand on Habad Street; from Chanukah to Purim with his second daughter. Passover he spent at his third daughter's house in Nachalat Shiva, and Shavuot with his fourth daughter in Mishkenot. But the High Holydays he always passed with his son, "because," as he explained, "he is my son." This earned his daughter-in-law the undying resentment of her husband's sisters.

In this way he lived out the last seventeen years of his life. And despite the best efforts of his children he was never welcome. He consumed vast quantities of food, for in old age he had regained the appetite of his youth; he hung around the kitchen and criticised the cooking. He rose in the night, prayed, ate, and woke everybody up. When he moved on to the next daughter he always made a point of comparing her unfavourably with the last, and did his best to set his children against each other. But they refused to quarrel with him, as it is also said: "Children who provide their parents with fattened poultry, but do so with ill grace, incur divine punishment."

Wherever he went he carried his secret box, which none of his daughters, and especially not his worthless sons-in-law, were allowed to lay hands on; he hugged it jealously under his caftan and slept with it lodged beneath his bed. He bumped into Elijah, in a field, under an olive tree: he asked him about the Messiah, about points of Law. He sat in the corner of the study-house and made his calculations. He walked to the Western Wall carrying his precious box.

It was a time of apocalypticism like any other. In the American colony they sat and sewed the flaps on the enormous tent in which Jesus, returning, would meet the lucky first five thousand of his followers. In the streets of the Old City missionaries dropped religious tracts which, being in English, were of no use to anyone except for wrapping and wiping. And in the various consulates the vultures gathered.

Reb Shalom returned home at the end of his days' wanderings wild-eyed and exhausted, sat in a corner of the salon and muttered to himself. Late at night my grandfather would wake to find him, bent by the light of the moon over his secret book. He was lost in the labyrinth of his calculations, wreathed in the vapours of his own myth. The powers of the day were Amalek, the Emperor Franz Josef a Persian potentate. He lived in daily expectation of the armies of Alexander the Great.

War was declared: a few at a time those Jews who were Ottoman citizens were called to the flag; the rest were deported wholesale by train to Jaffa, and from there by battleship to Alexandria. Shemariyah the young son of the beadle, Leib Itchka the wagoner and the boy who swept out the study-house were all taken to the corvée. The conscripts were set to work cleaning roads and latrines, and building the railway between Sulea and Lod. Many who had done little more in their lives than turn the pages of a Mishnah were set to carrying rocks, drinking rainwater and sleeping in the mud. The rain was relentless, and the dry weather brought scorpions. When they approached the captain's tent to request a day's respite on the Sabbath the captain drove them off by pelting them with stones.

Between El Arish and the Egyptian border the soldiers were caught in sandstorms which raged all night: the privates had no tents, and in the morning each man would dig to find where his neighbour was buried. The fine sand blew into their ears and noses and even into the officers' pocket watches, so that on their return to Jerusalem Zweiger and his colleagues were inundated with work. Then the soldiers were suddenly recalled, and retrieved all their watches unmended and unpaid for.

My grandfather went walking and saw that hunger was in the streets, the children were pinched with it and the old men nearly transparent from inanition. Nevertheless they continued to make their way painfully to and from the Western Wall. The streets of the Old City were full of filth and soldiers and promissory notes from the Austrian post-office which had been shut down and its papers sold off for wrapping cheese and halva. Now everybody's business was common knowledge: the sums they had borrowed and the interest paid.

Day after day the fellaheen streamed in from the villages to queue patiently at the barracks near the Lion Gate, where they were issued with second-hand uniforms and a ration of boiled rice and marched off southwards, leaving their orchards to rot. On the third of February my grandfather received his call-up; he packed his phylacteries and prayer book, a volume of Exodus with commentary and Ohlendorff's *English Grammar,* and walked like a blind man to his hiding place.

He tried to hide at first in the House of the Hand, but after a day or two Zweiger got frightened and made him leave again. "In any case," he said, "why should I stick my neck out for that factionist?" So then he hid in the attic of his sister-in-law's house in Mishkenot. The attic was small and cramped, reached by a short ladder, with one broken window stuffed up with rags. If he removed the rags and craned his neck he could see the little synagogue where poor street pedlars gathered to pray on Sabbath eve.

All day my grandfather sat at a rickety table and read Exodus, or *The Book of the Covenant*, or Dostoyevsky in Yiddish. Every so often he walked up and down the room. From time to time he pulled out the few torn pages of Ohlendorff's *English Grammar* that he had stuffed in his pocket and tried to teach himself the language which, he felt increasingly, was most likely to be of use to him.

It was then that my grandmother began to sell off those precious volumes which Shalom Shepher had received from Isaac Raphaelovitch, and which he had handed down to his own son on his wedding day: the sixteenth century rabbinical treatise, the commentary on Genesis, the decorated copy of the Zohar, all were sold for a song and lost forever, books for bread. But the children were still hungry, flour and sugar were almost unobtainable, and every day the rumours ran back and forth: the English were firing off Gaza, a Turkish battalion had taken the Suez Canal, an American ship was offering passage to Manhattan.

My grandfather thought of going to America.

At night the faces of his wife and children came to him in dreams, he tossed on his pallet bed and his stomach tore. He was crippled by fierce headaches and indigestion. Fear woke him trembling in the small hours of the night.

He sat at the table and fantasised about America.

What would he do in America? A little teaching, a little journalism. He would supplement his income by dealing in Torah scrolls. He would do just the same, in fact, as he did here in Jerusalem, for wherever a Jew travels he can make a little Jerusalem for himself.

That was when my grandfather said to my grandmother: "Sell the samovar." Sell the samovar, she repeated to herself. People are starving and he wants them to buy a samovar. But she wrapped up the samovar in a blanket and took it round to the house of Hannah Raisl.

Hannah Raisl, whose husband was too old for the call-up, twisted her face and said: "It's a little fancy for us. Why don't we ask Leah?" And Leah the second sister was brought. Leah pretended never to have seen the samovar before.

"What a fancy one!" she said. "But it must be a nuisance to clean. Look how the dirt has got trapped in the fluting. A piece like that asks for dedication. Let's see what Sheinah Gitl thinks."

Sheinah Gitl thought she didn't much care for tea from a samovar, but that Dvoirah might be interested. Dvoirah said: "So Joseph wants to go to America! What would his precious Dr. Herzl think?"

My grandmother did not then care to trouble her last two sisters-in-law, but carried the samovar to the Street of the Jews, where she sold it to a broker at a knockdown price. And after that date she had nothing more to do with her husband's sisters.

As for the American ship, it proved nothing but a myth, the sums required to board it simply legendary, now one hundred napoleons, now two, now three; but when it finally set sail on its illusory voyage it carried a host of passenger aspirations, all of which sank out there in the deep heart of the Mediterranean.

That year a plague of pilgrim locusts visited the country, brought by an east wind which should have swept them into the sea, but a west wind sprang up and they dropped down on the fields and vineyards and the orange groves around Jaffa and stripped everything. In Jerusalem there was typhus: at the Bikkur Cholim hospital they cut up the tent of the five thousand to make sheets for the sick and wounded, and in the graveyard down by the Mamillah Pool Shalom Shepher held entire conversations with Elijah, who promised him that the Messiah would be coming, that the Messiah would be coming very soon. He shuffled back to the tenement pale-faced and delirious, collapsed on the divan and refused to eat.

Consumed at last by the Jerusalem in his soul, he lay on my grandmother's couch a withered husk, no more alive than the shroud in which he would soon be buried.

Instead of booking passage to America my grandfather spent the money from the samovar on forged papers which would enable him to leave the city clandestinely by car. Late at night, wrapped in his wife's shawl, he left his attic and walked the brisk distance along the Jaffa Road. There at the city's edge he waited until dawn.

Towards noon the car finally drew up, several hours late and already crammed with people. My grandfather slipped in among the first. Full to capacity, surrounded by weeping women, the car started its engine and drew off.

It was when he was already squeezed into the back, his packet of provisions crushed beneath him, that Joseph detected a face among the crowd: that of Schonbaum the printer, whose expression was strangely harried as he called out: "Reb Shepher! Reb Shepher! Your father has passed away!" Then the doors were closed and the blinds drawn down, and the car set out on its journey from Jerusalem.

Chapter nine

Back at the bungalow, Saul sat by his radio in a frozen molten state, clam-shut and volcanic by turns, his rheumed eyes blazing at me over the matzo pancakes. "You think I can eat?" he fumed. "That professor, when he came thieving here, he also took my appetite."

"I think you should eat something," I suggested equably.

"You are all right! You don't care what happens. Now Cobby, that *pisheke*, with his usual cleverness, tells everyone he wants to give it away. But does he consult the rest of us? No. He's so generous with other people's money."

"But they will study the Codex. Don't you want the Codex to be studied?"

"To hell with the Codex! If they want to study it let them pay for the privilege!"

He rose in the spittle of his disgust and left the room.

I remained at the table, finishing up the pancakes; for a wild moment wishing I had taken a package holiday in Tenerife. A minute later there was a tap on the glass. It was our watcher again, his face at the window like a daytime ghost.

"Please," he began, as soon as I stepped out of the door, and glancing back anxiously he ushered me out of sight.

"*Gveret* Shepher," he resumed, as soon as we were safe. "Please allow me to introduce myself. My name is Gideon Ben Gibreel."

I made to shake his hand but, of course, he did not offer it. He did, however, bow, regarding me with a sideways, diffident look, like a half-tame bird which is hoping you will give it crumbs and not harm it. He was thin and tall; his face at once foreign and familiar, his skin the pale olive of an Oriental. I liked his eyes: they were green, compellingly clear, and I had the strange sensation of having looked into them before, long ago perhaps, in some previous life.

"I know who you are," I said. "You were at my uncle's place."

"That's right. Your uncle is kind," he confessed, "but unfortunately he was not able to offer me the sort of assistance I am looking for. Your other uncle," he looked sheepish, "refuses to speak to me."

"I'm not sure how useful I can be to you."

"Nor am I," he laughed lightly, under his breath. "But perhaps—you see, I need to see the Codex."

"In that case you should apply to the Institute."

"I already did," he spread his helpless hands. "I must say they're being very obstructive. They refuse to allow anyone without your uncle's authorisation. And meanwhile your uncle sends me back to them. Apparently there is some question mark about the ownership." His expression as he said this was droll, as though a joke he alone was aware of added some weight of irony to his words.

"There seems to be some disagreement, yes."

"It's very unfortunate. I have particular and pressing reasons. And I have come a long way. If they had only allowed me to look, I can assure you it would have done no harm. Now—"

"Now?"

He glanced about anxiously. "Now there will be all sorts of interested parties."

I took a deep breath. "Mr. Ben Gib—Mr. Ben Gibreel—"

"Please." He smiled, showing a perfect set of teeth. "Call me Gideon."

"I'm afraid I really don't know what I can do. I'd very much like to see the Codex myself, and what with all the confusion I still haven't succeeded."

"But you will see it," he urged. "You are of the family." Again that sidelong expression. "They will let you in. Your ancestor, Shalom Shepher, was a great scholar."

"So I've been hearing."

"A great *magih*—a scroll-checker. You know what is a *magih*?"

"Yes," I replied, somewhat irritated, "I know what is a *magih*. Look, I think I should ask my uncle about this."

"Yes, but after all, perhaps it would be better not to trouble him again...." He continued to smile, but regarded me sadly, one might have said with compassion. "*Gveret* Shepher. This is no longer a private family matter, I'm afraid. On the contrary." He turned abruptly, sweeping his silvery caftan in the dust. Close to, I could see in its fabric a kind of Cyrillic stripe, the symbolism of which was lost on me. "Tell me about the Codex. Is it very old?"

"Quite old, yes."

"And it is written on vellum?"

"Yes."

"And with three columns?"

"Yes, but—"

"And with full *masorah*. But what about the colophon?"

"The professor thinks it is a forgery. He also thinks the book is textually corrupt."

"Yes: he would think that." He tossed his head in a slight, imperious manner. "*Gveret* Shepher, I am here to tell you. It is not a forgery. It is not corrupt."

"How do you know?" I demanded.

He didn't reply at once, but gazed out across the abandoned lot, tracing a circular pattern with his toe. I had the impression he was toying with me. Or perhaps he was still unsure whether to trust me. "Your uncle is so concerned about the value of the Codex," he said eventually. He looked me straight in the eye. "But tell me, if you will, the answer to these two questions: where did the Codex come from, and how did it get here?"

"I don't know," I admitted. "But someone will."

"No, *Gveret* Shepher. Nobody knows. Nobody knows the truth except myself." He allowed this declaration to hang briefly, but there was no trace of complacency in his mild expression. "Whether you too can be trusted with it is your own choice."

I didn't reply; I had decided to feel sceptical, and I was annoyed, too, by his superior tone. "I am sure," I said stiffly, "that everything will become clear. The Codex is being examined by various experts."

"Ignoramuses. Their approach is quite wrong."

"That's as may be. But for now," I reminded myself as much as him, "it's out of our hands. There isn't very much we can do about it."

He accepted that; for a moment we stood in silence under the cypress trees. A slight breeze fluttered his robes: I could smell the dry earthy smell of cones and dead evergreens, seventy years' worth, crushed to a fine powder beneath our feet.

He smiled then, and I felt with a sudden flood of conviction the deep kindness sitting behind his eyes. "You are right," he said at last. "We will have to be patient. All is not lost yet. We will bide our time."

He turned and fled swiftly back across the square.

Chapter ten

Nine miles out of Jerusalem, on the broken road through Bab el Wad, they raised the blinds and looked out. My grandfather took in his first view of the landscape beyond Abu Ghosh: hills and valleys, rocks and shrubs. The odd soldier. Near Deir Ayub they stopped and bought oranges. Two German aeroplanes passed low overhead. A troop of Turkish horsemen appeared like a mirage among the valleys.

The only true evidence of war was the long succession of wagons, crammed with children, furniture and household articles, travelling in exodus from the coast to the interior. The British had already fired on Jaffa; Tel Aviv was being evacuated. Here on the road to Jerusalem were the mundane consequences: a slow trail of refugees whose silence and fixed gaze bore witness to their suffering. On top of a heap of cushions, chairs, rugs and featherbeds a trio of Turkish women passed in grim state. Suddenly the pile toppled, taking them with it.

Throughout most of the journey my grandfather sat with a shoulder in his face and an elbow in his ribs, crammed up against the hard corner of the car. The smell of bodies was overpowering.

Whenever he tried to adjust his position he received an angry poke, so he just kept still as best he could, although he was in agony. A Bukharan with the eye of a vulture kept watch on him the whole time.

"Did you want to change places, Jew?"

"No, thank you, I'm comfortable where I am."

Just before Jaffa the car stopped. The journey had taken three hours. The driver pulled up before the police checkpoint, a few passengers slipped out and skirted the town, and after a half-hour's walk my grandfather entered Tel Aviv: a few white houses among the sand dunes.

Nursing his aches and pains he waited outside the Hotel Rosenberg for the car to take him on to Petach Tikvah.

A young man about his own age, wearing white shoes and with the look of an artist, stopped and leant against the wall next to him. He gestured to the street, which was full of goods and people. "It's all over with here!" he said.

"For the time being."

"That's right! For the time being!" The man smiled at him sideways. "If you're in need of anything, now's the time to buy. I can sell you a can of gasoline for five francs. A few days ago it would have fetched a hundred!"

My grandfather thanked him but had no need of gasoline.

"Sugar, then. I have a head of sugar here and you can name the price."

He was grateful, but had no need of sugar. The young man pushed off from the wall impatiently and moved on.

The car, when it arrived, attracted a crowd of curious onlookers. It was still an unusual sight in Tel Aviv, and in that respect, he observed with satisfaction, Jerusalem was in advance of the first Jewish city. He climbed aboard to glorious isolation. For a small sum the driver had agreed to take him on alone to the settlement.

Enclosed in the car, with the blinds drawn and the heavy smell of sweat still lingering, he thought about the words of Schonbaum, about the face of Schonbaum, about the words he must have misheard and couldn't believe. He was still numb to the tidings. The car jolted and stopped, the whine of its wheels spinning against sand. They both got out, and with one shovel between them, succeeded in digging it free. Joseph pushed and the driver revved the engine. A little further on it got stuck again. The road was buried in sand. "It's too dangerous," the driver said. My grandfather set off on foot for Petach Tikvah.

He walked until night. The landscape around him, of undifferentiated orange groves, bare sand and scrub, seemed hostile and alien. It lent him no clues. Even his small parcel of belongings had grown heavy; sweat ran under his arms and into his eyes. He stopped under a tree to pray the evening prayer. The chanting of the liturgy calmed him somewhat. At last, out of the gloom, a pair of wagons approached: two Galilean farmers who had come down from the north to assist with the evacuation from Jaffa.

"Is this the road to Petach Tikvah?" he asked.

They looked at him strangely. "No," one said. "This is the road to Chaderah!"

He sat down with his bundle by the roadside. He felt like weeping.

"We know a watchman's shelter near here where you can stay the night."

He shook his head. "I have to carry on to Petach Tikvah."

The two men touched their donkeys and moved on. Soon afterwards another wagon came by, driven by a young Jew in an open shirt with a kerchief around his neck. He was heading from Kfar Sabah to Petach Tikvah. Appearing out of the darkness with his small lantern, he had the glow of a ministering angel, although he was plainly one of the godless generation. He smiled, showing a phalanx of white teeth. "Climb up, friend!" My grandfather climbed on board and sat beside him.

"You've come from Jaffa?"

"No, from Jerusalem. And yourself?"

"From Tiberias. What do you do in Jerusalem?"

"I am a teacher."

"A religious teacher?"

"A teacher of Hebrew and arithmetic."

The man turned to him and smiled again: his teeth shone out of the darkness. "Now that is the sort of teaching I approve of. Do you read literature?"

"I read Bialik."

"Only Bialik?"

"I have a particular fondness for Dostoyevsky."

"Ah! Dostoyevsky. But not Tolstoy?"

"I'm also fond of Tolstoy."

"Good. I am fond of Tolstoy. And of Spinoza! You don't disapprove?"

"Why should I disapprove? I myself have a great appetite for Spinoza."

"Then we approve of each other. If you're hungry there is fruit in there."

My grandfather looked at him: he was bareheaded and without beard or sidelocks, but his expression was honest and open. These were the young idealists whom the greybeards railed against, but my grandfather was a true child of his generation, and could see nothing to criticise in this rustic, sunburnt, energetic Jew. He reached down and took an orange. "You are very kind," he said.

They entered the settlement around midnight. The town was swelled with the numbers constantly arriving from Jaffa, and wagons drew up hourly en route to and from the north. The Yemenites came barefoot, the women carrying their children, the young men pulling cartloads of belongings. Joseph slept on the ground beside a rabbi, two old women and two hens which the rabbi loved like children and wouldn't be parted from. By morning the hens had each produced an egg.

"We are the Children of Israel on the road of exile," the rabbi said. "We know the heart of the stranger." And he presented my grandfather with one of the eggs.

Immediately on his arrival he sent three letters, one with the car to Jerusalem, two with other travellers, to inquire after the welfare of his family. He did not dare to hope that Schonbaum had, by some accident, been misinformed. That same evening a mass meeting was held in the synagogue. Mr. Dizengoff addressed them: they must move north. Kfar Sabah was full. Chaderah didn't have good air. They would go on to Karkur; from Karkur the whole of the Galilee would be open to them. The settlers there were ready to receive them. A hundred Galilean wagons were standing by.

My grandfather scribbled a note to Dizengoff: I will take any work that is offered, even at a wage of 5 francs a week; even if it is in the Galilee, I will go anywhere.

As he waited by the door a farmer approached him.

"You're a teacher, aren't you?"

My grandfather admitted that he was.

"And you've come from Jerusalem?"

He confirmed that he had.

"The Turkish Commander is in town," the man said. "His boy burst into the synagogue this afternoon demanding chickens. They're searching the marketplace for deserters, but you can hide with us for the duration. They'll move on, and then you can eat with the family."

My grandfather didn't know how to thank him.

"Teach my youngsters and it will be a fair exchange. Teach me and my brother and I might even pay you money. I understand you have family in Jerusalem."

"A wife and five children," my grandfather said.

"Well, from time to time you might be able to send them something. The war can't last much longer. The English will be here within a month or two. In the meantime, we can sit it out."

So the note to Dizengoff stayed in my grandfather's pocket, and he took up residence behind a false wall in the farmer's loft. From there, through a chink in the boards, he could see the wagons leaving in ragged convoy, heading in a thin trail to the north; he also watched for an hour as a couple of Turkish soldiers hung desultorily about the farm, barking peremptory orders and picking their teeth. But the soldiers soon left, and the wagons also; my grandfather remained, wondering too late if he had made the right decision.

On the third day of his confinement the farmer climbed the ladder and brought him a note: he recognised immediately his wife's handwriting.

"News from home?" the man inquired as he opened it. "I hope all is well."

Joseph read in silence. He drew a slow hand across his eyes.

"My father is dead," he informed him.

"I am very sorry."

The man respectfully withdrew. Alone in the loft, the letter at his feet, my grandfather tore his garment and recited the mourner's kaddish.

Chapter eleven

Fania was cooking latkes in the kitchen. She plunged a damp hand into a bag of flour. "That Sara Malkah!" she spluttered. "What a nutcase—what a *meshuggenah*! Making trouble for the whole family."

"Not a *meshuggenah*," Cobby countered, since they must argue. "Just an unhappy woman. You know, I think she's doing it to get attention."

"She certainly got that."

The flour was full of black weevils. Fania both saw and did not see them. She frowned for a moment, then tossed flour and weevils hissing into hot oil.

That very afternoon, the madwoman in question had made her preordained descent on Cobby's and Fania's flat, where she would touch nothing lest it render her unclean, not even the buzzer on the intercom; she stood, feet apart, in the middle of the rug, her body poised like a prize fighter's, her head emblazoned with a silver wig, and with one terrifying index finger accused us of everything.

"Thieves! *Goniffs*! *Schnorrerim*!"

I sat side by side with my uncle on the sofa, and for the first time in years, felt like a fully paid-up member of the family.

In a nutshell, the case boiled down to this: she, Sara Malkah, the aged and litigious daughter of my great-aunt, Hannah Raisl, demanded the Codex as her just inheritance. It had never really belonged to Joseph Shepher but was the rightful property of her father, the unpalatable Zweiger.

How it fell into the hands of Zweiger in the first place, she could not categorically prove. Her claims on his behalf were outlandish in any event. Zweiger the great scholar, Zweiger the skilled maker of watches (who we knew for a fact never made but only mended them), Zweiger the inheritor of the vast library of Isaac Raphaelovitch (it's no wonder if the Codex lay unnoticed in the possession of such an ignoramus), Zweiger her father (may he rest in peace) was left the box and the Codex on the death of his father-in-law, the sainted Shalom Shepher.

And why was it left to him and not my grandfather? It was clear to anyone, said Sara Malkah. It was beyond retort. There was no way Reb Shepher would have left anything so precious to that freethinker, to that Zionist.

So he must have stolen it!

"The poor woman," Cobby murmured.

"The poor woman!" Fania repeated, ironically. As the weevils burned.

Now the TV people were really interested, and since he had done so well in the radio interview, Cobby was mesmerised by the prospect of cameras. Indeed, one would have thought Sara Malkah herself was preparing for a starring role in the projected mini-series based on these events, with her parting cliché of "I'll see you in court!"

Dinner was served: we made an odd trio at the head of the vast family table, whose satellites, children and grandchildren, had made off, most of them, for America. Cobby consumed his soup with a peasant hunger, gripping the spoon in his fist, his face close to the bowl; seemingly oblivious to the storm brewing beneath his nose.

I toyed with my glass. "Do you think," I asked carefully, "the Institute will be returning the Codex?"

"Returning it? Returning it to who?"

"To us. To you. I mean," I attempted with awkwardness, "will you be leaving it there for safekeeping?"

"Yes, yes, for safekeeping. That would probably be best." Cobby reached across for a piece of bread, tore it between his two hands, and thrust one half of it roughly into his mouth.

"You're not eating," Fania observed.

"No, I'm not very hungry."

"You should eat. You're too thin. Are you pining away?"

"Why on earth," I smiled stiffly, "would I be pining away? But when do you think," I asked Cobby, "I could go and see it?"

"Go and see it? What—you don't believe it exists?"

Resisting Fania's attempts to push a latke onto my plate, I answered, "Yes, of course, but I only wondered if I could take a look. If you could ask them for me. I'd be very interested." I repeated the words ponderously, feeling myself caught in the coils of some bizarre time loop, for it was just as I had feared: my first request had been wiped from Cobby's memory banks.

"Why not? Yes, of course. I'll ask Shloime. What good is a little *protektzia*, eh," he grinned and tapped his nose, "if you can't use it?"

"Even if I went there on my own?"

Cobby wasn't listening; he mopped up traces of soup with his rag of bread.

"Cobby. Do you think he would let me in?"

"Let you in? Of course he will let you in. You say you are my niece. Is it Fort Knox?"

I let out a breath and relaxed, having obtained the best answer I was likely to. With luck he would still remember our conversation in the morning. After dinner we sat together in the bluish light of the television screen; while Fania busied herself in the kitchen I tried to turn his mind to the subject which really interested me just now; more, even, than the Codex. My grandfather's war diary, which I had been translating, stopped abruptly when he reached Petach Tikvah. Did Cobby know what happened to him after that?

My uncle was vague about his father's whereabouts during the rest of the war. He sat back in his recliner, scratched the grey furze of his chest and speculated: "I think he hid in a barn in Petach Tikvah. Or" (shouting to Fania) "was that the time he went to Tel Aviv?"

"Who?"

"Abba. During the war."

"He went north with Dizengoff."

"No. He didn't go north."

"Well, who am I to know? Was I on the scene?" A clatter of pots and pans rose from the kitchen.

Most likely he hid somewhere, scratched a living from his teaching skills or from labouring in the fields, sending what he could to his abandoned family; while every day conflicting intelligence of the British advance raised his hopes and dashed them once again.

"He never went north," said Cobby. "What nonsense. He would have got trapped behind the enemy lines."

Cobby remembered those last days of the war. The Turkish army was in disarray: soldiers deserted in droves, and captured in handfuls, ran away again. A few were hanged as an example; it wasn't possible to execute them all. The fields turned white where the troops laid out their shirts for delousing. They stumbled through the streets of Jerusalem, half-starved and half-naked, begging for bread.

"*Ekmek, ekmek,*" he told me. "That's the word I remember."

He sat on the recliner in the breeze from the balcony, the leaves of the potted palm fluttering at his head. He might be in Monte Carlo, except that the stone-smelling air was so unmistakably Jerusalem; it was hard to imagine him transported from that past reality to this. He was old like a sea-worn relic, pitted and whorled with time. I tried to imagine him young. I thought of his picture in the album, his dark-curled head.

It was hard for them to accept that I had grown older, that I was my own woman now, no longer the little girl who hung shyly on her father's arm, or the grieving teenager who had buried him; the silent appendage of a domineering mother, whose only means of self-expression was to sing, sometimes, the Psalm of Degrees after the evening meal. It was hard for them to accept that I had made different choices, that I had different goals, that I refused to ride the tramlines of expectation, just as my parents did, just as their parents did before them.

"But where will it take you?" Fania had asked, when I described my academic work, my passion for texts, my long evenings in the library. "What's the use of it? Where will it all lead?" Hopeless to try and convince her of how I loved my work, or beyond that, how it was possible to live clinging to the present moment. "We survived through uncertainty you can't imagine," she said contemptuously. "We always made our plans for the future, though."

I told myself that it was doing me good, that this was one of the reasons I had come here, for the zest of a new perspective, to have my life dissected along with the bagels and herring in my aunt's kitchen. But more and more I realised what it was I had really come to discover: the answer to the question of why I was here at all, of what series of plans and accidents had led me to this breathing moment; of whether the history I had been hiding from these twenty years had anything to tell me about the nature of my own existence.

Sitting under the pink-and gold painting of the walls of Jerusalem, I turned the pages of the family album and examined the faces in which I saw now something of myself, now something of my brother or father—the pale line of the lips, the sullen slant of brow—faces, some of which I could identify, and others which even Cobby could not name for me, his memory now hazier than his cloudy eye, more shaky than the liver-spotted hand in which he held them up to the light for examination. I could see that my Aunt Miriam was beautiful in her youth, that my grandmother endured patiently but was exhausted; that Aunt Shoshanah, wearing her perpetual frown which was not deliberate but just an accident of physiognomy, seemed always to be squeezed into the picture like an afterthought. I remembered my father's mournful reprimand: "You must be nice to Shoshanah: she doesn't have any children of her own."

Cobby told me about the tragedy of her childless death, of how there was nobody at her deathbed to cry for her. "Well, you cried for her, I suppose," I said brittly, and turned the page on Shoshanah, unwilling any longer to look her in the eye (because I never was very nice to her after all) and I thought: If history is a text of sprouting stories, if it is a tree, does this particular branch of history end with me?

It was hard for me to accept that they had grown older, that so many faces from the past were dead, and the living ones denuded in a constant process which had nearly reached its end. I looked at my uncle: he stood by the table in the bright kitchen with its orange tiles, its cheeseboard with a picture of a cockerel and the calendar from a pharmaceutical company. He was a little stooped, he had a slight tremor and one cloudy eye. His glasses were mended with a sticking plaster. When he spoke I heard my father's voice.

For a moment I was caught in an eternal moment, and it seemed to me that rags and shadows of my father were present in the room: his gestures, the sound of his voice, the remembered contours of his cheek and chin. The shape of his mouth. My father lived on in fragments in his surviving brother, as once I imagined he would in the child I never had.

When I showed my uncle Cobby the photograph of Hannah, quite casually it seemed, he held it for several minutes in a trembling finger and thumb, pushed his glasses up his forehead, examined it closely, with the look of a man peering back through centuries to a time so distant it was all but forgotten: an era whose faces were nameless like those in a forgotten dream.

His father returned after the British took the city. One day he was out playing in the courtyard of the tenement and a strange-but-familiar man appeared. He had been ill, and when the man approached and embraced him he had been afraid at first: afraid of the *khappers* he had heard about, who used to come and carry small boys off to the Russian army. But then his brothers and sisters had tumbled out, shouting and crying, dancing and singing for joy: Father is back! Father has come home! And ever after he had felt a secret guilt, for not having recognised, for having feared his father.

His grandfather, Shalom Shepher—peace upon him—had long since been buried on the Mount of Olives. As for the box containing the precious Codex, my grandmother put it away in the laundry chest. For there wasn't time to think about such things just then. From the laundry chest it was moved to a lumber room, along with vast numbers of old letters and official documents and piles of newspapers which my grandfather would not throw away because they were printed in the holy tongue. Eventually it was transferred to the attic at Kiriat Shoshan, where it remained for nearly seventy years, until we went up and opened it.

And the truth unravelled like knitting to create a new present and a new past.

Part Three:
A Bang on the Head

Chapter one

I am a cipher, an appendix, a footnote to the history of the house of Shepher. A seed dropped by the bird of the diaspora, washed up with the dream of travelling on.

When my brother was born they named him Reuben Michael so that when he was older he could choose. For thirteen years he was Jewish Reuben to the boys at school; then he chose, and was reborn as Mike. Mike Shepher quarrelled with his parents, ran away to London and was never seen again.

They did not make the same mistake with me. They named me Shulamit to remind me that I had no choice. They took my education thoroughly in hand. For nine years I attended religious classes at the Talmud Torah, and my brain is now embossed with the black mosaic, the Hebrew Bible.

My father taught me to love the Hebrew language. The Hebrew language was like him: elegant, logical, concise. A word begins from a root, a mere three letters, and grows like a plant through seven constructs: I break, I smash, I am broken, I am smashed, I make shatter; I am caused to break down, I devastate myself.

What else did I learn? I learned that Jewish dishes should be washed under a running tap and that an ox and an ass may not be yoked together to plough a field. I studied the rules of salting beef and searing liver, and read that a limb torn from a living animal is forbidden food. I also learned to sing, in a voice which people said was the voice of a seraph, the psalms which celebrate the holy Torah and the songs which welcome in the Sabbath bride.

I was my parents' penance; my mother wore me like a badge of pride. Through me she gained the approval of the community. We ate *kneidels* and *kugel* and *kishkes.* We dipped our apples in honey on the New Year. And every few Sundays we would climb into our car and drive to the top of a hill from which we could see the whole of England spread out beneath us in a green patchwork, a panorama like Moses' from the top of Nebo: a beauty-spot known to locals as Surprise View.

Mine was a kind father but a melancholy man. All day long he worked at the factory, measuring lengths of timber with his thick fingers. He fed the timber to the jigsaw with his workman's hands. Sometimes in the evenings he would tell me stories, for in late middle-age he had remembered the stories of his youth: about Sandalfon, the guardian angel of birds, who was responsible for forming children in the womb, and about Metatron, author of the Book of Secrets and God's heavenly scribe. About Moses, who saw God through a clear glass and Elijah, who saw him through a darkened one. About the dangers of moonlight and about the resurrection of the dead. At weekends we walked the streets of our neighbourhood, stole raspberries from Mr. Mankin's garden, bamboo sticks from the municipal park. We picked up coins from the pavement and jewellery from gutters, and wherever we went I was taught the pleasures of being light-fingered and sharp-eyed.

There was also education by omission. My mother took responsibility for that.

In school we used very old geography books. It was an old school and everything in it was old including the teachers. In those days that was considered a mark of quality. One afternoon I brought my textbook home to trace the map of India. (In those days we only studied the countries of the former Empire.) My mother looked up the Middle East and found, instead of Israel, Palestine.

My father, who had been born there, was unperturbed, but my mother was furious. Palestine did not exist. It was a whim of cartographers, at best a historical accident. The children who used this atlas were being deliberately misinformed.

My teacher explained to her that the book was old.

That did not concern her, my mother said. If the book was that old it should say Judea. The point was that it was a lying book.

My teacher bridled and said that she would take it up with the headmistress. The headmistress wrote to say that all obsolete books would be replaced when the school budget permitted.

The religious studies teacher played it safe. She called it the Holy Land. This did not mollify my mother, who called it cowardice.

The truth is she had particular reasons for feeling sensitive about the world map, and these had to do with my father's citizenship.

When my father left Palestine in 1938 it lay under the bureaucratic offices of the British High Commission, licensers of shoeshines and donkey-carts, and ten years later amid gunfire and bombed buses and circle-dancing it became the State of Israel and my father was not a citizen of that land. In his passport it said 'British Subject' which made him a foreigner wherever he went. In Britain he had the right of abode, by virtue of his English wife and children. But he was not a Briton. Nor was he, as my mother blandly repeated, an Israeli. If anything he was of course a Palestinian, the citizen of a country which did not exist.

Before we dwell too deeply on the irony of my father's fate, a Jew and a Palestinian, a subject of the British Empire and a citizen of nowhere, let us remember that he could have returned to the country of his birth. All he had to do was present his credentials to the kindly immigration officials at Lydda airport, and we could have become (in due course, and by proper verification of our Jewish origin) a family of Israelis. In this sense he was not a genuine Palestinian; more a Palestinian by default. But my father (or was it my mother?) never wanted to emigrate just yet. (When he did return, as I have already indicated, it was in a lead box, but that did not faze the authorities. They are used to their people returning in coffins.)

My father lived in England for thirty-four years. During that time he applied for citizenship on three occasions. I think of my father's bouts with the British immigration authorities as a kind of boxing match in which he couldn't find his gloves. Three times he was refused. The first refusal was a punch in the stomach. The second was a slap in the face. The third was a blow to the head, from which he did not recover.

I did not know anything about it at the time. I did not know anything until Uncle Saul, sitting at the kitchen table in Kiriat Shoshan, dropped it on me like his other bombs. "Your father did not love your mother," he said; and then: "Do you realise that this country England, which you claim to love so much, denied your father citizenship three times? That three times they humiliated him, a punch in the stomach, a slap in the face, a blow to the head, to say nothing of what they did to us, the suffering they made here, so that we were forced to blow them up with bombs?"

But. That is another story.

For as long as I could remember the blue and white tin of the Jewish National Fund had stood on our bookshelf next to the Sabbath candlestick, and framed on my bedroom wall was a treeplanting certificate for a tree in the hills of Judea I had no memory of planting, nor of contributing towards in any way, except perhaps by being born. I could have told any teacher the exact location of Jerusalem, the lira exchange rate, the translation of El Al Israel airlines which stands for *To* the Promised Land *On* the wings of eagles, and a hundred other pieces of trivial information to prove my exotic origins, which mattered much to me. But the blue and white map on the tin, which was as familiar as my own face, was home-but-not-home, and the map in the atlas, of the Britannic crone dipping her claw into the Atlantic ocean, this too was home-but-not-home: to choose between them was already impossible by the age of ten. My mother taught me that the love of Zion was a virtue, while the love of Albion was drenched in guilt; but she herself was divided. Her favourite poem was 'O to be in England,' but 'Next Year in Jerusalem' was the prayer which moved her most.

She never allowed us to forget that we were strangers in a strange land. Yet when she disembarked at Haifa for the first time, in the summer of 1954, she had been disgusted by the squalor and backwardness of the Jewish state, and shocked at the number of Arabs still living there. It was the greatest disappointment of her life, and she never forgave herself for it. Probably she knew then that she would never emigrate, yet to acknowledge this would have been an act of impossible betrayal. So she maintained the myth of intention, and lived the life of an alien in her heart. We stood on the hilltop and gazed at Surprise View; I said to my mother: "Isn't it beautiful!" And she replied, in the few words of Hebrew she had ever mastered: "*Aval zeh lo shelanu.* But it isn't ours."

Meanwhile we lived always on the point of departure, putting our lives off until the next summer and the next, while those who were apparently braver or richer or (was it possible?) more committed than we, pulled up their tent pegs and saddled their camels for the Promised Land.

My father once had a plan: he wanted to go to the Negev and farm tomatoes. He bought a book on tomatoes and bided his time. And time passed and he did not go to the Negev. Time passed and methods of tomato farming changed. One night he sat at the kitchen table with my mother and my mother said to him: "That plan you had, to plant tomatoes in the Negev. You're never going to do it, are you?" And my father smiled at her and said: "A man has to have a dream."

But soon afterwards my father died with his dream intact, and was flown back to the Land of Israel in a lead coffin. And five years later my mother died also and was buried beside him, on the Hill of Rest outside Jerusalem.

Chapter two

I am travelling by taxi through Tel Aviv, on an evening flushed and heavy with the threat of rain, down wide boulevards, down narrow streets choked with fumes and traffic. We weave our way through back alleys and between bollards, past endless apartment blocks, small pharmacies, jumbled groceries, little electrical shops. We pass by bald lots, scrublands, dead cars, shanties; by new malls adorned with Hollywood stars. My driver is sweaty and blond; he speaks into several telephones. He steers with one finger. We are quite lost.

"Mountain Street off Miracle Street. At the top of the hill by the television tower."

He has never heard of Miracle Street, but he won't admit it. His finger is confident. His finger is full of pride.

This is the city which was founded on sand by Zionists, and look what it has become. A tangle of dead ends and one-ways, unexpected barriers and sudden pavements. A labyrinth designed to fox the visitor. A city which began as a dream and grew dense, like a jungle; which began white and is now a general grey. The white visions of the dream have turned dark with salt, a hot moisture hangs in the polluted air; the air pounds with the noise of traffic and work, sirens and horns and the hearts of hundreds of thousands of people.

Tel Aviv is not like Jerusalem. No temples were built here. No messiah will come. In all the vistas of history it is nothing but dunes.

The nights in Jerusalem are cool; the nights in Tel Aviv are mild and sweaty. Jerusalem air is full of pine and spices; Tel Aviv air is full of tar and sand.

Once a Jerusalemite always a Jerusalemite. Yet how many Jerusalemites flee to Tel Aviv. If I lived here I couldn't choose between them. My soul would belong to Jerusalem, my body would belong to Tel Aviv.

My driver is quite lost, but he won't acknowledge it. Only after performing a sweeping three-point turn, he grins at me over his shoulder, presses a switch on the meter and declares: "I turn this off."

We are high up, at the head of the city. Far below us lights are coming on along the promenade. Beacons illuminate the tops of the tall buildings. Strings of lights decorate the border of the black sea. The city is glimmering in a perpetual carnival, dancing on the edge of the watery abyss. My driver takes me confidently round in circles, up blind alleys, down dirt tracks, down roads which terminate in three no entry signs.

He throws up his hands and says: "This is as close as I make it. I let you out." I pay him, laughing, and run the last few steps up the darkening yard. My aunt greets me at the door: an emotional embrace which chokes us both.

"Shula! Little Shula! Is it really you?"

We look into each other's faces and know that we have both aged.

The apartment is cool and spacious as I remember it, full of plants and glass, unglazed ceramics and African wood. There is a verandah hung with ivy and a window overlooking a sea of twinkling lights. A big old television which is rarely watched and an ornate piano which is never played. Innumerable objects, knick-knacks, curious souvenirs. A great wallful of books of all kinds and sizes: albums, catalogues, encyclopaedias, ancient dictionaries and compendia, poetry and airport novels, presentation volumes and peeling paperbacks, the biography of Picasso and the Little Red Book of Chairman Mao.

The walls are covered with paintings I have not seen before, vibrant and colourful geometrics, landscapes so minimal they are almost abstracts. A cheerful jumble of experiments. My aunt Miriam always wanted to paint. Instead she got married, had children, became a schoolteacher. Those ambitions receded into the past. Now, in her widowhood, she has returned to her first love and become an artist.

The verandah window is open, and somewhere below, I can guess, is the open sea, obscured now by the tall blocks which grow denser year by year; but the sea's breath is in the air which blows very gently through the apartment from one side to the other, from the open verandah to the open kitchen window which looks out over the suburbs to the distant hills.

Now I sit once more in that comfortable kitchen corner, while she trots to and fro from cupboard to stove and back again, resembling a Shetland pony with her slacks and her thick-soled shoes, the little plait which she swings back characteristically over her shoulder; and while she fiddles with various small battered pans I gaze at the tiles with donkeys which I still remember, and the high shelf stocked with my late uncle's range of cherry brandy and liqueur, meticulously dusted and untouched from year to year.

"What about all this with the Codex, ha? Now my cousin, Sara Malkah, is phoning me up. Saying it should be theirs and that my father stole it." She punches me lightly on the shoulder. "What have you walked into, Shula, eh?"

My aunt Miriam has become old, but she retains that air of a small, tight ball of inquisitive energy, her head thrust slightly forward, frowning with the pressure of her inquiry: alert as a bird, but much more intellectual. Even her smile is a frown, spreading up from the corners of her mouth and rippling her forehead into a hundred furrows.

"So tell me, Shula, are you still singing?"

"No. I'm not singing any more."

The table is filled with food: olives and pickles, houmous and Turkish salad, white salt cheese and bread with poppy seeds; various aubergine dishes and a dish of chicken cooked in sugar and vinegar. I eat and Miriam watches, her own plate embellished with a half tomato which she never touches. She sips from a cup of hot water as she talks.

She was my father's favourite sister. I can see him in her kindly, slightly simian features; she has a way of standing, sometimes, which is exactly his. I see his ghost in all her gestures, the way a brother lives indefinably in a sister, or a mother in a son.

"And how is life treating you—what are you doing with yourself these days?"

I smile at her. Of all the family she is the one I can talk to, confide secrets, have a heart-to-heart. She will be pleased and amused to hear that, in my own way, I have followed in the family footsteps, become a denizen of the library and a devotee of text: fully exploiting our natural bent for fact-checking and minutiae. In a previous generation, in a different skin, I might have been a scroll-checker or a scribe; now I am the secular equivalent, employing my own eagle eyes to uncover clues and errors.

I admire her library, and tell her about mine. I have a seventeenth century Dutch bible, I tell her, the crown of my collection, with windmills, a sabre-bearing lion and a snatch of bowdlerised Hebrew on its frontispiece. I have a first edition Bialik I found on the internet. I have books at home in England I would miss like children if I stayed away too long. I tell her, too, about my academic work, my baulked career; my endless search for the pristine Scripture. Miriam watches me keenly in my enthusiasm.

"Your arrival is timely, then," my aunt remarks.

I almost tell her about my encounter with Ben Gibreel, but on the point of speaking I stop myself. And in that moment I feel myself enfolded, drawn into the secrecy of a collusion which has barely started yet.

Instead I reach into my pocket and without speaking, I place the photo of Hannah on the table. Surprised for a minute, she peers and picks it up.

"Where did you get this?"

"The family album. Do you know who it is?"

She handles the picture like an artefact; the eye she casts over it is keener than ever.

"That's Hannah," she replies, and smiles at me sadly. "She nearly got married to your father once."

Chapter three

In this mythical history I have called my father Amnon, because in the Bible Amnon followed the voice of his desire and when he had achieved, no longer wanted it. My father followed the voice of his desire and still it taunted him, until everything he tasted turned to ashes in his mouth.

As a child he created the adult he would become. He had a large, pale mouth, the skin on his lips was brittle and in winter the lower lip split right down the middle. When this happened he couldn't leave it alone, he had to keep stretching and squeezing it till the blood bubbled up crimson. He did it in bed, and left red kisses all over the pillow. There was never any doubt as to which pillow was his. Sometimes, by keeping very still, he managed to create a bubble of dried blood on his lip with which to disgust his brothers and sisters.

Other methods were: turning back his eyelids; holding his food in his mouth and yawning; making facial warts out of chewing gum and hair.

He was sensitive about his ears. Like his brothers' ears they stuck out like jug handles, almost at right angles. For years he tried unsuccessfully to train them flat. He slept on his side or he pinned them back with bandannas and chewing gum. Nothing worked. Eventually, as he grew up, something altered itself—the shape of his head or maybe the shape of his ears—and they flattened back into nothing extraordinary. But the fact remained that his ears were the curse of his youth.

His nose, by contrast, betrayed him in later life. It started out unexceptional enough—no Greek or Roman sculpture, it is true, but all the same, a quite acceptable nose. Only when he got older did it start to swell, black hairs grew out of the nostrils and a constellation of enlarged pores opened up across the top. It became what he called a prize potato of a nose. He could joke about it, but the transformation of his nose was mortifying.

When my father was five years old he received a bang on the head which very nearly killed him. According to family legend it was nothing less than a miracle that he survived.

At this time the family was living in a tenement along the Jaffa Road. A four-square tenement built like an army barracks, with one tunnel entrance which was locked at night. A fortress of a building whose high verandah ran around the top storey like a gallery. Steps ran down on stone buttresses from the upper floors. In one corner was a tiny synagogue. In the courtyard, a single privy and a well.

My grandparents rented a two-roomed apartment on the upper floor of this tenement: one of these, divided by a curtain, was the children's room. The other was salon, dining-room and study; their parents slept there on a foldaway divan.

My grandmother cooked on the verandah winter and summer. She stored the household water in an old stone jar. She hung out the washing across the narrow alley, where it was sometimes knocked down by passing camels. She scrubbed the clothes with blocks of yellow Nablus soap.

On winter mornings the boys went up to the little synagogue and roasted potatoes in the ashes of its dying stove. These they put in their pockets to take to the Tree of Life School across the Jaffa Road.

It was November, the month of the shooting rains. The street below the tenement was like a river. Bubbles burst from the surface of the Jaffa Road. Grooves and wadis were carved in the back alleys. The courtyard of the tenement was filled with pools.

My grandmother was making *cholent* on the verandah. My father was playing on the back balcony. He was trying to draw water from the flooded gutter, using an old shell case fastened to a length of string. The string was not long enough, so he fetched a footstool; leaned over the rail, and fell without a cry.

It was Silber the student who found him. He lived below my grandparents, in a one-roomed cellar of the tenement: he was unmarried, a devoted scholar, and was to die of tuberculosis at the age of thirty-six. Though harmless, he was not popular with the inhabitants of the tenement, chiefly because of his habit of remaining long hours in the one privy reading the *Yiddische Zeitung*. Though the children threw stones at the door he would ignore them, and emerge in his own time, unruffled, smoothing the pages of the *Zeitung* with a sinuous hand.

He was returning from shopping when he found my father, his precious life-blood running away in the gutter. His first impulse was to stop the blood. He plunged his fist into his bag of coffee and pressed it in trembling handfuls onto the wound; then he picked up the unconscious boy and ran with him, on his long legs, all the way to the Righteous Gates hospital.

They did not expect my father to recover. The skull had cracked open, laying bare the brain. Meanwhile the coffee and blood mixed together into a paste which hardened into a black sticky crust, and the crust solidified into a fragrant helmet over my father's wound, so that the doctors could not remove it without causing further trauma to the brain. The coffee led to an infection and for three more days my father lay delirious while Silber sat reading the *Zeitung* by his bed.

But after a week he woke from his delirium to the cry, A miracle! His miraculous recovery marked him for a special life. The scar on his forehead remained a sign of the miracle: a sinister image of the thread by which his existence hung.

When he was very small his mother would dress him in an English sailor suit with short trousers and a buttoned panel in the front, and later he graduated to a Norfolk jacket with a white wing collar, knickerbockers and black stockings and a pair of heavy leather shoes. His pockets were always bulging, full of mischief: a tin whistle, a handful of sweets stolen in the market; fivestones, a lamb's tail; a dead beetle wrapped in sandwich paper. He only stole what grew naturally or was unattended, and whatever lay unclaimed became the object of his kleptomania. He stole flowers for his mother from the Bukharan gardens, and figs and plums from under the noses of the Arab watchmen. He was a gangster hero to his generation, settling disputes and demanding loyalty, buying sweets with his lunch money and selling them at a profit during classes. He was a gambling racketeer: there were bets laid on fivestones and cockroach racing, and every summer the big bee-flying tournament. Later, when he was better off, there was interest paid on loans. He received the Yiddish classics by mail order: *Journey to the Centre of the Earth* and *The Adventures of Sherlock Holmes*, *Tevye the Milkman* and *The Hunchback of Notre Dame*, kept in a locked cupboard and loaned out at a *grush* a week.

From the age of five he attended the Tree of Life School, where the rebbe beat time to the liturgy with a notched stick which he brought down regularly on the children's knuckles. All morning he would watch the shadow move on the sundial of the tall Clock House across the road from the Tree of Life School, and the hands on its two clocks, one for Arabic, one for European time, slowly marking off the hours of his incarceration. No matter what time he looked at them the two clocks never agreed. The rebbe conducted; the children musically repeated:

El—melech—ne'eman!
God—faithful—king!

until the liturgy was carved into their souls like the names in the ancient planks on which they sat.

When he was nine years old he had an argument with the rebbe. He criticised Jacob for tricking Esau out of his birthright, and the Lord God for approving the deception. The rebbe, in a fury, sent him home, where he spent the afternoon making noodles with his mother. On his return to school next day the rebbe demanded an apology.

"God was a trickster!" the boy repeated. "I still say so and I won't apologise!"

His teacher then locked him in the broom cupboard for an hour and there, in the rag-smelling darkness, he lost his faith.

After that he was willing to indulge in any amount of blasphemy for the edification of his schoolmates: making up rude rhymes based on the liturgy, the *Shema* said backwards at breakneck speed, and writing the name of God on a piece of paper, which he would then tear up and wait for the divine wrath to descend. After he lost his faith he performed this act frequently in the presence of witnesses, and to the best of anyone's knowledge he was still waiting.

But the family was not of the most Orthodox: the boys wore their sidelocks short, the merest tuft that could not be noticed, and on their heads they wore the *casquette* or peaked cap in substitution for a prayer cap. Though my grandfather kept the commandments he did not interfere with his children's opinions; but he did expect them to observe the Sabbath. He let them visit their friends on a Saturday after services, though he had no notion that Cobby sloped off to a meeting of the Socialist Youth or that Amnon ran all the way down to Beit HaKerem, flung off his *casquette* and played football with the heathen.

When my father was twelve years old they moved to the new bungalow at Kiriat Shoshan. From then on, each night the children would make their way home from school across the mile of rocky ground to the new district, past the morgue of the Righteous Gates hospital where the dead lay in the darkness, lighting their route with a candle stuck inside an orange peel. In summer the land gave up its snakes and scorpions; in spring it bloomed with a brief rush of flowers. They were familiar with everything that grew: cyclamen, anemone, milkweed, mandragora.

At night my father would keep the watchman company on his rounds of the neighbourhood, walking the starlit streets until the small hours; he would return chilled to the bed he shared with Saul, climb under the quilt and pull the warmest part of it to himself, leaving the skinnier boy to shiver on his own. The next morning, tucking in the sheet, he would sneak a read of Saul's latest verses.

In the summer of his eighteenth birthday he took his first lone trip to Tel Aviv, rattling down in the old bus from the hills to the plain, his gaze fixed on the unfamiliar landscape or on the inevitable sign, No Smok, No Spit. He wandered like a tourist among the white buildings. He walked on the seafront and admired the Casino with its striped awnings and its two round banners, like curious windmills, perched atop a Moorish balustrade. Peeping through the fence between the men's and women's beaches he spied on plump *Yekkes* and skinny Yemenites, on fat ballebustahs sitting on the sand in their brown hose. Since he had never had the opportunity to learn to swim, he strolled on the beach in his shoes and gazed, a landlocked Jerusalemite, at the blue vision of the sea with all its distant promises.

He had completed his senior studies, but on the handwritten diploma in which he was awarded an Alpha plus for Talmud and an Alpha for Literature he received, unaccountably, a Beta minus for Biology, and since Biology was his favourite subject this was a terrible blow. His plans wavered, his confidence was shaken. Nothing his father or mother could say would rally him. His whole future vacillated on the pivot of a Beta minus.

That winter he rode up to Tiberias and passed a frigid interlude of three weeks in Saul's bachelor flat, a hole so dismal even the walls wept, at the top of a building running with cockroaches and stray cats. Saul's door was identified by a grinning concave wound, created by successive tenants who had discovered that because of its warped frame, it would only open with a kick. On the ground floor, near the entrance, the landlady lurked all day with a stinking mop, and whenever the brothers passed she would remind them: "You can pay for that door, you know."

The visit was meant to be one of reconciliation, but since neither brother acknowledged there was anything to reconcile, it only served to confirm their frosty relations. Sometimes they played chequers, but these were games of such venom and subtle rivalry they could hardly be called amusements. Saul worked in the evenings, his head bent over an untidy heap of school exercises. Amnon went walking by the Sea of Galilee. The water filled him with a strange, mesmeric calm, and for the first time he understood what held his brother spellbound in that place.

He returned to Jerusalem, but he could no longer bear the stultifying atmosphere of Kiriat Shoshan, where the streets were quiet all day and his father, in his tremendous industry, drew all the energy of the house into himself. He lay on the couch in the salon and read the newspaper; through the open door of the verandah he could hear the sounds and the silence of Kiriat Shoshan: the voices of children, the tinkle of cattle-bells. The place was always the same: always the same concourse gathering outside the synagogue, the murmur of distant prayers; the air black with religion. Sleep and ignorance was the only answer. The newspaper and the couch were his, he floated away with them like a man on a raft; he was incommunicado.

When he opened his eyes in the afternoons he would find his father standing sadly over him, or seated at the big table dealing with his correspondence, the sound of reproach quite evident in the scratching of his pen; and he would lie there unmoving, reluctant even to breathe, a leaden weight hanging in his head. His father said nothing, he said nothing either. The words hung between them, no less telling for having remained unspoken.

"So tell me, *nu*, what are you going to do with your life already?"

"There's nothing for me here. No opportunities."

"Don't tell me opportunities. You had good opportunities a year ago and you passed them up."

He walked down to the Old City and lingered by the Jaffa Gate, watching the Arab porters who waited for their burdens or lifted them up with the help of a thick band wrapped around their foreheads, bending double under their enormous weight. He thought then that he would have liked to be a porter, to choose his burdens as they came to him. He thought: Even a porter is able to choose his burden, but I can't decide which load I want to lift.

He knew then that his childhood was truly over. It was time to begin a new phase of life. So he collected his few belongings and left Jerusalem, climbed on the bus and went to Tel Aviv.

Chapter four

This morning, in the queue behind me at the checkout, he was there again: an anomaly in a silver caftan and a halo, under the strip lighting of the Supersol.

I had the distinct impression he was following me.

It had been strange to find myself in this gleaming supermarket, which, landing like a craft from outer space, had all but obliterated the site of Kneller's once famous grocery. I remembered the grocery from my earliest childhood: full of boiled sweets, obscure tins and dusty boxes, its upper shelves lined with industrial pickle jars, its proprietor hunched unaffably behind the counter, squinting at the inevitable copy of the *Daily Post* and listening simultaneously to the radio news, or listening to the news and leaning over a battered volume of the *Talmud Bavli*. If you could not see what you wanted he would disappear into a mysterious back room, a sort of Aladdin's cave from which he would emerge eventually, not with the exact item but with an approximation of it so close you didn't feel you could refuse: it was the thing you wanted, distorted by a dream. Later, as he grew old and frail, he employed a succession of young boys and girls to do the heavy work of the store, and one of these could usually be seen arranging merchandise in the back room according to a strict blueprint. He extended credit beyond what was reasonable and retained the same mouldering stock for years on end, but despite this he kept the business going for more than four decades. His shop, with its single low-energy ceiling fan and its smell of stale bread and vanilla, was a focus and landmark in Kiriat Shoshan, whether to the children who raided it for sweets on their way home from school, the women who carried their baskets there daily or the men who lingered to talk over community matters with Kneller in his capacity as treasurer of the Tent of Joseph synagogue.

In later years, it is true, locals patronised his store more out of a sense of loyalty than out of need, and they felt always, as soon as they stepped into its scented interior, as though they had been transported back into a redolent past. This was more true than they knew, for the shelves were filled with historical artefacts, and Kneller himself was a relic of great antiquity. Every year when we visited my father would hear unfounded rumours of his death. He would say to my aunt: "I'm very sorry to hear that Kneller is dead." "Kneller is dead?" she would cry. "Who told you such a thing? I saw him only yesterday outside the synagogue." And true enough, Kneller would still be alive. This rigmarole continued for a decade or more: the old man survived his first death by a good few years, and never suspected how often he had risen from the grave, until one summer when my aunt announced: "I'm sorry to tell you Kneller is really dead this time."

Now his shop, too, was gone: replaced by an anonymous supermarket, its shelves sleek, its two tills operated by gum-chewing checkout girls.

Outside on the pavement, my friend accosted me, keeping pace as I walked quickly up Rabbi Kook Street. Sharp noon shadows flicked over us one by one. "I don't mean to harass you," he said. "It's just," he laughed nervously, "you're the only one I find approachable."

I raised an eyebrow at him, sidelong. He had no difficulty keeping up. In fact, he was remarkably fit for a religious scholar.

"You're different from the others," he added.

"Yes," I said, "I am different. I'm an outsider."

"Then we're alike. I am an outsider too."

I kept on walking and I shook my head. "I'm not your sort of outsider."

"How do you know you're not? You don't know anything about me."

"And you don't know anything about me."

"I never said I did. Your problem," he declared, "is that you judge by appearances."

I stopped, and took a good look at him. He was smiling gently; his eyes twinkled. His curls, slightly windblown, gleamed on each side of his face. I knew, somehow, that I was falling into a trap. "You're religious. I'm not," I said. "We can both judge that much from our appearances." He just went on smiling, so I pursued the point. "You're a religious man," I said recklessly, "and I'm a non-religious woman. That much, I would have said, is pretty obvious."

"We're not as different as you think."

"More different than you seem to think."

"You are not non-religious."

"Ha!"

"And we are both alone."

"I am alone. You are not alone. You have your whole…organisation behind you. In any case," I added, "I'm happy to be alone."

"I never suggested you weren't. As for me…" He broke off cautiously, then said: "I am alone in quite a different way."

I didn't move from my place, leaning against the wall under a pepper tree. An early spring warmth was in the air, and the smell of warm dust, and a sound of vacuuming from the windows of the nearby flat; and I knew in my heart that I was enjoying this conversation.

"You like to argue," he said.

"Actually, I loathe arguments." I paused. We both had to smile at this. "I just don't quite understand what it is you want of me."

"Only your assistance." He hesitated. "Your co-operation. Your friendly co-operation, if possible. I really do need to see the Codex."

"Hmm!"

"*Gveret* Shepher—Shulamit. May I call you Shulamit? You think I am trying to trap you. You think I'm trying to get friendly with you for my own ends. It's true. I don't deny it. But I do find you a very interesting person."

"It's at the Institute. It's out of my power."

He ruminated, running his right index finger along his upper lip, in the pose of a student bent over the Mishnah. A shudder of unidentifiable origin ran through me. His eyes on the pavement, he asked: "Do you know the contents of the colophon?" Raising them, he fixed me with a gaze which was quite unnerving.

I laughed. "It's a fairytale," I said.

"Why a fairytale? Don't you believe in anything?" He spread his hands impatiently. "Your Codex, as you call it, is the rightful property of the tribe of Dan."

I could not help grimacing with embarrassment. "Yes, but it's a concoction, isn't it. A made-up story. That's what the professor thinks it is."

"A strange sort of professor who distrusts the evidence of his own eyes."

"On the contrary, a very sound sort of professor." I pushed off from the wall decisively, and walked on. "Anyway, how come you know so much about it?" He didn't answer; he was hanging back. I turned. "I didn't mean to offend you."

"No. It's all right." He gave a rueful smile. "Really. But I thought I'd better stay out of sight of the house." He indicated the bungalow, which was only a few yards ahead.

"Oh."

"I'll see you later," he quipped, and without waiting for a reply he strode off fast, clutching his striped carrier-bag of groceries.

Chapter five

Jerusalem, The Holy City, 17th Cheshvan

Our Dear Son!

We have your letter of November 1st. Receive our blessing on your appointment to the post of Teacher of Hebrew and Arithmetic, that you should work hard, and advance successfully, and succeed from there to find your way in life, in a manner which will give your parents satisfaction. No doubt it is, in your eyes, a humble beginning, but don't forget that your father also began from such a humble position, as it is written, And let them not have cause for shame through me, and let me not have cause for shame through them. And let us say, Amen.

On receiving your letter we set aside a special file for you, the third that we have had cause so far to open. In it we have put your letter and a copy of this, our own reply to it. The first two files are already bulging. See to it that yours isn't to be found wanting. Some effort on your part will be required for that, since I'm not as young as I was, and won't be writing in the way I used to, every week, even when I got no reply from my children, and the file filled up mainly on my own account. Now I'll only reply to each letter I receive.

Of course, one must pay heed to another important factor: that is to say, the content of the letters. They must contain, exclusively, good and cheerful news. This may not prove so easy to achieve, especially because of the tendency we have often noted, towards melancholy and dissatisfaction; nevertheless we hope it will be the case.

All is well here. All the family send their warmest greetings.

Blessings from your mother and father,

Joseph

P.S. Write and tell us how you're getting on.

Jerusalem, THC, 8th Nisan

Our Dear Son!

We read with interest of your application for the post of Sanitary Inspector of Foodstuffs in the Municipal Health Department. Certainly the post is not without its importance, but will it offer sufficient intellectual stimulus? Teaching, though less adventurous, will always provide challenges for the mind. We feel sure you will act for the best, and wish you every success in this new venture.

It's a pity you aren't getting satisfaction from your teaching job but they did offer you better positions a year ago and you turned them down.

All are well here. Nothing to report. A dealer in books called by, a Persian Jew, asking after valuable volumes. But as I informed him, your mother parted with all our rare books during the War.

Miriam is waiting for your letter. She asks me about it almost every day.

It seems Ben Zion will not be able to travel from Boston for Passover. You, of course, will come for the festival.

Greetings and blessings,
Joseph

Jerusalem, THC, 14 Tammuz

Our Dear Son!

We thought you were coming for the Sabbath, but you didn't come. From the tone of your letter it is apparent that you haven't got any substantial source of income in Tel Aviv just now, and it also seems that you are suffering from a lack of basic necessities. Why, then, do you stay in Tel Aviv? Come home and stay with us until you are able to decide your future. Perhaps in the meantime you will find some teaching work of the same kind you are doing in Tel Aviv.

It pains us to see you in this situation. If the private students you are seeing really are trying your patience, have done with them for your sake and for theirs. Above all, come home and let's talk about it, and reach some arrangement for your long-term future.

Miriam is still asking about her letter. Enclosed is half a lira. We thought you might be in need of a small sum.

Greetings, blessings from all,
Joseph

This is the city my father came to: a city of straight streets and regular lines, pale blocks and newly planted trees. The White City, little Tel Aviv. A city like an architect's plan, unreal: where today there was sand and tomorrow was a paved avenue. A café on every corner and at the end of every westward street, the blue surprise of the sea. A city which rose like a dream, which twenty years ago had been nothing but dunes. A wedding-cake city with turrets and balustrades and Turkish minarets, ornamented with mouldings from the Alfred Willard factory at Valhalla: neo-gothic, neo-classical, Eastern and romantic, baroque, rococo, art nouveau. A city where a German immigrant could sit on a Viennese verandah and gaze across at a Moorish or Italian balcony. Everything was dazzling, everything brand new. They didn't know, then, how in time the balustrades would rust, the mouldings fade and crumble; the city built on sand being essentially built of sand.

This is the city he came to: a sallow Jerusalemite who couldn't swim. Walking unsteadily on the fresh pavements, his sight dazzled by the oceanic light. He lived hand-to-mouth, holed up in a small bare room on Gordon Street, the inevitable scrawled notice tacked up in his window: *Man Lehrt Hier Hebraisch.* A room with a sink and a small vestibule. A folding table and a folding bed. All the Simple Simons, all the dummkopfs, all the choice imbeciles who poured off the European ships at Jaffa in their tight jackets, headed in a relentless stream towards his door.

"I break, I smash, I am broken, I am smashed, I make shatter."

Hour after hour he sat and gazed out of the window while his pupils stumbled through the declensions of the regular verb. To them he seemed to possess an infinite patience, a rock-like calm unusual in a young man. They clung to him like an oracle, a soothsayer, in this strange continent, this new beginning.

"I am caused to break down, I devastate myself."

When they were gone he would walk north to the mouth of the Yarkon, beyond there to the site of the new port and the Eastern Fair, out into the orange groves beyond the city. Or he would stroll down the beach as far as Jaffa, sit on the sand in his shoes and watch the sun of desire set in the seas of his ambition. He would close his eyes and feel the sea breeze on his face, run his finger repeatedly over the parchment of his dry cracked lips. Long after dark fell he walked himself to exhaustion, unable to quell the restlessness which filled his body.

He had quickly given up his teaching post, attempted another and resigned that too; he had sent in his application for the post of Sanitary Inspector, but then withdrawn it: the title smacked too much of alienation and boredom, and besides, behind the white façades he knew that Tel Aviv stank through all its houses and restaurants; he had no desire to earn his crust by poking his nose into all the infested corners of the city. Other, similar openings passed him by: he seemed only to exchange one slavery for another, and always the next one seemed harder than the last. But it was hardest of all, he thought, for his poor students, with whom he was fast losing patience, and if it wasn't for his arrogance in wanting to improve his own situation as well as theirs, he would have scorned them and their few poor coins long ago.

Sometimes in the summer afternoons—which were often empty of any occupation—he would lie on the beach in his clothes and absorb the heat of the sun like a true lizard; his limbs would grow heavy, his head begin to bake; he would feel the pull of his scar as the skin on his scalp tightened. It seemed to him then that he would turn to lead, lie there for ever in the aching heat: he wished he might never return to the small suffocating room and his next pupil.

Miriam says that after the summers in Tel Aviv he would be quite blond, his lashes and eyebrows fair, his skin golden. His lashes were long and light, almost like a girl's. When he returned to Jerusalem for the holidays they hardly knew him: he mounted the steps of the verandah like a radiant Adam. She fetches a photograph from her family album and gives it to me, saying, "That is how he was."

I hold the photo between my finger and thumb: this fleeting image, this youthful, shining vision of my father. After less than a week in Jerusalem his tan would fade and his hair visibly darken, he would lose the golden glow of Tel Aviv and reacquire the sallowness of a Jerusalemite.

Chapter six

"So tell me," I said to Gideon, "what's it all about?"

I leant against the wall of the synagogue. The trees were restless; it was a breezy day. Rain threatened to fall at any moment. Together we gazed up at the black lettering:

> With God's Help, the Stones of this House were Laid
> To Honour his Memory, the Tent of Joseph.

It was named for my grandfather. But the name of a later benefactor had been added in letters twice as big, and the old dedication was faded, pushed aside, like a thin pauper by a fat millionaire.

"Tell me about it," I said. "I'm prepared to listen."

Instead of replying Gideon looked away, into the middle distance where the same woman was wheeling the same pushchair round and round the square. I had seen her glance at us, I had noticed her calculating. An odd couple: Gideon in his caftan, I in my jeans.

Thirty years ago Reuben and I used to play here in the dust. We tossed fivestones and collected treasures: flower-heads, a dead butterfly, bits of glass. We climbed the walls and chased the dustbin cats which were always too canny and too quick for us. We played on the five leapfrog tyres, of different colours and sizes, in front of the ice-cream kiosk at the heart of the square. We devised a game: leapfrog up from smallest to largest; step back down from tyre to tyre; run to touch the pepper tree, all within the count of twenty. The tyres had to be taken quickly or the hot rubber burned your hands.

We would play all afternoon, and then as evening fell a change would come across the neighbourhood: shutters would open, radios were turned on, movement would be seen on the various balconies. A woman in a red flowered kimono watered her geraniums; a man in a string vest emerged, lit a cigarette and scratched the wire-wool on his chest. In the cool box of the house the adults would be stirring: Saul shuffling into the kitchen in his vest and slippers, Batsheva emerging, winding her long grey hair into a knot. Shoshanah would call our names from the verandah, a narrow, nervous figure in a green sheath dress.

As soon as night drew in and lights appeared in the neighbourhood, we would open the French windows to admit the evening air. The sky was dark blue, and the trees on the square black; beyond them glimmered the lanterns of the little synagogue. The family would forgather in the salon. Batsheva sat tatting in her rocking chair; my father lay full length on the sofa with his shirt undone. Slowly, on her walking frame, my grandmother approached, assisted by Shoshanah: a slow, infinitely painful, shuffling tread. Gently she was lowered into her upright seat. As light as bone, as brittle as dead leaves, she remained a fragile vessel of tenacious life.

So we would sit together listening to reports of skirmishes on the border and shelling in the north; of rhetoric in parliament and speechmaking in America; of the weather in the desert, on the coast and in the Galilee. From every window the same reports emerged, as every household in the district listened to the evening news.

"You don't want to tell me about it. You'd rather remain mysterious."

"I'm mysterious! You're the mysterious one."

"I'm not in the least mysterious. I'm completely up front. I don't shuffle around the bushes in a caftan and sidelocks watching people, asking questions which don't have answers—"

"Ha!"

"—making obscure allusions, throwing down challenges—"

"Have I thrown down a challenge?"

"That, precisely, is what I want to know."

We sat down then, I at one extremity of the bench, he at the other, like two bookends. "Well," said Gideon, "maybe. Maybe I have."

The rain blew in fitful gusts, a barely-felt dampness. I circled my knees with my arms. The woman with the pushchair turned back indoors.

Gideon pulled a squashed packet of Time cigarettes from somewhere under his caftan. "Do you mind?" he asked. I shook my head. He cupped a match with his long hand and lit up. He drew his first smoke with elegant concentration.

"I often ask myself," he announced, "why I am here."

"You ask yourself that?"

"Why not? Don't I have a right to ask that question?"

"Well. . . ." I shrugged. "I just thought you'd have all the answers ready."

He grinned sardonically. "I mean, I ask myself why I am here in Jerusalem. Why was I chosen? Why was I the one? I'm not really equipped for this kind of mission."

"What mission would that be?"

"Sometimes I think it was meant. And sometimes I think it was a complete accident." He looked at me sideways. "I mean, of course, my being here in Jerusalem. I don't really mean to be mysterious. I'm just unsure how to tell you about myself."

"Try beginning at the beginning."

"The beginning. . . . The beginning, as they say, lies beyond the Sambatyon."

"Meaning," I translated, "a very long long way away."

"Yes," he suddenly smiled. "That is how you take the phrase. An old folk saying. Only in my case I intend it quite literally."

I laughed out loud. "You're crazy."

"As you like." Gideon kept silent for a minute and, dumbstruck, I did likewise. "Tell me," he resumed at last, cigarette poised, rearranging his caftan with long fingers, "do you know the story of your great-grandfather and his journey to the ten lost tribes?"

"My uncle has been telling it to me, yes."

"You think it's a folktale, a bedtime story?"

"I think it's a bit of a tragicomedy."

"Yes. I can see how your uncle might turn it into that." A pause. "I wonder if you have ever thought," he went on carefully, "that there might be some truth in it?"

"Never. Not for a minute."

"You are a rationalist?"

"Always. Absolutely. And an atheist."

"There are no chinks in that rational armour of yours?"

"None," I declared, a little too forcefully.

"Strange," said Gideon. "I had you down as a spiritual person."

"How do you figure that?"

"I can see it in your eyes."

Our eyes met. In the variable light his were sea-green and steady.

"Well," he sighed. "It's possibly my mistake. In any case, I have my own good reasons for believing the story to contain some truth. Not to mention what might be written in the colophon. But of course, the majority of people will take your rationalist stance. It's only to be expected. As for the Codex—it will be acquired by somebody, someone it doesn't really or rightly belong to—and as for its secrets: we can only hope they will remain unsolved."

"What secrets?"

Gideon glanced at me out of the corner of his eye. "Oh—trivial things. The true location of the Holy of Holies. The date of the Last Judgement, the end of the world."

"Oh, *that.*"

"Nothing atheists need bother themselves with. Only I, of course, can't leave such matters to chance. For three generations we have been trying to retrieve the Codex, but we were never sure of its whereabouts until now. Now it's my responsibility to keep it safe. Return it to its rightful owners. And I'm running out of both time and options. Which is why I was rather counting on your support." He glanced at me. "Are you feeling all right?"

"Just a touch of indigestion."

"Hmm. So you see," he continued eventually, "I do wonder sometimes about the fate that brought me here. While you, of course, have to struggle not just with the reason for your being in Jerusalem, but with the accidental nature of your whole existence."

"Yes, well, I—"

"No sense of purpose. I feel sorry for you for that."

I sat up abruptly. "There's no need whatsoever for you to feel sorry. I absolutely do have a sense of purpose. The struggle is the purpose. I'd rather struggle with the meaninglessness of my existence than have all my answers handed to me cut and dried."

Gideon's smile did not waver.

"You're getting wet," he said.

"It doesn't matter."

"Yes, it does." Holding his cigarette in his mouth, he removed his caftan in one swift movement, revealing the white high-collared shirt and trailing religious fringes underneath. "Here. Why won't you let me put it on?"

I had backed off by instinct, but it seemed rude to refuse, while he held the coat out in an almost conciliatory gesture. Reluctantly I let him place it around my shoulders. It was like being enveloped in the distant past. The coat was warm and heavy. It smelt musky. It smelt of a strange man's body.

"There. That's better." He regarded me, head cocked. "You know, it suits you."

"Gideon," I said, and my teeth began to chatter. "Why *are* you in Jerusalem?"

He looked surprised. "To acquire the Codex. I thought you knew that."

"No," I replied, "I didn't. I thought you just wanted to have a look at it."

He showed not a flicker. "No," he said. "I'm here to take it back."

"Right," I said. "I see." I sat in silence awhile inside the alien coat. The rain had begun to fall harder. I was trembling all over, but not with cold.

Chapter seven

Tel Aviv, 8th June 1937

My Dear Ones!

I just received your letter, and I am truly ashamed. It really is too long since I have written. Since I wasn't the first to write, I will at least be prompt about replying.

You ask about my current situation. Really, I have very little to report. I could give you my news, but in order to call it news, it would, I suppose, need to consist of something. And since it consists of nothing, it is very difficult to find words for it. If we leave aside eating, drinking and sleeping, there isn't much left to tell you. However, I can tell you that I am in good health, that "the day is short, and the work is great, and the labourers are sluggish"—the reward however, is not much—in this regard we must diverge from the dictum of the sages. You were right, Father, when you taught me to "find yourself a teacher"—if only it were so easy as to find students—I am in harness to all the dunces of Europe, but my one comfort is that I'm not sold to them in slavery for six years. And moreover: one goes and another comes, and that's a comfort too.

Of course I have no intention of leaving Tel Aviv. Should opportunities arise, I am far more likely to stumble across them here, if you will not read too much into that 'stumbling.' But regarding my plans for the future, I'm afraid I haven't given them much thought. I'll wait for better and more favourable circumstances.

I read not a word in your letter regarding the situation at home, and I request that in the next letter, even if it be written in anger (undeserved, naturally) you'll find the space to add a few words about that too.

Please tell Miriam she will receive my letter soon.

Yours,

Amnon

Tel Aviv, 15th August 1937

My Dear Ones!

I am very sorry that you felt troubled by my last letter. If I thought that such would be its effect I would never have sent it, in fact I would never have written it at all. It was the product of an idle moment and an idle brain, I merely felt obliged to produce something, and a piece of silly nonsense was the result. Really I am not as depressed as I seem—nor am I so very short of money—I was only joking. I tried to kill the devil with a broom, simply because there was no gun in my hand.

At this moment I am lying on the beach at Tel Aviv. I've taken the great step of removing my shoes, but I haven't yet paddled in the sea. The sun is beating down without mercy and I have to get up soon and give an hour's teaching, but just now I doubt if I could ever move my legs again. My body is melting with the heat and my head is full of conflicts and I can't concentrate. But the commandment is given: Go forth and accumulate—money that is, so I must obey my Maker.

I cannot accept the sum you were so kind as to send. Believe me, I have enough and those few coins are not needed or wanted by me. Will you be hurt if I return your gift? The truth is I have no right to it. Your kindness does me more good than anything else.

Accept blessings in the name of

Amnon

Tel Aviv, 2nd September 1937

My Dear Ones,

I am hurrying to write this before I come to Jerusalem—I hardly know what feelings are churning inside me. One moment I am happy and the next miserable. One moment life seems at an end and the next, it is just beginning. If I could explain myself all would be well—but I won't write any more nonsense—I will merely bring myself to Jerusalem, to your door, and then you will see for yourself what words cannot get over.

I do not mean to frighten you with this—merely to ask, if I might bring a friend with me to Kiriat Shoshan? I have no doubt at all that you will say yes, so be pleased to expect us both, right on the noon, precisely three days from now—"And may the Redeemer come unto Zion, and let us say, Amen!"

Until then, accept the blessing of

Amnon

She had come to him for lessons, in the hot little room off Dizengoff Street which carried in its window, along with a hundred others, the scrawled notice "Man Lehrt Hier Hebraisch." She came at three o'clock and Mr. Wasserstein at five. She wore a thick winter coat, the lapel of which still bore traces of the stitching from her yellow star.

Her name was Hannah Entenmann. She was a violinist. She had climbed on the boat from Hamburg carrying her violin. Now she lived with her uncle above a dry goods store, not far from Ben Yehuda Street.

Her uncle carried a bald dome of a head between two fronds of hair: a dry, sceptical, dismissive man. She worked in the shop in return for bed and board and wiped the snotty noses of his five children. She learned Hebrew and practised her violin. She was polite, studious; she always did her homework. She addressed her teacher formally as 'Mr. Shepher' and always took care to look him in the eye.

Mr. Shepher discovered he had a regular need for polish, string, ribbon and light bulbs from Entenmann's dry goods store near Ben Yehuda Street. At first he used to find her behind the counter; then Mr. Entenmann popped up with his fronds of hair.

He lured her out. They sat in the square under the sycamores and learned the words for *sun, heat, thirst*. He tried to make her laugh, but she would only smile.

Once he persuaded her to play for him. In the back room full of dust and furniture and rolls of linen behind the dry goods store she played for ten minutes as though he were not there. She was a young woman in love with a violin. He was a young man in love with her.

She wasn't pretty. She had dark hair; dark ambiguous eyes. Rough fronds of hair fell across her pale face. She wore the thick coat in the heat of spring, and removed it reluctantly when summer came. She was polite, smiling, formal. He had to uncurl her, little by little, like a hibernating animal.

Sometimes he had to cancel Mr. Wasserstein.

The new words she was learning took on a particular accent in her mouth, an accent he was already familiar with—it was around him all day on the streets of the city, it came back at him from all his pupils—and yet strangely hers: softer and more melodic, oddly distorted and individual. He made her repeat phrases, read paragraphs from books and newspapers. When she stumbled he made her read again.

He tried in vain to correct her pronunciation.

Once she did not turn up for her lesson, and he sat there panicking for half an hour before walking to the dry goods store and discovering she was ill. Then he went down to the market and returned with melons, grapes, flowers. Mr. Entenmann accepted them with a sardonic look.

They misunderstood each other. She didn't appear at the appointed time. He went looking for her on the promenade, in the theatre, along Dizengoff Street, anywhere he might find her in the small city. When he returned he found her waiting in the stairwell of his own building.

They learned, in Hebrew and German, how to say *embarrassed.*

All that summer they played the friendship game. When she did unclose it was sudden and complete and all at once, in the cramped hot room with its entangled sheets and its tall shutters turned against the sun and poor fat Mr. Wasserstein sweating on the steps outside, and by the time they emerged Mr. Wasserstein had gone, he had cancelled himself (in the correct declension); so they went and drank iced tea at The Snows of Lebanon Café.

When he first took her to Jerusalem she wore a blue polka-dot dress and a brown embroidered headscarf and her hands were long and brown over the Sabbath candles as she made the benediction. She had a large wart on her index finger. Miriam remembers it well because at the moment she saw the wart it seemed to represent everything she felt, fourteen years old and full of jealousy, about the woman who would steal her favourite brother. She sat dumb in the corner of the salon as they laughed and talked, as the family grew more charmed and more enchanted; she looked at the index finger and thought: Witch! Later she wandered out onto the verandah, where the light from the Sabbath candles fell in long gold lozenges through the slats of the French windows, while a deep stillness had settled on the Sabbath square; she looked back at the happy gathering and thought that everything, now, had been irrevocably ruined.

"It was just selfishness," she says, smiling at me over her cup of hot water. "I was in love with him, pure and simple. I know one shouldn't admit such things, but...." She shrugs her shoulders. A moment later she adds: "It was all quite innocent, of course."

Eventually he came out to her, on the dim verandah, which was no doubt exactly what she had wanted; he asked her why she didn't join the company. She sulked and wouldn't speak; when he tried to touch her cheek she turned away. He hesitated a moment in the half-light. A moment later he went back indoors.

"That's when he made his choice!" Miriam tells me, laughing.

"Not much of a choice, I grant you, but…" She looks meditative. "Of course, a man can never really choose against his sister." Later she watched from the verandah as they walked around the square: she saw how they stopped for a smoke in the shelter of the synagogue. Three years younger and she might have told on them. By the light of the synagogue lantern she saw them kiss.

At the close of the Sabbath Hannah played for them all. She stood on the black-and-white tiles in the middle of the salon and they sat, appreciative, on dining chairs and divans, under the paintings of Parisian streets. What did she play? Miriam can't remember. None of them had much understanding of music. But she felt then, under the shell of jealousy, the sense of something less negotiable: the first intimation of a hidden life.

Oh, we all loved her, she says, we all liked her! Even I liked her in the end. I remember I asked her once to bring me one of those hats from Tel Aviv, and she brought it the very next time, she didn't forget! She was so cultured, so talented. She taught me to play a bit of violin! Yes: we were never in doubt, Father was so certain; and then it was, "When will they get married? Have they set a date?" Who would have thought it would be so different: Who'd have thought things would turn out the way they did?

They didn't know that he was also waiting; they didn't know that he was puzzled too. She was always hidden, always hard to discover: a dark-eyed, nervous and elusive doe. The she-deer in the streets of the white city. The thing impossible which he must pursue.

Chapter eight

I came in through the kitchen door and Saul was waiting for me. Lurking, scorpion-like, in the passageway, and without his radio: a warning in itself.

"Where have you been?"

"Nowhere." I shrugged my shoulders. "In the square."

"By yourself? In the square?"

"By myself. Excuse me. Could I come by?"

He moved aside at once and followed me. "I've seen you together," he said. "You have been seen."

I took off my sandals; rubbed the soil from my feet.

"You've been seen with that *frummer.* That Oriental."

"Yes." I smiled. "He's an interesting bloke."

Saul's face crumpled with petulance and disgust. "What for do you want to talk to that *goniff*? You know why he's here? Hunh? You know why he's here?"

"I think I know why he's here. Though I don't see why you're calling him a *goniff.* I'm not aware that he's stolen anything yet."

"*Yet!* she says. He's not stolen anything *yet!*"

"He's mad as a mongoose. I rather like him, though."

"She thinks it's funny, *noch*." He confronted me, nose to nose. I noticed, not for the first time, his unwashed odour. "You don't know these people. You think you know these people? I know these people. Cobby thinks he's so clever, calling up the radio, now the television; you go up there too now, poking around. Why don't we just go out and tell the whole world? Here, come, take it, take everything. Free, gratis. Like a free-for-all."

"Yes. Why not? What are you afraid of, Saul?"

"What am I afraid of? She asks what I am afraid of." He seemed to think about it, and to have no immediate answer. The question of fear seemed altogether too huge. "You come out here," he said. "You come out here. Just like your father. After twenty years." He was breathing stertorously. "What would you know about to be afraid?"

Chapter nine

Jerusalem, THC, 8th Adar

Our Dear Son!

We trust you returned safely from Jerusalem. Saul reached Tiberias without mishap.

The pleasure of your company was only partly diminished by the knowledge that we are not to see you again until Passover. Since this is the case, I am doubly grateful for the photograph of Hannah, which I have taken the sentimental step of enclosing in my wallet, mostly for my own contemplation, but also to show on occasion, should anyone care to look at my future daughter-in-law. It really is a very attractive portrait, but that is hardly surprising, since the subject has qualities which show to better advantage in a formal setting than in a casual snap.

Your presence and Hannah's was especially appreciated, on a day which for me, as I am sure for everyone, was filled with the warmth of family togetherness, the joy of being united, and a genuine sense of peace. To the holy glow of Sabbath was added the radiance of loving hearts, and I can say with full confidence that we truly entertained the Sabbath Bride.

I can add on behalf of Saul (I am sure he would not contradict me) that Hannah's setting of his lyric was very sweetly done, and if he did not acknowledge as much at the time, it is only that his embarrassment, of which you are so well aware, inhibited him from showing a proper appreciation.

Please thank Hannah again for the apple cake.

Blessings and greetings from your mother and father,

Joseph

Tel Aviv, 25th February 1938

Dear Ones,

You told me to write as soon as I was fixed up with work, but that hasn't happened and I haven't written, the fish slipped out of my fingers once again; what am I to tell you? For a long time I thought, I haven't the right to be happy, and yet for a few months I was happy nevertheless; now however I am restless again. You will say: There is no pleasing him. But what do I have to be pleased with, when my situation is so without hope, and every way I turn I find nothing but frustration? But I will not dwell on these matters: it's only that I promised to write you a letter, and since I must fill it with something, I offer what comes to hand. You will take my complaints on the chin and think "It's only Amnon."

My problem right now is a spiritual one. Which is to say: I am in the East and my heart is in the farthest West. Which is to say, in ordinary language: I feel a strong desire to go to England. The hitch is, my heart is in my body and my body doesn't have wings: a burden with nothing to bear it.

Now I know that if I could only obtain the wings, I would fly without hindrance into the horizon. If you object that the horizon cannot be reached, I will have to reply with the restlessness of youth, that that is for me to discover; but in any case, without wings one cannot attempt the journey.

Nor need you fear I will fly too close to the sun: my expectations will be quite humble. I wish only to be free to improve myself. And where else have I the chance of doing so, if not in England? She will take me, at least: I am after all her subject. So when I set down again it will be on solid ground, even if it is marshy English ground, which could not be more unforgiving than what I am used to here.

If I change sand for mud, and sunshine for English fog, that will be my responsibility and I will make the best of it. I only wish to take my opportunity.

Now I must go back down into Egypt again, which is to say, I must return to slavery: Mr. Wasserstein is my task-master.

By the way, Hannah has now joined the same treadmill as me, except that teacher and pupil alike are both more talented and more enthusiastic: they make better music with the violin than I ever did with the irregular verb.

Pass on my greetings to everyone: the little Bubaleh, the Maidaleh and so on—also to the big ones whom I'm afraid to call by nicknames....

What do you think of my chances if I took off now, before I am too old to flap my feathers? Answer me.

Blessings,

Amnon

Jerusalem, THC, 29th Adar

Our Dear Son!

We received your letter of 25th February.

Its contents in toto: you haven't found a fixed job. You don't like teaching private students any more. You want to go to England. You don't possess the wherewithal for the journey.

The conclusion to be drawn from this summary seems clear: It's therefore necessary to endeavour to obtain resources. We for our part are prepared to do this. The situation is difficult right now, but we will do our best to borrow the money.

So for your part: work out the cost and fix the minimum sum required, and we'll set about the task of finding it. Naturally, it is first and foremost necessary that you have a fixed intention; but above all, that you work out the cost.

Warm blessings and greetings, especially from Mother.

I await your detailed and decisive reply.

Your father,

Joseph

Tel Aviv, 4th July 1938

Dear All,

We've had a day pregnant with disturbances here, as you have in Jerusalem. Right now the street is relatively quiet. I stood at the police checkpoint, earlier today, at the junction of Allenby and Carmel on the Potsdam Square, where you can lean against the barrier which blocks the way (like the one at the junction of Jaffa and King George Streets in Jerusalem) and with your back to the law enforcers and your face to the populace you can watch and listen to the arguments among the passers-by. You don't have to strain your ears—everyone raises his voice in this city, it's a true city of shouters, one language answers another, nobody really understands, but that doesn't discourage them, they only shout the louder. They blend together into one great babel we call the Potsdam Chorus.

Important questions are buzzing on the corners of the square just now, so the noise was greater than usual there today. The pundits on the benches along Rothschild Boulevard express their opinions as loudly as they can, that the time has come to react, to throw away the policy of restraint, and I'm sure that if an "Araber" happened to fall into their hands there in the shade of the boulevard and the comfort of the benches, it would be the worse for him; but meanwhile they just shout (which is in itself a species of restraint), in order to make themselves heard over all the other shouters.

Meanwhile I'm putting off the evil hour, and under these circumstances there is always an excuse, before applying my brain to marking papers. The matter of my journey I've also put off for the time being, for various reasons I'm trying to ignore.

Write and let me know how you are. And peace over all Israel.

Yours,

Amnon

Jerusalem 19th Elul

Our Dear Son!

What's happening with regard to your journey? Doubtless you are making use of your free time to settle all the arrangements. The visa you can obtain on the strength of your letter from the university, but I'm reliably informed that if you don't send your application soon, it will be too late to sit the entrance examination this year. You still haven't let us know the details of the deposit required. Look into it and let us know so that we can arrange it now and not leave everything to the last minute. I may be able to get it through a businessman I know.

The sooner you get to London the easier it will be for you to settle in and find work before your studies begin.

You mentioned something about wishing to study law. In our opinion it would be better if you studied engineering.

Regarding Hannah we are asking you again: a) If she is remaining here then don't go without her complete agreement—in this case, we're sure you haven't considered doing otherwise. b) If she is going with you—get married here first.

Why don't you write anything about how you are?

All is well with us, thank God. Everyone asks after you, especially Miriam.

Blessings,
Joseph

P.S. If there is no danger on the road, come to us for New Year.

Jerusalem, 24th Tishrei

Our Dear Son!

Today we received the letter from the university. If there is no danger on the road, come immediately.

Your father,
Joseph

In those last months there was a certainty about her, a deep and settled calm. She seemed more self-contained than ever. Even as he lingered and vacillated, changed the date of his departure twice (it would be too late now to enter the university—he would have to reapply in 'thirty-nine) she was cool and assured, businesslike even, helping him fill in forms and pay fees, meet deadlines and make the necessary applications, listening to his doubts and agonies with a serene expression. He thought she had changed somehow in those final months, that she dressed or did her hair differently, maybe she had gained gravitas from her teaching work, or her face had aged slightly, indefinably, the way faces do. She had got rid of the coat and the beret too, the one she was wearing in the picture she had given him, so that the image he carried was already out of date and ever afterwards, no matter how often he referred to it, he would be troubled by an awareness of its differing in some infinitesimal way from the woman he had left behind.

She began bringing him treats that spring: cracknel from the market, the yellow beans he liked, a bagful of carob pods—the poor man's chocolate. She continued to study hard: she brought home poetry books, Tchernikhovsky and Bialik, as though to acknowledge they wouldn't have time for these things later. They read German together. They promised they would teach and learn by letter.

They spent a lot of time on the beach that summer. Her hair turned coppery, her eyes very blue. She looked healthy at last: she lost the pinched look with which she had first come to him. Her brown hands, searching through her shoulder bag for fruit or sandwiches, looked strangely unfamiliar: the hands of a native.

In the evenings she stood on a chair and played the violin. Watching her from the bed, he was fully aware that he did not yet know her secret, that there was still something she was not telling him.

He asked: "Will you come to England? Will you marry me?"

She answered: "I will not go to England. I can't marry you."

"Why can't you?"

"I'm telling you. I just can't."

She promised to write to him.

All that winter, in the English rain, his hair darkened and darkened, from the golden halo of the summer to a dim mid-brown; he lived like a monk and wrote letters and the letters were returned unopened; he waited for her letters and nothing came. His hair darkened and his skin turned pale, like the skin of a man who lives underground, like the face of an old saint on the wall of a church; and he walked through the maze of grey streets, in the wind, in the rain, he wrote and waited and the letters did not come. The family said: We have seen and heard nothing from Hannah. At the music school they had no news of her.

And then one day he sat in the library, and read in the paper that the virtuoso, Otto Rosenberg, the well-known violinist, had escaped Germany and was en route to join his fiancée in Tel Aviv.

Then he wrote no more letters and no more letters were returned, and eighteen months afterwards he married my mother.

Chapter ten

And now," says Miriam, "would you like some serious cake?" And she brings out from the refrigerator a boxful of elaborate gateaux.

I eat and she watches, cupping her glass of hot water with both hands: she has digestive problems, she explains, she can't eat much. Added to that she has headaches and circulatory problems, but she works hard, keeps the flat clean, cares for her plants; battles old age to the best of her ability. It's no picnic! We Shephers live long lives, and life, worst luck, is something you can hold on to even when your health is shattered.

The kitchen is immaculate, the little pans and dishes neatly stacked, leftovers saved carefully in a cut glass bowl. Everything is clean, faded, scrubbed to a dull sheen: old and respectable, well worn and perfectly usable. I am held in a moment of safe, absolute reality.

"So she was already engaged," I say, "when she came to Palestine."

"So it seems. She dropped no hint of it."

"Maybe she thought," I say carefully, "her fiancé might never escape."

"It's perfectly probable that's what she thought."

"But still," I explore my gateau, "it might have been better to be straight about it."

"Your grandfather," says Miriam, "was very upset."

I turn to the open window, where the city still twinkles in its nest of darkness: a map of gems beneath our bird's-eye view. The sky reflects the bloom of illumination; too bright to show its own network of stars.

"So they never married."

"They never married. Of course," Miriam smiles, "if they had, you wouldn't be sitting here now."

"Of course...." I maintain my gaze; attempt to hold, for just an instant longer, the shiver of a strange new revelation, along with the unclutchable, the idea: the notion of my possible non-existence.

"But they loved each other."

"We were never in any doubt," says Miriam, "that they loved each other." A silence. We are both thinking of something. The air between us grows pregnant, like a thundercloud.

"But tell me," Miriam says briskly, "something about you. How do you live now, who is special in your life?"

I return to the cake; take up my fork again and continue eating.

"Oh, nobody in particular."

"There used to be someone, I thought. Daniel, was it, you once wrote me about?"

"It was a long time ago. It ended."

"And nobody now?"

"Nobody." I turn to look at her. "There never has been anyone but Daniel."

We have tumbled with such speed into the present that Miriam seems momentarily contrite: in her eagerness to leave one painful subject behind she has blundered, perhaps inevitably, onto another.

She places a hand on mine. "Do you want to talk about it?"

I look into her sad, aged, kind, experienced eyes.

"Yes," I reply. "Yes, I think I do."

Chapter eleven

Somewhere in the heart of this file is a letter, a long white letter in a small black script, written on pages torn from a school exercise book; copied once onto blue airmail tissue, sent out in an envelope across three thousand miles; read and reread, reread and preserved; kept in a drawer, taken from the drawer; thrown onto a bonfire and risen, like a blue butterfly, on a plume of smoke, before igniting, flaming for three instants and turning into ash.

Somewhere in the midst of this file is a letter, held back for some reason though I can't guess what, put aside for some purpose I will never know. Perhaps it was this one:

Our greetings, our heartfelt rejoicings, our warmest love go out to you on the long-awaited birth of your beautiful son.

Or perhaps it was this one:

Yesterday I walked down as far as the Mandelbaum Gate, a distance which gave me some opportunity for reflection, as well as a pair of sore feet—thinking of the strangeness of this division, of the road which ends in ruins and barbed wire, cutting off, it seems, all access to the past—to the scenes and locations of my childhood in this wounded Jerusalem. All those scenes are vanished, most of those people gone. Of course, it is a life which was dying long before war killed it—for a long time I had hardly visited the Old City. But it is strange and symbolic, to be cut off by fortifications from the streets of one's past, from childhood, when so little of the future seems to lie ahead of one.

Or was this the letter my father put aside, kept separate, referred back to sometimes:

She came to see us on the Sabbath past. Her visit, needless to say, was entirely unexpected. She looked well, and to me pretty, though despite the kind welcome she received she seemed ashamed; I tried my best to put her at her ease, and I am pleased to say she grew, in time, less awkward. Saul says we should not have welcomed her; but the hurt was ours and yours chiefly, and not his, and I must say I cannot subscribe to such a harsh and unforgiving attitude, toward circumstances which were not entirely of her making, and misfortunes by no means entirely her own fault.

She is back teaching at the music school, and some time since obtained her qualification; she intends to audition for the philharmonia. She did not speak much of her private life, nor did I see fit to ask her, since she evidently came only to reconcile, and out of a genuine wish to see how we all were.

She did, of course, ask after you, and I told her you were married; and she asked me to convey her congratulations, and all her good wishes for your happiness.

She did not give her address, but I believe she is now living in a flat on Trumpeldor.

My son, you must follow the path that you have chosen. To say you did not choose it is to lose volition. The mistakes of the past are the foundations of the future. We must build on them if we are not to be destroyed.

Your mother and I have not and never will reproach you for the choices you have made.

Somewhere in this file is the precious letter. If I read them a thousand times I will never discover which.

My grandfather died of a seizure in the winter of 'fifty-six, broken at last by the Jerusalem in his heart, when the city was still divided, when barbed wire ran from Sanhedria to Ramat Rahel.

Chapter twelve

Late on in the evening Miriam's grandson drops by, a big, broad-shouldered youth in uniform whom I last remember as a little boy. A square-jawed giant in enormous boots. It is hard to believe that, in the space of two generations, this bird has produced this beast.

He sits and fills the corner of the kitchen, mops up the remainder of the food, demolishes the gateaux. He asks me laconic questions about myself. His voice is monotone; he has a languid confidence. Mostly he wants to know about the price of cars and electrical goods in the UK.

I wonder who he is, this relative of mine who bears no resemblance to me, nor, so far as I can make out, to any previous Shepher. He is long-limbed and athletic; he has a headful of dark, bristling, close-cropped hair. He is sleepy-eyed. The little boy I remember was blond and delicate; he chased butterflies in the back yard of my cousin's apartment. He ran a bright beetle over his gentle hands. He showed me where kingfishers sat in the remnants of the old orange grove.

Now where he was bright he is dark; where he was once light he is now heavy. I ask him questions and our conversation runs into blind alleys and dead ends of secrecy, classified information, drilled-in reticence. I stumble like a civilian on an assault course. I am at a loss.

Sprawled on the long gold sofa in Aunt Miriam's salon he is impressive, like a Greek statue, but utterly unknowable, a member of an alien race. He chucks peanuts into his mouth and talks in hard, clipped, resilient sentences. They glance off me like ball bearings, I can do nothing with them. I take them up sometimes, try to mould them into more meaningful conversation; but my sentences are absorbed in turn like data into a vast databank.

Aunt Miriam sits at the far end of the sofa wearing a half-admiring, half-amused expression, as though she were not in the least surprised at having produced this prodigy: on the contrary, she fully recognises this new manifestation of the Shepher clan. And as I watch him I begin to recognise familiar features: the long pale lips, the prominent ears, the way he crosses his legs or scratches his right eyebrow with his little finger. It is as if the fragments of a loved face should flicker in the depths of a hologram.

"It was Yigal," Miriam tells me proudly, "who found the Codex."

"Yigal found it? Really. Is that so."

I can tell that I am as much an object of puzzlement to him as he is to me: a foreigner, a soft-handed amateur. A sentimentalist, even. I am far too interested in the past for him. Yet his gesture mirrors mine exactly as he strokes his jaw and says: "If I weren't an Israeli I wouldn't see the point in being a Jew."

With one phrase he dismisses the whole conundrum of my existence. "It's a strange thing," I reply. "There are Jews who can't much see the point of becoming Israelis."

He shrugs his shoulders. He's almost impervious. But inside the soldier's shell I glimpse the vulnerable boy.

He says he has a friend who can rent me a car cheap.

He is a powerful being. He descends, clears platters, dispenses practical wisdom. And when he has finished he kisses his grandmother briskly, shakes my hand, and disappears once more into the humid night.

Chapter thirteen

When he has gone I tour the walls of the flat.

There are strange images here, glimmering and labyrinthine: a tumble of grey quadrangles, a series of pale blue archways one inside another. What seem to be hillsides stepping out in purple, one above the next. Suggestions of cities, suggestions of ruins. Among them, familiar pictures I still recognise: a seven-branched candelabrum, a gold-embossed Ten Commandments, elaborately scrolled and embellished with the word 'East.'

There is a studio where my aunt works, in long quiet stretches, in serene and methodical peace. Though time must be short now, she remains unhurried. She tells me she is never lonely. That there are barely enough hours in the day.

I think of my own ambitions which lie rusting in my throat, the voice I had once, which is no longer what it was.

I am tempted to try a few notes.

I think of the wrong turnings and procrastinations, the caution and failure to choose; of the sheer fatalism which has made me what I am. Of a life lived in the constant expectation that something is about to happen, that some miracle is waiting to occur. The same courage of misconception which drove my father. The illusion of destiny: that fatal Shepher urge.

Chapter fourteen

In the middle of the night I am woken by an unexpected storm.

Thunder bursts like a bomb. The room lights up. Rain sweeps against the open window. I get up to close it, and the whole sky is violet.

The air is smoky and tropical. A scent of burnt fuses hangs over the haze.

I am thrilled and full of longing.

I want to see dull brick and a pale skyline, washed-out country, bare hedgerows and a rutted lane. I want to feel English weather, a November mizzle, a gust of east wind, an estuary fog.

Home, home, home. The distant darkness and safety.

Aval zeh lo shelanu.

Part Four:
Surprise View

Chapter one

When Moses ascended Mount Sinai he found the Lord God affixing crowns to the letters of the sacred text. "Lord of the universe!" said Moses, "why are these crowns necessary?" God answered: "In times to come the learned will expound from each letter dozens and dozens of rulings." Moses then turned and found himself in the house of study. He sat down at the back of eight rows of scholars and listened carefully as they argued points of Law. The argument was abstruse, and despite occasional references to the Torah of Moses, Moses failed to make head or tail of it. He tried to follow the debate, but after some time he realised he hadn't understood a word.

Moses was nonplussed. He was filled with a crushing sense of his own ignorance. He crept from the study house disconsolate.

Why was Moses so disturbed by this incident? A fundamental point had been made clear to him. It was not until he sat in the study house that he realised the paradox of truth enshrined in language, the glittering nature of the human mind which reflects back, from each sacred word, six hundred thousand facets.

He foresaw then, in a split second of revelation, the potential for a Torah which had once been no more than a heap of letters to be slowly transformed, letter by letter, in a process of perpetual reinterpretation.

An abyss of possibilities opened up beneath him. He was seized by a sudden sense of vertigo. Just as he was about to fall he felt the wings of God's presence bearing him up.

"Lord of the Universe," he said, "was this Your intention?"

"Be silent," said God, "for such is My decree."

Chapter two

The rain pours at an angle, chased by wind, into the threshold of the apartment block, which provides virtually no shelter. We huddle close to the buttons of the intercom.

"This isn't much of a meeting place."

"There's nowhere else to go."

Rain drips down our faces. Gideon is standing about six inches away. I can smell the raw dampness of his caftan.

"Is this permitted?" I ask.

"Is it what?"

"Nothing." I edge away. "I didn't expect this weather."

I look out at it, sweeping abruptly across the deserted street, bouncing from the leaves of the oleanders; raising pockets of dust from the dry pavement.

"We can't stay long like this."

"No. We can't stay long."

He seems in no hurry, however, and it might be my imagination, but it seems to me that he has once again moved closer.

"My uncle isn't at all happy," I say.

"What does he have to be unhappy about?"

"You."

It wasn't my imagination: he has moved closer. I can feel his breath, warm in the cold air. His eyes, green as weed, have turned watery in the disturbed light.

"You know what they are saying about the Codex."

"No. What are they saying about the Codex?"

"They say it's a rogue copy. A variant version."

Gideon smiles faintly.

"Doesn't that bother you?" I ask.

"No. Does it bother you?"

I shiver; my thin shirt is getting wet. Still I strive to keep a distance between us.

"Yes, it bothers me," I say at last. "It bothers me that it doesn't bother you."

"Because you want to believe in absolute truth. You don't like the idea of there being versions."

"No," I protest, confused. "That's what *you* don't like. *You* want everything to be absolute and certain."

"No," says Gideon. "You're wrong. I don't want it to be so. I know it is so." He brushes the rain, ineffectively, from his caftan. "That is the difference between us." Suddenly he draws so close to me I can feel my breath stop, my heart seizing. "What if I were to tell you that your Codex—this 'Shepher Codex' as they're calling it—is as far as I am concerned the purest, most perfect Scripture in existence—the absolute Ur-text—the original?"

"I wouldn't believe you," I say; and add, hesitantly: "I don't believe such a version ever existed."

Just then, a man with a newspaper over his head rushes up, glances at us both, and puts his key in the lock. We move apart. He dashes into the dim vestibule and slams the door.

"You have to decide," Gideon says. "Time is running out."

"Decide what?"

"Whose side you are on."

"I don't know what you mean."

"Don't play games any more. It's me or them."

"I'm not playing games. I don't even know who you are."

"Yes, you do. You know it very well."

"Tell me then."

He stares, but he doesn't answer. For a moment we face each other, shivering. Droplets of rain hang from his eyelashes. In that moment I recognise his eyes. Just for a flash, like a name I have forgotten.

"I need your help," he says.

"To steal the Codex?"

"To steal it back. Your ancestor stole it first."

"You're saying my great-grandfather was a thief?"

"I'm saying he was part of a long family tradition."

For fully ten seconds we stare each other down. My heart is pounding. I haven't felt this way for as long as I can remember. "All right," I concede at last, and it is only with difficulty that I keep my voice steady. "So I've pinched a few library books in my time. I won't deny it. But this is something different. This is huge."

"I think you have it in you."

"Why on earth," I say, "would I believe you? Everything you've told me is preposterous."

"Not nearly so preposterous as what you are thinking now."

I turn my collar up. "I have to go."

Still we remain standing. Wind rattles in the intercom; dust swirls in the corners of the porchway. There is something fevered about it: a hectic, foreign wind.

"If you let them keep the Codex," he says, "it will be lost forever. They will fight and wrangle over it forever."

I think I might lose myself then, to the compulsion in Gideon's eyes, insistent as they are, and yet so gentle. I turn away, to escape that subtle plea.

"You know the truth," he repeats. "You have to help me."

I hunch my shoulders and run off into the rain.

Chapter three

She first laid eyes on him at a meeting of the Jewish Youth Guard. She was eighteen years old. He was twenty-three. She forgot instantly that she was engaged to be married.

It was her first winter in London. She had bought red gloves in celebration, to match the lipstick which (a girlfriend told her later) didn't really suit her. She sat at the far side of the circle, catching his eye throughout the singalong.

The girlfriend, Marlene, would tell her that she should wear a deeper shade, a sort of mulberry. She had dark hair, dark eyes, honey-coloured skin. She wore a polka-dot buttoned blouse. Her figure, fed on years of dripping and cocoa, was loose and sensuous.

"Who is he?" She nudged the girl next to her.

"Who is who?"

"The one with the eyes."

"Which one would that be?"

"The one looking at me."

She had been born in a northern terraced house with a cardinal red step and a midden at the back, but ever since she could remember London had been her promised land. As soon as she left her home it became no more than an exotic memory to which she could never return.

Much later, when the house, the street and the neighbourhood were gone, she could only piece together a mosaic of images: the Yorkshire range she used to rub with blacklead once a month; the lace curtains which had to be washed each week; a pair of brass candlesticks her mother had brought from the shtetl. The shape and colour of the cobbles in the street; a glimpse of jewels in the bottom of the beck, which turned out to be only broken glass.

"Oh, him. He's just arrived from Palestine. His name's Amnon."

On the street they called her the scholarship girl. She attended the high school; she took elocution lessons. She could recite the sleepwalking scene from *Macbeth* with all the gestures and ask for a loaf of bread in French. She was different from the rest of them.

"He's a bit of a dish, isn't he. I'd get in quickly there if I were you."

She had asked her father once what it meant to be Jewish. They were in his workshop down by the railway line, taking his beloved motorbike to bits. They had stopped for a mug of tea; he sat on a high stool and his face was spattered with oil. A Jew was like a wandering spirit, he said. A Jew was a scapegoat, but they weren't the only ones. He had wanted to go to Russia and be a Bolshevik, but he had had to stay here and marry Mam instead. Now he was going to damn well make his pile. Suffering was a brotherhood, but some time everybody had to leave their family behind and get on; which was presumably why he had changed his name from Haim Losowsky to Harry Lister. Dad had believed in the socialist utopia, but now he said it was every man for himself. On the one bookshelf at home he kept a copy of *Das Kapital* alongside the novels of Jack London which he read again and again, but nothing was left of his ideals except the revolutionary songs he sang to himself while shaving, interspersed with the arias of the great operas which he loved.

She sat in the circle, raised her chin defiantly and sang the Zionist Workers' anthem with a clenched fist. Her eyes fixed on his lips: wide, pale; one with a scar in it.

We swear it, we swear it
Our oath mixed with blood and tears
Enough, enough, in exile to stay!
Take courage, take courage, to battle for freedom
With courage, with courage, go forth to the fray!

Not surprisingly, he didn't seem to know the words.

Dad was an Englishman in every way now. He even had an English accent. Lister was like Lister Park in Bradford and Joseph Lister the famous surgeon. Dad wore a tweed waistcoat and a flat cap, he had three pipes in a bracket on the mantelpiece, Shorty, Blacky and Special, and it was her job, Hazel's, to choose one for him when he came in from work.

The Listers were proud to be English. Sometimes, when the motorbike was in one piece, they took trips into the countryside and went camping and fishing. Mam and Hazel rode in the sidecar, Mam wearing a blue gauze headscarf to protect her hairstyle and nursing an enormous handbag in her lap. Hazel felt the wind blowing in her face and thought: I'm free, I'm free, I'm free. It was the kind of sensuous delusion which would mislead her all her life.

"Shall I introduce you?"

"No, thank you. I can manage that myself."

In the year she was fourteen she had kept a careful record of her reading and counted up one hundred and six novels. She was devoted to the classics, a slave to romances of the English countryside. To sit in a meadow, reading a description of a meadow, was her idea of heaven.

Mam believed in practicality over beauty and said that that was what it meant to be poor. So Hazel's hair was cropped just below her ears in a sensible style, her heavy brown stockings were darned at the heels and her figure thickened with meals of bread and dripping and cocoa. Mam could neither read nor write, but she saw that book-knowledge was the ticket so she encouraged her daughter to learn. She kept all her school reports in an empty chocolate box along with her swimming certificates, that God forbid she shouldn't drown some day. And she egged her on to go to the Jewish youth group even though it was full of Zionists and fanatics, because who knows, she might meet a nice young man up there and maybe, one day, get married. Hazel Lister had the face of a heartbreaker, and up at the youth group she broke the hearts of any number of nice young men. But she was too good for them all: she packed her certificates and took herself off to London. She rented a room in a hostel with fifteen Jewish women and found a job as a shorthand typist at the Hammersmith Palais de Danse. She threw out her brown stockings and bought her first nylons.

At this time she still believed that London, like the rest of the world, was a riddle that could be solved. If she was bold enough the city would open to her like some complicated flower. She did not realise that the mystery would remain and that she would merely get used to it. All this life, this dynamo of things happening, would eventually become no more than a noise at the back of her head.

But at first it was just like reading a book. Like all egotists, she imagined her life as a drama in which she played the starring role. To sit in a café, reading a description of a café, was her notion of experience.

"Well, don't take too long about it or you might miss the boat."

She was her own woman now: she had tamed her hair into a smooth helmet with a garland of shining curls, and she wore tailored dresses with buttons down the front. Her northern accent had disappeared. She was a chameleon, matching the London gentility accent for accent, holding her own with the Cockney working class. She smoked occasionally, imitating the divas she saw at the picture houses, smiling at men through curtains of drifting smoke. She practised her expressions in the mirror: the strong bow mouth, the arched eyebrows and above all the soundless, thrown-back laugh, conveying a sexual knowledge she had not yet acquired. In time these unnatural expressions would become automatic: thirty years later, when they were long out of date, she would still be using them.

She had graduated from the classics to the modern novel, but she found the characters perplexing. Their motives were never clear; they neither loved nor hated, and their stories ended in mid-air. She began to suspect that either the author was being deliberately obscure, or that she was not as intelligent as she had thought. So she gave up on contemporary fiction and retreated to the classics.

She was perpetually in love. Romance was essential to happiness at the age of eighteen. Marriage was only essential to happiness after the age of twenty. That was why she broke off so many engagements. There was Danny the long distance runner, Yaacov the joker and Leon the intellectual. There was also a wages clerk at the office where she worked, named Margaret: a tired, wise-looking woman with a cloud of pale hair, whom she worshipped in secret. Danny had proposed to her with a curtain ring and she had accepted, but she never expected him to take her seriously.

And now there was him: this bombshell. Who was he, this stranger with the eyes of a poet and the hands of a labourer, whose single eyebrow, angry and concise, seemed to follow her about the room? She didn't know how to react; she was embarrassed. The circle broke up at last, but she didn't approach him.

"Hazel, you haven't met Amnon. He's our new Hebrew teacher, just over from Jerusalem."

They shook hands. He smiled and said: "You have a strong voice."

"Really?"

"Oh yes. I hear your voice louder than all the others."

That night they walked out together in the London fog: she in her button-down collar, he in his second-hand coat. She with her filmstar gestures and he with his bicycle clips. She would recall afterwards how they talked and talked, but in fact she remembered wrongly: it was not he who talked but she, endlessly chattering as they threaded the north London streets, while he shrugged his shoulders or muttered: Yes, I also…trailing off into a gesture because he barely understood a word. When they returned to the house the meeting had ended; he twisted his bicycle clips and under the streetlight asked to see her again.

They met a week later at the Dominion cinema on Tottenham Court Road. She was afraid she wouldn't remember what he looked like, but the moment she saw him, hunched nervously against the wall of the picture house, there was no mistake. She remembered the eyes and the coat. And the hunch. He kept flicking her glances, persistent, irresistible. She never could remember what it was they saw: whether it was John Mills or Paul Muni. They sat in the third row from the back and he never once touched her. He seemed to be surreptitiously mending the seat in front. It was only afterwards, when they emerged into the rushing January night, that he gave her a sudden kiss and thrust a cinema ashtray into her gloved hands.

The next day she called Danny and cancelled their engagement. It was a typhoon, a tidal wave. There was no withstanding it.

Three weeks later she packed for Stamford Hill. She found him in the tiny kitchen, cooking omelettes. As he cooked he smoked; he was wearing old trousers and a torn vest and she fell in love with him at once because no man she had known had ever been able to cook omelettes before.

Chapter four

Hurrying down the Jaffa Road I catch sight of him, striding ahead with purpose in his long coat, a black fedora on his upright head. I had never realised before how tall he was. How striking. He moves through the pavement crowds like a charmed being, like some regal figure from another age.

It proves quite difficult to keep up with him. I dodge barrows and puddles, children and strollers; run up against lamp-posts and into bus stop queues. Once again I lose sight of him; then he reappears, turning into a sidestreet that leads to Mea Shearim. I hover at the corner, dart across, then follow. He never turns around. He never notices me.

I ask myself: What are you doing? What on earth are you up to with all this cloak-and-dagger stuff? A sudden giggle escapes me. I pause, I clutch my side, I catch my breath.

He has entered a dingy little shop next door to a study-house: a mean, shabby place with cellophane in its window and a tired, dusty display of faded prayer books, children's primers, grubby skullcaps and long-unsold religious artefacts. Lurking under the archway opposite, I can just make him out in conversation with the hunched, grey-headed proprietor.

They seem to be talking at length, animatedly; evidently they know each other well. The shopkeeper reaches under his counter and brings up a small tower of textbooks. Gideon flicks through one with his elegant fingers. The old fellow claps him affectionately on the back.

A Hasidic gentleman wearing a foxfur streimel eases past me in the archway, throwing me as he does so a look of mingled puzzlement and suspicion. I smile awkwardly in return, and make as if to be moving on my way. When I look back at the shop Gideon is leaving, taking his pile of books with him. I wait in the shadow of the wall until he disappears.

Biting my lip, summoning up my courage, I cross the road and push open the door of the shop. An alarmingly loud buzzer announces my entry.

The shop is not as small inside as it seemed from without: its frontage is meagre but its bowels are deep, like those of all the best bookshops. Peering past the counter I can see that it goes back a long way, and that its walls and floors are crammed with hundreds of spines: spines wide and narrow, colourful and dark, lettered in scarlet or embossed with gold, boxed in distinguished sets or slipped in singly, waiting to be discovered. All, I can see, are of a religious nature; some are beautiful; all give off that tantalising whiff of new binding, fresh ink and paper, that scent akin to wild mushrooms picked at dawn, which for me is always associated with a gift; with love. The last thing Daniel gave me before his departure was a book of Amichai.

The proprietor, seated reading behind his counter, a large black skullcap on his generous head, looks up at me with surprise, but greets me without hostility.

"*Shalom*. Can I help you?"

"I'd just like to browse, if I may."

"Please. Be welcome." He indicates the shelves: a wide, beneficent, invitational gesture.

Under the remarkably good lighting I peruse the shelves: my mind is on something else, my heart is beating hard with my intentions, but I cannot help being distracted by the feast in front of me. Many of the books I recognise: numerous Scriptures, of course, Hebrew bibles, prayer-books and spiritual guides; tiny, exquisite psalters; commentaries by Rashi and Ibn Ezra; vast arrays of Mishnah; collected volumes of Maimonides. There is the Zohar here too, and works on the Kabbalah; Saadiah Gaon's *Book of Beliefs and Opinions*; and one I have long wanted to study, Judah Halevy's *Kuzari*—his Book of the Khazars.

I reach it down and open it. The proprietor nods at me. He has a broad, kindly face, wise eyes, a nose plump with sensitivity. "Plenty to go at, yes? Not for nothing did they call us the people of the book."

I move towards him.

"Actually, I was looking for something in particular. That book your previous customer just took away—I forget what it's called—"

"The Hebrew primer?"

"Oh! Is that what it was." I am disconcerted.

He reaches under the counter. "No. It's as I thought. There are none left. It was a special order he made. He's taking them back for his people there in Baku."

"Baku?"

"In Azerbaijan. That's where he comes from. On the Caspian Sea." He emphasises the word *Caspian*, as if to distinguish it from the Mediterranean or the Sargasso. "The Communists didn't let them have Hebrew books there for the longest time."

"Really? I didn't know that."

"So now he's taking back primers to help them learn." He shakes his head. "Such a pity. Such people. Did you see him? Like a giant, a Samson. A *shayner Yid*."

"He certainly was very striking."

"Ancestry, let me tell you. Do they have ancestry! An ancient community. More than two thousand years old. Some say they're descended from the, you know, from the lost tribes. Some say from the Khazars." Again he shakes his head. "Now look what they've come to. Tsk! A crying shame. Back in Krasnaya Sloboda, where his family come from, before the Communists they had eleven synagogues. Now there's only one. But a Jewish town. Completely Jewish. When the Sabbath starts the whole place shuts down."

"Amazing."

"The Nazis never got to them, thank God! And all through the Communists they hung on to their religion, even when they couldn't remember it all. They circumcised their children. They never forgot who they were." He sees my look is keen, so he continues: "They don't always call themselves Jews, sometimes they call themselves Juhuru. Mountain Jews. They lived cut off in the mountains for centuries. A proud people. With their own traditions." He leans towards me confidentially. "You know what? He takes his shoes off when he enters the synagogue. That's what these Mountain Jews do."

"Fascinating."

"They call him Gideon. Gideon the Danite. You know why? He says his family is descended from the tribe of Dan."

"And do you believe him?"

The old man shrugs. "Who knows? Sometimes it's not what people are that matters. Sometimes it's what they believe themselves to be."

I glance back over my shoulder to the door of the shop, through which my mysterious friend has so lately left: mysterious and now a little less mysterious, and yet in another way still more so; and I think, you are right, old man, you have a point there. Perhaps you are even wiser than you know.

"So," he places his palms on the counter, "would you like me to order you the primer?"

"Oh—no thank you." I smile. "I don't really need it. But I would like to take this." I hold out the copy of *Kuzari*. He raises his eyebrows slightly, as if in acknowledgment of the coincidence; takes it, dusts it down and wraps it up. The paradox of my existence has been that by teaching the Scriptures I have been enabled to feel nothing about them. Analyse, dissect, historicise, yes, but at a distance; it was never personal. Now, like a lava crust, the lid is lifting on those long years of suppression.

As I emerge from the shop onto the grey, derelict-looking, deserted street, I clutch my parcel to my chest and feel an odd sort of comfort: almost a resolution. I am pleased with my purchase; full of the latent challenge which comes from acquiring a new volume. New vistas are opening up before me. I am buzzing, deep down in the pit of my stomach, with an excited thrill.

Chapter five

An exchange of photographs: my mother's demure snapshot for my father's Palestinian identity card, now defunct, in which he sported a mafia-black shirt and swept-back hair and looked, so Marlene said, like a member of the Jewish Resistance. The identity card, once produced on demand for British policemen on street corners in Jerusalem and Tel Aviv, went into my mother's handbag along with a jumble of lipsticks, sugar lumps and used handkerchiefs. There for thirty years it was gradually effaced, transferred ceremoniously from one handbag to the next until it was finally laid to rest in the family album.

Her own picture was slipped into a compartment of my father's wallet, into a leather frame already occupied by the photograph of another woman. She, Hazel, was witness to the event: the old picture held down by a grubby thumb, the new one slipped over the top of it. They made rather too cosy bedfellows for her liking.

"Who is that?"

The wallet already closed, and behind his back. "Who is who?"

"Is it your sister?"

"Who? My sister! Yes."

She didn't believe him.

Those tissue-paper letters, covered in black calligraphy she couldn't read: she wondered who they were from. He had translated a letter from his father once, full of exquisite and old-fashioned turns of phrase, but not all the letters were written in that tiny curlicued script. There were others in a round hand; and she had caught sight of the writing on the front of a certain envelope, sloping and intense: Return to Sender. He had delivered a letter once on their way to the pictures, thrusting it into the red box as though he were angry. His sister again? Somehow she doubted it.

Her jealousy was a creature she fed on fragments, a thin mean animal in the dark of her mind, and whenever it began to die she would revive it with memories, nourish it on resentments, so that thirty years later it was still lurking there, running back and forth, ready to spring at the least provocation. A black headache waiting to possess her. She went through his drawer, hunting for evidence, discovered three handkerchiefs, meticulously paired socks, an education certificate, a flotsam of found and stolen objects: cufflinks, buttons, screws. A novelty spoon filched from a West End café; a dead watch picked up in a tube station. Even his hand razor said nothing about him. His possessions were a man's, impersonal; they might have belonged to anybody.

She fed her jealousy on bits and pieces: snatches of conversation, a glance, a smile. A smile in the wrong direction, a meeting of eyes; a conversation which was too absorbing. She watched for signals, read his body language. The nuance in his stance, the tone of his laughter.

"What is the matter?" he'd ask, and she would turn away, snub him in front of the whole company. She would put on the frost, the way she'd seen done by Garbo or Bette Davis, arching an eyebrow, thrusting out her chin. She gave him the silent treatment. She flirted with Danny and with Mervyn from the Zionist Youth Guard: he didn't seem to notice, didn't seem to care.

Back in the tiny flat with its rusty cooking ring, its dodgy electric fire, she raged at his turned back while he fried sausages, spat accusations along with the cooking fat; made threats to leave him, to love somebody else.

He didn't turn around as he said: "I think you should go with Mervyn. I think Mervyn would be good for you."

"Or Danny!"

"Or Danny. Danny would be good for you too."

"You don't give a damn who I go with!"

He only laughed; and she fell to tearing the pillow with her teeth, or beating his back, or throwing the hairbrush at him. He cooked his sausages, and served them up with a helping of fried bread, a piece for her and a piece for him; and they ate together at the tiny table, he in his vest and she in her cami-knickers.

He had arrived too late to enter the university, and in addition to teaching had taken on a shift at a bottle factory. She went on with her secretarial job. They worked, returned, quarreled, slept and worked; all through spring and into the early summer she wore him down with scenes and tragedies. Still each night they clung on to each other in the narrow bed originally meant for one. He hung close to the edge; she rode pillion. The bed was like a small coracle in a vast uncertain sea.

The day the war started they were out walking in the country beyond Chingford. A man shouted the news to them from his passing car.

"Get down! Get down!" he shouted. "Don't you know war has been declared?"

They jumped into a ditch, but after five minutes, seeing nothing had happened, they climbed out again and made their way back home.

With the war coming something changed in him: he clung to her more closely, talked of love, declared himself in a way he never had before. He seemed more isolated and more vulnerable, reporting monthly to the police station with his identity papers stamped 'Alien,' watching nervously as German friends were interned. The authorities spared him that fate, but he was refused for the forces, obliged to stand back as others fought his cause. It was that, perhaps, after all, which broke him the most: not the loss of communication with his family, which was now almost too painful, or his failure to enter the university, flung from his reach by the exigencies of war, but the definitive loss of manhood, the confirmation that it was too late for him now; and the jobs he must work at, menial, tedious, numbing, low-paid, degrading.

So he didn't object any more when she laid claim to him. He didn't ignore her when she spoke of plans. He relaxed under her grip, he ceased to struggle. When she mentioned marriage he no longer joked.

With the start of the blitz his evening classes were cancelled; they couldn't afford the rent on their attic flat. They moved from Clapham to St. Albans and from St. Albans to Southend on Sea. She worked as a secretary for the Refugee Commission. He got work loading wagons and planting trees.

The spring of 'forty-one found them in Henley-on-Thames, living separately for propriety's sake. By now he was jobless, paying his rent out of his meagre savings, surviving on handouts from her secretary's wage. He had reached a dead end: all his life seemed to have been chasing him to this last bolt-hole, this respectable boarding-house on a respectable street, where he lurked like a fraud in his airless, frilly room, stuffed to the cornices with furniture and cheap chintz; knowing he was living on his last shillings, counting the days until the farce ended and he would be cast out onto the street, to wander as he had been meant to, to fall into dereliction and to die, finally, as somewhere inside himself he had always intended. It was the just penalty for a great failure of judgment.

Every day as spring ripened into summer, he met her at the riverside when she came out of work. She looked cool and cheerful, as though she had just stepped out of a boating song: beautiful, and at ease, and dressed for the weather; while he slouched in his dark winter trousers, his one pair, mended at the seam. She smiled when she saw him, showing her perfect teeth: and he would absorb, for one instant and perhaps longer, something of her relaxed radiance.

Every evening as the summer deepened, as the leaves darkened and the grasses grew; as the blossom gave way to foliage and the buds on the willowherb bloomed and turned to feathers, they walked by the river and sat and watched the swans; she talked about the future and he listened; and when she talked of marriage he did not demur.

Chapter six

Day after day, religious men come to the door of my uncle's flat and plead with him to allow them one glimpse of the Codex. Men in black coats, men with silver beards, men with fervent eyes and dark glossy sidecurls. He has to send them away: he has to tell them that he doesn't have it.

It was never his intention to make mischief. He wished only to bring honour to the family name. He still thinks Sara Malkah may be amenable to reason. His innocence is touching in a man who has lived so long.

He stands at the desk in his study, shuffling through heaps of papers and muttering to himself. He is looking for something; I think he has forgotten what. His cupboards are full of documents: box files and ring-binders, cases and envelopes, wallets and folders. He classifies everything, he throws nothing away.

"Ah, here is what I wanted. No it isn't."

Because of the warm dry climate in which they are kept, these memoranda themselves have begun to perish. The paper is yellow and friable, ribbed with strange markings, as though it has survived a fire. There are letters here which have turned ochre with time, which are coated in dust, which make no sense to anyone except perhaps some long-dead solicitor or accountant. Things he has kept "just in case," "because you never know." He would like, when he dies, to leave behind a full record. All he will leave is this bonfire of chaotic words.

He tosses out an old photograph: my mother and father on the dock at Haifa, my mother in a white dress, my father in a Homburg hat.

"Somewhere in here," he mutters, "is a letter from that lawyer."

Cobby has his own theories as to where my great-grandfather spent his two years' disappearance. They are no more provable than any of my own. It's easy to imagine him crouching in some dim genizah, turning the stiff pages of the ancient books; or, having stumbled upon some remote community, lingering awhile to correct their Torah scrolls. He might have fallen ill again and, giving up his quest, lived for a few months the life of an anonymous peasant. Or, straying off-map into the Caucasian mountains, he might have discovered there a remnant of the ten lost tribes.

Cobby, a rationalist, is not inclined towards this last theory. He doesn't believe in the legends of the Sambatyon. There are no mysteries in this world which are not solvable, no lost peoples hidden in the hills.

He cannot explain definitively where my great-grandfather obtained the Codex which is now the source of such tribulation to the family Shepher. Perhaps he didn't bring it back from his journey at all. He might have been entrusted with it by some nameless stranger. He may have stumbled on it in that vanished genizah where he spent his missing years.

I, on the other hand, am not quite a rationalist. Or if I am, it is only with reference to the present day. The present is sceptical, but the past, for me, is full of miracles. Or if not miracles then at least mysteries. Or if not mysteries then possibilities: moments of revelation, portents which come true.

So I am willing to imagine that my great-grandfather travelled on a distant journey: that his journey took him to the country of a Jewish tribe. That he lingered among them, examining their holy parchments, and that when he left he smuggled away with him this precious souvenir.

He carried the Codex back to Jerusalem in his bundle. And when he reached Jerusalem he fell into a strange malaise. Some put it down to chronic tuberculosis; others to gnawing hypochondria. Others suggest a softening of the intellect; others an inexplicable loss of faith.

Or perhaps, I theorise, he became mesmerised by that gap between language and revelation, by the imperfection of language as against the perfection of the Word. Perhaps he was paralysed by the implications. Because if God could allow versions, if God was unable to prevent mistakes, what did that say about divine power—what became of the concept of divine truth?

Cobby says: "I know it's here somewhere." He rifles through his heaps of paper and mutters to himself and shakes his head.

I look down at the photograph, at the wisps of paper which moment by moment are turning into dust, and I think: it is as true for the false evidence as it is for the genuine. Bit by bit time leaches it away. We are left with nothing more than the flotsam of our own findings. We settle for inventions, half-lies, speculations, myth.

Chapter seven

My parents were married in the summer of 1941, with a rose, a thin ring and a witness off the street.

The rose was a gift from my father, stolen from somebody's garden on his way to the registry office. It was white, and therefore a symbol of surrender as well as love. The ring was the best he could afford, and twenty years later had worn so thin he was obliged to replace it. That, in my father's eyes, was poor economy.

These are the few details we can still envisage: he had had a haircut. He was dressed in his only suit, and a tie he had borrowed from an acquaintance ten months earlier and never returned. His shoes were old, but polished to a high lustre. All his life he was a great polisher of shoes.

Mrs. Busby, his landlady, said that he looked most handsome. Apparently she had forgiven him the indiscretion with the mushrooms.

The evening before, as a mark of special favour, she had served him a plate of grilled mushrooms for his supper. My father, who had never seen or tasted mushrooms, was forced to dispose of them in the

W.C. He had no idea that they were expensive and difficult to come by. Mrs. Busby met him emerging, the empty plate in his hand.

But it was his wedding day, and she had got over it. She even shed a tear as she handed him his hat. Her own son, Billy, was with the forces. She didn't know when he would next be home on leave.

She twitched back the curtain and watched him cross the road. He might be a foreigner but he was still a gentleman. A real handyman, too, about the house. His girl was pretty, of course. "But she'll run to fat," Mrs. Busby said aloud, stabbed by a moment's jealousy. "I can see it in her calves."

So my father crossed the road and disappeared around the corner. Now he was lost to Mrs. Busby's sight and, if she but knew it, lost to himself. He walked quickly, a man with a destination, but his mind was blank. After the incident with the mushrooms he had felt dreadful, he had tormented himself all evening and most of all he wanted to cancel this craziness and go home. For two and a half years he had been hounded by an irrevocable decision, a decision which now seemed to have been taken in the distant past, but on that last night he had realised that it is not decisions which are irrevocable, only deeds.

Now he was going out to do the deed.

It was then that he stopped in his tracks, beside the white rose bush. Was it possible that he could turn aside even now, unmake the future he was weaving for himself, change his fate? No. He saw the white roses which hung over the garden wall, took one between his thumb and forefinger and wrenched it off. A woman knocked angrily on an upstairs window. He smiled at her and tipped his hat, took the rose and continued on his way. He was so happy and so desperate.

No photograph was taken of the occasion; no-one ever described it to me. Yet this is the image I have of him, walking to his wedding. A man without family or wellwishers. A man with a ring in his pocket and a sad smile. A foreigner alone in a foreign country, carrying to his marriage a simple gift of truce.

Chapter eight

Gideon says: "What?" It is only then that I realise I have been staring at him.

We are sitting together in the Atarah Café on Ben Yehuda Street. Outside the rain falls with relentless steadiness. The smells are a mixture of fresh coffee and sweet cream and damp outerwear. The windows have steamed up.

I start, and he smiles. He is watching me too, with his weed-green eyes, his cheek resting on the palm of his left hand. With his right hand he taps the ash from his cigarette. I have been examining the creases in his cheek, just under his eye; I have been wondering exactly how old he is.

"Nothing," I lie. I shift uncomfortably in my seat. The remains of my cappuccino have turned cold. It seems to me that Gideon can see through and is capable of reading every fleeting thought on my traitorous face. There is no ring, I notice, on the hand where his cheek rests.

Maybe they don't wear rings in his part of the world.

"You looked miles away," he observes, with a knowing expression.

He does not know that I know; I have told him nothing. Perhaps he fears pricking the bubble of his mystique. But if anything, now, he seems more mysterious. Less knowable for having so clear an origin.

"You haven't said yet," he adds, "whether you believe me."

It is my turn to smile then: as if believing really were the point at issue. As if I were capable of believing anything. There is something more crucial than that, a feeling I can barely frame in words. Something powerful and akin to instinct. Smilingly, under control, I answer: "I know I like you."

"I like you too," says Gideon. And lays his hand on the table. He doesn't touch me, of course. But his ringless hand lies there, like a sort of approach.

I draw back. I look away, out of the greyed-up window. "You haven't told me," I remark, "anything about your family."

He shrugs. "There's nothing to tell. I have three brothers and four sisters. All of them married. What would you like to know?"

"You're not married yourself?"

Gideon grins. "I'm the black sheep." His grin widens. "I'm the despair of my mother." After a moment he asks: "And what about you?"

"If my mother were still alive," I reply carefully, "I suppose she would wish I were married."

"And what do you wish?"

"I wish I could be happy with what I have."

"And what do you have?"

"Myself. My work. It should be enough."

"It should, shouldn't it?"

I shift again, restless under his all-seeing gaze. I can find no refuge from my rising feelings. "There's nothing to be sorry for," I mutter. My feelings are like a tide climbing in my throat, cutting off my voice.

"I'm not sorry," says Gideon. "I'm glad I met you."

I almost rise in my seat. From somewhere close by, from somewhere at my back, a whisperer is repeating in my ear: He only wants the Codex. He is only trying to manipulate you. "You do know," I say abruptly, "that by letting you have the Codex I would be parting with the one thing which really matters to me. The one thing which might rescue my whole sorry career."

We confront one another then. We regard each other. Gideon's face is graver, sadder than I have ever seen it. Mine may be on fire. "Yes," he replies, serious, "I do know that. Don't imagine I am ignorant of what I ask of you."

"If it is a variant version there is nothing I would like better than to sit for three years or so and analyse it."

"Absolutely. But do you think your relatives will let you?"

"If it goes back with you to—to wherever, I won't even have that possibility."

Gideon is silent. He plays with some crumbs on the table: his fingers are long, elegant; an artist's fingers. "Who knows," he murmurs, almost inaudibly.

"I won't," I say briskly, a cold wave rushing in, "and you are asking me to make this sacrifice."

"I am simply asking you to do what's right."

We both fall quiet; there is no more to be said. The bustle and noise of the café around us increases and seems to invade our intimacy; the clatter and press of people seems to want to edge us out. The thought of returning to that bleakness fills me with desolation. I want to remain here with Gideon, arguing if necessary. So long as we argue I can at least stay with him.

He looks up suddenly and his face is radiant, laughing. "It's a gift, isn't it," he says. "This secret we have with each other. I'm sure when we first came here neither of us expected this."

Chapter nine

The workshop was cold, flimsy, nothing more than a makeshift shelter cobbled together from blocks and corrugated iron; the floor was of concrete, the roof had a hole in it; it was the sort of place you might herd cattle into. Lonely, like a beginning, a bandsaw stood in the middle of the floor, surrounded by a light pool of wood shavings. In other regions stood a drill press, a mortiser and lathe.

"Rescue job." Dad pointed with the bowl of his pipe. "Cobbled together out of salvage from a bombed out factory. Put it together myself. Runs like a bird."

Amnon looked suitably impressed. He got down on his haunches to take a closer look. He was interested. The machine brought out the latent engineer in him.

Dad wore a bottle-brown overcoat and a trilby; he was experimenting at present with a thin moustache. The moustache made him look bosslike, magisterial: it had the effect he wanted to achieve.

Amnon ran his fingers over the mechanism, the grey motor housing and the blade.

"Mind your fingers."

He stood up; regarded the equipment doggedly for a minute.

"Would you know how to use it, do you think?"

He shrugged and pouted. What was there to learn? Not much, he imagined. He would take to such procedures like a duck to water.

"I learn quickly," he said.

"I'm glad to hear it. We've more elbow room in here than we need right now, but give us time, give us time and we'll fill it. We'll have this whole place bristling with machinery." Dad chewed on his pipe, which was unlit: the workshop had been burnt down once already. He placed a hand patronisingly behind Amnon's arm. "Let me show you the yard." They stepped outside into the bare compound, where a few heaps of timber stood seasoning in the rainy air.

"Supplies are still difficult, of course," he said. "But things are improving. And they'll be wanting furniture. All those growing families, all that new housing. You mark my words. From here on in it will be up and up." He looked down then, surreptitiously, at his son-in-law's hands. In a split second he assessed them: strong, clumsy, but a good worker.

They walked back through the rain, past the tarred shed stacked with carcases, toward the small office which was little more than a prefabricated lean-to. There under the warm glow of an electric bulb—the day was already fading—Hazel waited for them with the tea made.

"I tell you," he said, "it's the entrepreneurs now who will make the money. What this country needs right now is enterprise. You have to be on the ball: grab your opportunities. You can take risks and be a winner or you can sit on your wage packet and stay a worker. Twenty years from now we'll all be capitalists."

He followed the young man into the factory office: inside it was warm, probably too warm, and stuffy; there was the smell of paper and typewriter ribbon and the burnt dust of the electric heater. Rain trickled down the windows and pattered on the thin roofing; there was something comforting and safe about it. Hazel met them with smiles and mugs of strong tea. She wore a cream high-necked blouse which suited her and her hair was fastened with a purple ribbon.

"So, did you see everything?"

He could tell she was eager. She possessed a new confidence here, on her home ground; she had relaxed back into something of her former precedence. She was still the scholarship girl. She had fallen again into the old partnership with her father: she talked to him boisterously, in an accent Amnon did not recognise.

"So, what do you think?"

She had brought him up north like a trophy, like the spoils of war brought back from a far battlefield to dazzle the home tribe. They had had nothing, nothing at all: only her brown suitcase filled with buttoned dresses and his battered valise. They had seventeen pounds nine and sixpence between them. Dad had been quiet and circumspect at first; he removed his pipe and shook hands in front of the mantelpiece, and looked his new son-in-law slowly up and down, as if to assess with one gaze his entire character. Mam had been less restrained, shoving him a bowl of chicken soup, asking him a battery of leading questions; when he had gone upstairs to wash his hands she took Hazel aside and muttered in her ear:

"He's good-looking enough, but what for did you have to take up with a bloody foreigner?"

Now he would start working on the shop floor at a wage of four pounds a week. He learned to use the bandsaw and the surface planer. He inspected the blades regularly and brushed them clean. He maintenanced the belts and oiled the pulleys; he worked on the old unguarded bench saw and lost the tips of three fingers. He stood by the boiler and ate bacon butties, washing them down with mugs of amber tea.

All day he worked hard at the bench saw, rough-cutting and thicknessing and ripping down to size. He planed and edged and faced the lengths of wood. In time he graduated to the jig and mortiser. He learnt to use the spindle molder and the lathe. He turned out stools and tables for the public houses, heavy three-piece suites for the rising middle class. Armchairs and sofas, dining chairs and tables, to fill the cohorts of new houses springing up like mushrooms in the aftermath of war.

The men took to him and called him 'Arry, but they knew he wasn't really one of them. It wasn't just his status in the business: it wasn't just that he was the boss's son-in-law. He worked harder than they did, he was cleverer than they; he would stay late in the shop, working a two-hander with Dad to fulfil the orders. He talked in a strange, dental accent it wasn't always possible to understand. They could feel his foreignness; they could sense his difference. Though he acted the part they knew he didn't belong.

Maybe, too, it was something in Dad's attitude, jocular at times but always a little condescending, which told them something they couldn't articulate about his standing there: never fully the manager, never quite the boss.

Hazel sat on a stool in the flimsy office and did the wages and wrote up the books. She gained weight; she let out her buttoned dresses. She wore full skirts and polka-dot shirtwaists. At night he fell into bed next to her exhausted. She clung silently to his redolent back.

Downstairs, in the drawer of the kitchen tallboy, his education certificates turned brown and gathered dust.

They moved to a brick through-terrace on a rent of ten shillings a week, with a coal bunker in the backyard and a cinder path. They acquired a refrigerator; they purchased a secondhand Hillman Minx. He was losing his hair; hers grew out, grew long and lost its shape.

They drove to the seaside, ate fish and chips under a bandstand and huddled together in the freezing rain. It was their first real holiday. They drank tea from a thermos, chafed each other's hands and gazed through the streaming window at the grey unenterable sea.

What did she think then, as she looked into his eyes and saw that something of their intensity had vanished (the evidence is in the photographs), that they had acquired instead a permanent wistfulness? The eyes of a poet who will never write any poems, whose achievements will always be held inside himself? But maybe she didn't see; or maybe she looked at his hands, which were hard and callused, ingrained with perpetual oil (the tops of three fingers missing), or the lines of his face, drawn by hundreds of hours spent toiling at the lathe.

It was all she had ever wanted: a house with a bathroom and a washing machine, a garden with peace roses and a patch of lawn.

Children; though all she got was blood, repeated trauma, the series of lost half-formed brothers and sisters who sometimes visit my dreams. She wanted sunshine and safety, a lounge with a skater's trails carpet and coffee afternoons. A house in the suburbs with white pebbledash and a blue-and-pink Vauxhall in the drive.

Dad said: "He'll never be Hepplewhite. But he's a hard worker. Clumsy; but I'll give him full marks for effort."

He was losing his hope along with his hair; he was growing older. She looked in his eyes and saw that he had aged. His teeth were yellow; his temples were touched with silver. He developed shooting pains in his head and back.

One night out of many he worked late at the factory. Alone in the big workshop he fixed a damaged band saw motor.

As he worked he thought about his life.

Life, which had seemed so broad and full of choices, had chased him down into this narrow place. A narrow, chafing place from which he could not extricate himself.

If he looked back, if he tried to identify the process by which he had come here, it seemed to him sometimes as though cosmic and omnipotent forces had conspired to ambush him. He had been driven by necessity, trapped by war, ensnared by economics, duped by love.

In the days of his youth he had made one irrevocable decision. Through one moment of energy he had changed his fate.

There was nothing he could do about it. He knew that as he dismantled the electric housing, as he disconnected and reconnected wires. The silent machines, attached like dogs each one to its own belt and motor, bore down on him with their sheer dumb reality. The smell of woodshavings mingled with his own sweat.

There was after all something satisfying in this manual work, in being alone here in the big workshop, oil on his hands and sawdust in his hair; alone with the big machines which were like him, dirty and dogged, used to hard labour, silently enslaved to their situation.... He hooked up the band saw to the motor of a redundant lathe.

It was ridiculous to say his life was ruined, when he had a wife who loved him, a business and a house, when anyone might well ask him, What more do you want? What more did he want other than the impossible, to change history, to go back and unmake the fabric of his life?

So as he worked the argument turned in his head, back and forth, positive and negative, as he twisted the wires and fixed them into place; as he picked up the spanner, as he grabbed the live plug, as a bolt of electricity shot through him and turned him instantaneously into a throbbing conduit; as the force of the current flung him like a rag doll across the workshop, supine and aglow, his veins a pure stream, negative-positive, positive-negative....

What ran through my father's mind then, at the moment of his near-death? What revelation struck him as he flew? No revelation, but a concrete pillar, which knocked the hot plug, smoking, from his hand. He fell and lay unconscious in the woodshavings for half an hour.

And what a calm half-hour that must have been, plunged into the abyss of pure forgetfulness, when my father lay sleeping on the workshop floor, at the true centre of his life, believing he was dead.

But then he awoke and, realising he was alive, staggered to his feet. And battered, burned, exhausted, unresolved, he closed up the workshop, climbed into his car, and drove home shakily to his sleeping wife.

These are the words which absorbed my father's youth: butt joints and lapped joints, router and sander, butt chisel, shave hook, gouge. Caught as he was in the geometry of choices. Fixed in the vise of a deed he could not change.

Chapter ten

Moses was complaining to God. He said: "The greatest day of my life was the day I climbed Mount Sinai and received the Torah." God said: "Even so." Moses went on: "Do you know which was the worst day of my life? That day the Children of Israel fought the Amalekites at Refidim. I had to sit on the mountain and keep my arms in the air all day. When they were up, we were winning, but when I let them drop we started to lose." After a pause he continued: "I couldn't join the battle. I couldn't do anything except sit there. You didn't give me the energy to fight, but you made me responsible for the death of my soldiers, when I didn't have the strength to hold up my arms any longer." God considered and said: "Aaron and Hur were there to hold your arms for you." Moses said: "It was the most humiliating day of my life."

Why was Moses so distressed by this episode? Because it revealed, in microcosm, the truth about his existence. He as an individual possessed no power. He was neither more nor less than a conduit for the power of God.

His responsibility was great and so was his weakness. At that moment Moses was gripped by the paradox of his own free will.

All is foreseen, say the rabbis, yet freedom of choice is granted. A man will be guided the way he wishes to go.

Chapter eleven

The Ben Or Institute is a stone pillbox in a collection of stone pillboxes of varying height in one of the western suburbs. A three-storey building in the heart of a quiet avenue, next to a small public garden where I eat sesame bread and takeaway coffee in the afternoon sun.

Inside, the stairwell is dark and imbued with the smell of old paper (I have never liked lifts, and in twenty academic years my habit of using institutional stairs has kept me mountain-climber fit) and at every landing is a view, through a grimy, grilled window, onto the mass of cypress outside. The library itself is on the third floor, strip-lit, utilitarian, stuffed to repletion, and comfortingly familiar to someone for whom every library is a home-from-home. A few bespectacled readers, a few religious students, glance up at me briefly as I pass. The door to the office at the far end stands open.

"Miss Shepher. *Shalom, shalom.* Come in, please take a seat, make yourself comfortable."

Shloime Goldfarb, assistant director of the Institute, a large man in an untidy shirt, bald head part-covered by a blue prayer cap, religious fringes trailing from his waist, smelling of underarm sweat and full of business as he sits back expansively behind his desk, is still talking on the telephone. Shelves stuffed with books and folders and box-files spilling paper, some of them faded and dusty, others freshly dated, fill the walls; there is an ungrilled window looking down onto the park; a fan whirrs gently despite the earliness of the season.

There is a shambolic, academic atmosphere I am used to and like, which lulls me even in the immediate knowledge that I don't much like this man, loud, bumptious, full of himself as he is. He swings away from me in his chair as he talks, and examines his own fingers, and pats the prayer cap on the back of his head; laughs mirthlessly, but with a guttural depth resembling an earth-tremor, and finishes up, "*OK, Uri, b'seder, Shabbat shalom.*"

Then he slams the telephone down and shuffles a number of important papers, and then he deigns to turn his attention on me.

"So. Miss Shepher. What can I do for you?"

"It's Dr. Shepher, actually," I tell him. "I wondered," I say, "if I might look at the Codex."

"Yes, yes, that's right! Forgive me, I forgot. Your uncle spoke to me on the telephone." A ballpoint pen turns nervously in his fingers; he jots a few words and moves a letterhead. "So you're Cobby's niece. Well, I'll take you to the Codex. It's just downstairs. Please excuse me a minute."

The phone has rung again: he snatches up the receiver in his great paw, and turning his back, launches into a lengthy conversation.

I remain seated stock-still: my bag in my lap, my hands folded, I run my eye over the faded Hebrew spines: *Ugarit*, Yigael Yadin's *Hazor*; there are a few English books, and about thirty back copies of *The Journal of Biblical Studies*.

"*Loh loh. Ken. Loh. Az mah?*" Shloime gives a short bark of laughter. The old-fashioned alarm clock on his desk ticks lugubriously.

At last he bangs the receiver down again.

"*Nu*. Miss Shepher. I'm a busy man. Shall we go downstairs?"

What a charmer, I think. I'm sure his wife loves him. As I trail him back through the library like a new trainee I ask whether he has yet had time to make a thorough examination of the Codex.

"What—an examination? What do you mean?" His reply is so sharp I sense I have touched a raw nerve.

"I don't mean anything. I just wondered if you had found anything out."

He pulls open the heavy door and thrusts back the grille on a disquietingly old-fashioned lift.

"This isn't the Dead Sea Scrolls. It's a *keter Torah*. You know what is a *keter Torah*? A handwritten copy of the Bible."

"I know that." I step reluctantly into the lift. "I thought it contained a number of variants?"

"Well, yes," he replies, sweeping shut the grille. He presses the basement button and, standing beside me in the small cubicle, seems to regard me for a moment with increased respect. "There are a number of textual differences."

I brace myself as the lift begins to plunge. I can smell the increased density of his body odour.

"Of course, you must understand," he adds. "Until the question of ownership is resolved, we cannot release the book for further study."

"But that could take months. Or years!"

He shrugs resignedly. What can you do? It isn't in his power to settle the issue.

Within seconds we are in the basement of the Institute, and I am stepping out before him into a cool, cement-lined, well-lit corridor. Shloime dodges ahead of me and leads the way. At the end of the corridor, around the corner, in a small windowless cell with switchboard, intercom and television screen, a small, elderly man in uniform is drinking lemon tea.

"*Shalom* Dubi." At Shloime's brisk approach, the old man rises leisurely and rattles his keys. "This is Miss Shepher. She wants to take a look at the Shepher archive."

"Dr. Shepher," I say, holding out my hand. The archivist does not take it. He looks me over with indifference.

Beyond the archivist's cubby hole, against the long wall, a series of locked and barred alcoves resembles a Wild West jail: each contains two stacks of ticketed and numbered shelves; above each, a sliver of basement window, barred and locked, admits the natural light of the outside world.

The old man selects one and opens it; stepping inside, the sensation is not altogether agreeable. He hunches his shoulders, and waves a hand dismissively towards a line of storage boxes.

"Which do you want?"

I hesitate. "I don't know." Peering at the labels in the gloom, I see only a series of thinly-sketched, indecipherable hieroglyphs.

The archivist shrugs. "What—so I should know? You were the one who asked to come and see it."

"She wants to look at the Codex," Shloime intervenes.

"Another one for the Codex," the old man grumbles under his breath; but now he does, finally, come up with the goods: for, reaching out and removing one of the boxes, he places it on the table and opens it up; and there inside, at long last, is the Codex.

I hardly know what takes me as he lifts it out: a rush of something deeper than adrenalin. It is just as I imagined it: large, shabby and worn, its binding soiled by centuries of human oils, its pages poking roughly from the edges. A faint tooling, primitive and not very elaborate, decorates the light brown morocco. As he sets it down on the table I can hardly keep myself from touching it.

I sit down quickly, under the interrogation light.

"Thanks," Shloime says, and the archivist, with a grimace, wanders off phlegmatically to his den. "So," Shloime continues, without sitting down, "it is as you can see it, a manuscript of the Pentateuch in book form, fairly well preserved, three columns on parchment, full *masorah.* Really, I'd say, a very nice example." He opens it up: as soon as he begins to turn the pages I feel a shudder run through me; a violation.

"There was something about the colophon," I manage to say.

"Yes, the colophon," he repeats, flicking, roughly it seems to me, to the back. "A standard practice, to include an account of the provenance of the manuscript."

Together we look down at the few lines of script: the many abbreviations escape my knowledge.

"It's fantasy, of course." He shrugs. "They spin a tale in the colophon to give the book a better provenance. It's a common trick, you know—to make it seem more valuable than it really is."

"Really?"

"Yes. This one says—" he hesitates, translating—"it came from the shrine of the Lord in Samaria, carried into Assyria with the exiles, taken from there beyond the River Sambatyon. Property of the elders of the tribe of Dan."

"Quite a provenance."

"Well, you know," he shrugs again, "it's a tall tale. Obviously the book is nowhere near that old."

"I see." I smile ingratiatingly. "So you don't set any store by these claims of it having been taken from the ten lost tribes?"

He smiles back, twistedly. "You may like to believe in those bedside stories, Dr. Shepher. I'm a serious scholar. Look," he continues, abruptly turning the pages, whether out of compunction or in order to escape quickly from the ridiculous colophon, "I can show you one of the differences you mentioned. Here in Genesis." He flicks through to the passage, running his finger down the columns with a lack of regard for the book's sacredness and antiquity I find disturbing. "Here where it says '*vayitzer*,' 'and He created,' with two *yods*. In the usual version there would be only one, which, strictly speaking, is grammatically inconsistent." I observe, thrilled: the instincts of the generations rise up in me. "*Nu*. And so. *Kacha*. You really have to be a scholar to appreciate such things."

"Yes, I'm sure you do." I hazard: "So would you say, on the whole, that the differences improve the accuracy of the text or that they further corrupt it?"

He wriggles, as though I have inserted a snake down his shirt collar. "Improve, corrupt. Why do you speak in these terms? In terms of the Bible text, you have to understand, you don't always favour one reading over another. We analyse differences. Like scientists."

"Of course," I agree, dubiously.

"It doesn't change the meaning. It's like tiny differences in DNA."

"But tiny differences," I say, "in DNA—can't they make big differences in the whole organism?"

Again he offers me his twisted smile. "Hardly. Unless we're talking in terms of secret codes. And you strike me as far too sensible a young lady to be concerned with those." He straightens up. "Well. You enjoy yourself. You take your time. I must go back upstairs. Ask Dubi if you are in need of anything."

"Thank you very much. I appreciate it." He seems keen to rush off, so I add, perhaps too eagerly: "And would it be all right if I came back again?"

"Yes, yes." He waves me off, abstracted. My enthusiasm clearly bewilders him. "Come as often as you like. Just let Dubi know when you're ready to leave."

He disappears, leaving me to myself: alone in jail with this most wanted captive. I turn the pages; I fetch out the little Hebrew bible I have brought with me, to begin the long process of comparing and uncovering variants. I start to apply myself, but it's hopeless even to begin the attempt just now. It will be the painstaking work of months, of years. For now I will have to content myself with feeling; with touching, reading and exploring it.

I cannot explain what sensation passes through me as I sit there alone in the isolation cell: what current of recognition runs between me and this book. I had felt its soft tug as I talked of it with Gideon; now, in the austerity of the dungeon, it floods and overcomes me. The black, friendly letters of the Hebrew text seem more beautiful to me than they have ever done. I admire the work of the long-perished scribe, imagine him bent over it with his reed pen. I turn the perfect pages, feel the pleasure he has taken in his labour; wonder at its brilliance and clarity. It seems the consummation of all my researches: part and parcel of the discovery I have been making about myself.

I think of the chain of events which has led me to this hour, of the delicate balance of accident and choice, chance and deliberation which has brought me here, not just in my own life but down through the generations. I see them all now not as random acts but as the fixed constructs of a chemical formula: as if everything was meant, with an inevitability of pure meaning, to place me at this crossroads of my existence.

I think, too, of the choice I now have to make: of what it

means in terms of self-denial. It will be a perverse act, a self-defeating one; an act of madness even. But I am suddenly filled with the frisson of the idea, wicked and outrageous as it may be, with the sheer *chutzpah* of the intervention. With the mere thought of the look on Sara Malkah's face. Could I possibly get away with it? I am thrilled by the symmetry of the notion, by the sweet justice of stealing to correct a theft. And not stealing, in fact, but returning: restoring a property to its rightful owner.

To Gideon.

Gideon, with his clear eyes and his calm insistence, his strange otherworldliness and even stranger familiarity, his by now almost unbearably desirable presence: do I then, finally, believe in him? I have to choose to believe, even without hard evidence. Based only on the power of my own feeling.

And if that feeling is true, if I give in to it, what does that mean for the future, for my further choices? All these years I have kept my heart locked in a box, like the Codex my great-grandfather carried with him up and down the Jaffa Road: a heart in a box in an attic, now rediscovered. Must I examine it now, must I work out its errors, its imperfections? The beat of my heart is singing in my ears. There is still some piece of the jigsaw which is missing.

When I look up at last I see that the light has changed along the grim line of cellar windows; I stand up, stiff and unwilling, to take my leave. I leave the Codex out on the table, as I have been instructed: knowing that, on this first visit at least, I will not be trusted to return it to its correct place on the shelf. Repeat performances, I hope, will make this part of the routine. I step out of the alcove; adjust my shoulder bag. As I pass the archivist's cell I put my head inside.

"Thank you. I'm going now."

The old man, gazing at his television screen, nibbling tortoise-like at a filled pita, barely grunts and acknowledges me. I press the button and step into the lift, rise up refreshed from the bowels of the earth, and return without let or hindrance to the outside world.

Chapter twelve

I remember the white dress, how it hung in the bedroom cupboard year after year, waiting until she was able to wear it again, smelling of camphor slightly and a little of dust, beautiful and inaccessible, like a moment of youth which could never be recaptured. I remember how I used to pore over that photograph, the unbelievable image of my mother: svelte and radiant in a necklace of red stones, her eyes dark, her hair under the hat like a dark halo.

She was never comfortable here, right from that first visit, when she landed like a filmstar on the dock at Haifa. She never got over that first impression. Later she took Miriam aside in confidence. "I never expected," she said, "that there would be so many Arabs!" "Well!" said Miriam. "What did you expect?" She had looked forward to blue skies and smiling faces, green boulevards, white housing projects, manicured historical monuments: all the Youth Guard campfire songs come true. Instead she found poverty and foreigners, tension and bad temper, primitive plumbing and the threat of scorpions.

But most of all she was oppressed by heat: by white lines of heat which wound themselves like bands around her head and tightened slowly until her eyes and brain throbbed and she was forced to retreat into a darkened room. Heat which ran in rivulets down her midriff and the backs of her legs, trickling its way uncomfortably between her shoulder-blades; which only found relief at evening with the arrival of the mosquitoes.

At evening the babble of talk in the salon took over, she let it wash over her like waves across a pebble beach, sleepy, uncomprehending, feeling the breeze which blew in from the verandah; thinking that somewhere she had read a scene in a book like this. She observed and held back, noting the picturesque gestures, the obscure expressions. Even her own husband had gone native.

Everywhere she went she clutched her novel—a gold-edged copy of *Pride and Prejudice*—like a talisman to protect her against scorpions. She carried it on her trip to the beach at Tel Aviv and walked by the Sea of Galilee with it tucked under her arm. The family started to remark and laugh about it: this fragment of old England she clung to with such tenacity.

At night, in the dim guest room with its high ceiling, its pot-bellied wardrobe and its forest of family photographs, she watched while Amnon undressed in careful silence: unbuttoning his shirt, removing his watch, he looked like a stranger she was nervous of having married. He lay down in the darkness next to her. She remained still and frightened, wondering who he was.

"I was wondering."

"You were wondering what?"

"If you've forgotten how to speak English."

(Saul had smiled inscrutably when they were introduced, muttered a comment she couldn't understand. She had asked Batsheva later what it meant. Batsheva told her: "He says that Amnon always preferred dark women.")

In the morning he was gone before she awoke: off for a walk by five, in the cool grey of dawn, and when she emerged in the gold of nine o'clock there he was, seated on the back step, reading the newspaper in the light wind under the cypress trees. She wandered into the salon to find her father-in-law writing letters at the big table. He smiled; she smiled. She read her book in companionable silence.

Her knowledge of Hebrew was nearly non-existent. He had never completed his studies in Ohlendorff's *English Grammar*.

She tried to escape once, down the dirt track behind the house, only to find herself exhausted by the time she reached the bottom, weighed down by a sudden sense of vulnerability and fear. A man in robes and headdress was there tending a few goats, and feeling like a trespasser she turned and fled.

Later she would romanticise that moment, keep the image like a painting in her head: Arab Goatherd in the Hills of Judea. Something beautiful and safe, exotic and nostalgic; the myth reforming like ectoplasm the moment she was home.

All those summers she lay in the darkened room, nursing the creature of her black headache: I remember her still form, her voice out of the shadows when I brought her pills. A martyred, enervated, unfamiliar voice.

"Where is your father now?"

"I don't know."

"Go and find him. Tell me what he is doing."

"Batsheva says he went to Tel Aviv."

Summer after summer the dress stayed in the wardrobe, shouldered aside by tunics, by pinafores, by loud sundresses in orange and purple stripes; lastly by wide skirts and billowing smocks. It perished a little, grew a little grubby. Its lustre faded; it became a relic.

The dress moved on with us from house to house: from the through-terrace with the cinder path to the semi with the garden of peace roses to the villa with the brick driveway on the edge of town. Under her auspices we became good Jews, attending synagogue on alternate Sabbaths, keeping the festivals and the dietary laws. She threw parties and joined the Ladies' Guild, organised fund-raising galas and charity dinners; she wore black glittery evening gowns. Her smile flashed as white as plain china across the rooms where her gaze followed him like a hawk's. She watched him being made eyes at by the women from the Ladies' Guild, by Mrs. Edelstein and Mrs. Goldberg from the Education Board. He was still as charming, she was still as jealous.

(Dad had been cynical enough, when Hazel and Amnon set up The Outlook Furniture Company (Directors: A. and H. Shepher: "Built to Last…") "He's got no head for business," he said. "He'll always be a shop floor man." Long after his retirement he'd still roll up in his Jaguar to the brave new premises, to inspect trade, hobnob with the workers and remind Amnon that he'd taught him everything he knew.)

Little by little she had grown enormous, and the buttoned suits went out with the flowered shirt-waists. The hourglass frocks were flung into the dressing-up basket, along with the silk sheath, the cloche hat and the worn kid gloves. Like a butterfly in its chrysalis she was still beautiful, cushioned by her rounded lobes of flesh. Somewhere inside the great shell of her body, the girl that she once was waited to re-emerge.

I remember the white dress, how it hung in the wardrobe, summer after summer, year after year. A memory she clung to, a hope she would not part with; until one day I looked in the wardrobe and it was no longer there.

Chapter thirteen

Cobby has been in the bathroom for half an hour. Fania knocks for the third time. The light burns hotly through the glass panel above the door.

"*Nu*. What's happening?"

A rustle; a groan. A faint voice emerges: "*Yored li dam*." I'm bleeding.

"So let me in already."

Another groan, then silence. Fania shakes her head. "It's making him ill. This whole bible business—it's making him sick."

I retreat guiltily into the shadow of the study-bedroom.

"I wish he'd never found the stupid thing. Let it burn on the bonfire! Nothing but trouble for this poor family."

I sit on the bed in the darkness and say nothing.

I am thinking about the Codex. I am thinking about Gideon. My heart is a dark tangle of apprehensions. I carry my secret and I can say nothing.

Is it really possible, will I do this thing? Just now it seems laughable; I cannot imagine it. I try to smile off the idea, but my lips won't answer. I have to acknowledge it's no laughing matter.

Gideon says he is asking me to do what's right, but how can I know what is right in this unmapped country, this welter of questions, this unsolved mystery? My instincts are rusty; my whole life I have done nothing but play it safe. Now I am stepping out into the void, trusting to faith, hoping the voice of my heart alone will guide me.

I sit as still as I can; I hold my breath. In the grainy half-darkness I hear my own heart beating. I think if I concentrate hard enough, the answer will come, like a name on the tip of my tongue, or a word hidden in an anagram: some clue which is hovering on the edge of my vision, marginally, tantalisingly out of sight. The missing piece of the jigsaw. But nothing so categorical comes to me. Only my heart rushes me into action: I, Shulamit, who has done and felt so little for so long.

My uncle emerges at last from the hot little bathroom. "No, no, I don't want iodine," I hear him wailing.

Chapter fourteen

My parents bought a house in the district of Savyon. A small white house in an abandoned garden. They had it for five years but they never lived in it.

For five years they vacillated over practicalities.

I remember the saga of the house in Savyon: the small square crumbling pillbox of a house with its dicky water supply and its septic tank, its bad plasterwork and broken windows; its garden of dust and dead furze in which it sat sagging year after year, waiting for someone to come and lay claim to it. They whitewashed it once, inside and out, like a poor mad relative given a clean nightgown; and a tenant took it, a Mr. Martelli, for five rancorous months before he absconded with his rent unpaid. One single night we slept there on air mattresses, freezing and terrified, while lizards ran on the walls and rats scuttled. The taps coughed and brought up nothing. It was vandalised twice. It was a sick house with a crack in it, suffering from subsidence, and the advice of the surveyor was that it be demolished.

I remember the saga of the house in Savyon: the brown envelopes and shouting phone calls, the endless trips to the solicitor, the shunting from small office to small office on hot Jerusalem afternoons.

The fat black wallet which sat on my father's desk, bursting at the seams with

> legal letters
> builders' estimates
> rates accounts
> electricity notices
> tenancy agreements
> deadline warnings
> purchase contracts
> painters' bills

Year after year they intended to move out there, year after year they delayed and put it off. The house greyed and decayed; the garden grew rocks and scorpions. Newer, happier houses sprang up round the neglected site.

I remember the saga of the house in Savyon. How it lay dead on the market for years, how they couldn't wash their hands of it for love nor money. How they sold it finally for a knock-down sum, cut their losses and came away with nothing. Months after the sale the value of the land shot up, the shabby little house came down, and a six-bedroom mansion was erected in its place. Savyon grew into one of the most exclusive neighbourhoods.

"If only they had hung on to it," my uncle Saul lamented, "it would be worth millions by now." But how could they hang on to something which was so tangible, a dream made real in all its shabbiness and mundanity?

Years after we lost it we would dream of the house in Savyon: a shining white house in a garden of pomegranates. A bright perfect house in the midst of a gleaming lawn.

Chapter fifteen

Alone in the study-bedroom, I lean out of the window, breathe in the night air touched with cooking smells and incipient storms and petrol fumes, look at the squares of light shining from the other blocks, the red and white and gold pinpricks of a thousand other windows. I feel my aloneness, feel how far I have come, how strange and familiar it is here in this distant city.

My great-grandfather had a bizarre dream: he wanted to recover the ten lost tribes. He wanted to do it literally, by boatloads and on camel trains, over mountains and across deserts: to lead them like Moses, footsore into the Promised Land.

Now all these people are here and they talk of miracles, of magic carpets and the wings of eagles. But what I see is the messiness of miracles, the pragmatism by which prophecies are forced true; the bloodiness and desperation which makes dreams real.

I move away from the window and run my hand over the bookshelves, the papery spines peeling and faded from many hot summers: *Inorganic Chemistry*, *The Life of Louis Pasteur*, the *Drugs and Therapeutics Bulletin* from 1978. I pick up *Leninism* by Stalin and begin to read:

> Leninism is the Marxism of the
> epoch of Imperialism and the
> Proletarian Revolution in general.

A dead moth drops from between the pages.

I lie down on my back in the semi-darkness. I breathe in the dust of books and close my eyes.

Chapter sixteen

Many hundreds of years later, after he was dead, Moses was walking with God in the Garden of Eden. Moses said: "For hundreds of years I have wandered the Garden of Eden, and now I am unhappy because I am full of ignorance."

Then God led Moses to a pair of double doors, elaborately carved and higher than the tower of Babel. Moses passed through the doors and entered a library as vast as the sea, lined with rows of monster bookcases so tall the tops were out of sight.

He approached the head librarian, who was hovering at about shoulder height and entering new books in an enormous catalogue.

"I am filled with ignorance and I need to learn," he said. "Where shall I start? What do you recommend?"

"That depends on what you want to learn about."

"Everything," Moses answered.

The angel then set off in an easterly direction, and after a distance of several miles they reached the beginning of the library. "Why don't you start here," the angel said, "and work your way through. I'll be hovering around if you need me."

So Moses sat down and began to read. He worked his way

through the shelves systematically, leaving no book unopened and no page unturned.

Time passed. The assistant librarians glided noiselessly from aisle to aisle, while almost imperceptibly the aisles grew in length, materialising out of the distance and extending into the blue air.

He stopped one angel who passed him with a batch of new volumes, and asked: "Don't the books ever stop arriving?"

The angel smiled. "Oh no," it said. "Of the making of books there is no end."

"He who increases knowledge increases sorrow," another added as it floated by.

Moses went back to his reading and continued to work his way through. He read the Prophets and the Writings and the Apocrypha and the Pseudepigrapha. He read Josephus and Philo and Paul and Aristobulus. He read Mishnah and Gemara, Rashi and Maimonides. He read the Zohar and Nahmanides. Then he got his head down and read like a machine through the middle ages, and on into the seventeenth century and the eighteenth, through all the massacres and pogroms and blood libels and expulsions, through all the debating and philosophising and poetry and revolution, and when he raised his head and looked at the library clock he saw that seventy years had passed.

But he didn't want to stop then, so he put his head down again and started on the nineteenth century, and read about reform and enlightenment and nationalism and emancipation, and pogroms and blood libels and massacres and expulsions, and all the time the angel was adding books in armfuls and the end of the shelf retreated by the minute. But he didn't have a minute to stop and look, so he went on reading *Autoemancipation* and *The Love of Zion* and the memoirs of Shalom Shepher who travelled to the ten lost tribes, and *The Jewish State* by Dr. Theodor Herzl, and then without stopping he read on into the twentieth century.

When he reached the twentieth century he ploughed his way through dense texts full of arguments and statistics and white papers and commissions of inquiry which made his head spin. And he read about bombs and pogroms and murders and assassinations, until he reached the Holocaust. So then Moses read about the Holocaust for twenty years, and as fast as he read the books new books were added, until he wanted to scream.

Next he started on the Jewish state, and there were wars and bombs and massacres and expulsions, and songs and speeches and parades and circle dancing, and a lot of glossy picture books about Jerusalem. After he had been reading for a hundred years he began to feel a little tired, but he struggled on because he wanted to be up to date. And after he had been reading for a hundred and ten years he began to feel a little ill, his head swam and he said to himself: "I will just finish this book and call it a day." But as soon as he had finished that book he picked up another.

He glanced at the clock and saw that he had been reading for a hundred and twenty years; his head ached and his eyes burned like fire. Then he noticed the librarian hovering at his side.

"Why don't you take a rest?" the angel suggested.

Moses staggered to his feet.

"Say," the angel exclaimed, "are you all right? You look a little green."

"I think I'm going to be sick."

The angel moved back. "You go right ahead."

Just then Moses felt a rush of dry paper in his throat, he bent over and heaved. He vomited all the pages of all the books he had consumed: all the parchment and paper and glue and bits of binding, the fly-leaves and string and cardboard and embossed leather came pouring out of his mouth. When he had finished there was a knee-deep mess of half-digested books in the history section.

"I'm terribly sorry," Moses apologised.

"That's all right," the angel assured him. "You're not the first one to overdo it. Isaiah did exactly the same thing. You go home. I'll get one of the assistants to clear up."

So Moses stumbled from the library of the netherworld, and returned to the Garden of Eden, which is the place of ignorance. And he wept bitterly.

Chapter seventeen

I rest my two hands on the low wall in front of me, take a deep breath and gaze out over the panorama of the city. "It isn't real," I say.

"Unreal," Gideon agrees. He turns too, and takes in the view: immediately below us, the deep fissure of the valley; the cluster of flat-roofed housing which is Silwan. To the right, the Mount of Olives. Away to the left, the walls and golden dome of the Old City.

"You can hardly believe you are here."

Gideon only shakes his head slightly. His eyes are abrim, their greenness spilling over: too full of emotion, perhaps, at the sight of all this, to express anything. It is a vast thing to contemplate, at once too mythical and too actual; altogether too beautiful. Jerusalem lies shimmering like a beauty the centuries have fought over.

It seems an instant of consummation, a moment of shared feeling: a deep, unspoken, nervous fellowship. Jerusalem lies spread before us in all its splendour, its indifference and its vulnerability. It is just hills and a city. Neither can express what it might mean to us.

"Excuse me, please, I wonder if I might trouble you?" A voice breaks in and shatters our alliance. We move apart; Gideon looks at the ground. "Would you be so kind as to take our picture?"

"Of course," I say, taking the camera: a little while is spent explaining the mechanism; I snap the fat woman and her thin husband against the immemorial backdrop which despite everything, is still not quite a cliché. When I turn back to Gideon he has moved away some distance. I go up to him where he stands under the cypress, moodily scratching patterns with his toe.

"So," I say.

"So."

Suddenly we feel nothing. The view is a picture postcard, drained of all meaning and feeling. Another whirlwind stop on the tourist route.

I look off, into the distance, into the sky. "If I were to do it," I say.

"Yes?" His tone is non-committal.

"I wouldn't be able to do it right away."

"No; of course not."

"I don't know if I'll be able to do it at all."

"No."

"I'm still not sure I even want to do it."

He tosses a pebble he has been fingering, hard at the ground; a puff of dust spurts up. I wonder if I have succeeded in making him angry.

"Maybe you shouldn't do it."

"Now you feel bad for asking?" I smile a little.

"Now I feel bad for asking." He swings away. "Does that make you happy?"

"You shouldn't feel bad. I believe you. Doesn't that make *you* happy?"

"I don't know." He grimaces. "It worries me."

I laugh. "It worries me too. I think I might be starting to lose my marbles."

"Your what?"

"Never mind. There are other things to consider. My family, for instance."

"Don't think about that," Gideon interrupts. "It isn't as if you'd be betraying them."

"No?"

"No," he says, with conviction. "Quite the opposite." He looks at me intensely, straight in the face: there is some meaning in his look and his words which is only now, vaguely, beginning to dawn on me.

"I need to know my own reasons," I continue slowly.

"What reasons?"

"Such as," my voice slows, chokes; I think it will grind to a halt, "that I might be doing it because of you."

Still he is looking at me, and I am gazing back: a quiet has descended all around us. Over the hills and the city, over the land, falls a lid of impenetrable, waiting silence. "That's as good a reason as any," Gideon answers.

He smiles at me then, and I am comforted. Always I am consoled by that gentle smile. I seem to have known it from a long time back: there is something heartbreaking in its familiarity. I trust it utterly, and yet I want to cry. What is it about Gideon? I ask myself. Seven paces away, he makes me tremble. For all my longing it might be seven miles.

I shake myself; feel the urge, like a dreamer, to rub my eyes. "What?" I ask.

"If I am to be your reason, let me be your reason."

Then out of nowhere the secret comes to me: softly as a snowflake the piece falls into place. And yet I can hardly comprehend it. It's something in the face, it's something in the eyes. It's the laugh or the gestures; it's nonsense. It's something and nothing. We stand facing each other under the cypress trees.

"Whatever you decide, I am in your hands. But remember," his voice is calm, and quite unhurried, "my time here is limited, and so is yours. You can't sit on the fence for ever, Shulamit."

He says nothing else; I say nothing either. There is no more to be said; still we are reluctant to go our separate ways. We should shake hands, embrace, touch each other somehow. Nothing is permitted. We should kiss.

As though suddenly out of patience Gideon spins on his heel and makes off through the trees.

I stand and watch him go; watch until his form is a distant blur, striding purposefully back to whatever secret place he has emerged from. Then I turn also and stumble with heavy steps toward the road, where the car waits to carry me back to the city.

Chapter eighteen

It is told of a certain father who had a son: when the boy failed to learn his lesson from the Mishnah, the father threatened him with dire punishment; the boy, terrified, ran off and drowned himself in the nearest well. When the time came to bury the child, the rabbi said: No rites are to be withheld; we must not treat him as a suicide. A father should not threaten his own son. Either he should punish him there and then, or keep his mouth shut and say nothing. And they buried the boy with full ritual.

I am remembering a night in August. A night of sudden change and mild, shuddering winds: the leaves of the rose tree scuttling against my bedroom window. A long time, nearly thirty years ago.

That night my brother was out, I didn't know where, and I sat up waiting for him because my father had locked the door and gone to bed, saying he could stay out till morning if he wanted to, he didn't care for that matter if he never came back. But I knew that Reuben had left without his coat, that he only had a few coins in his pocket, and now, at midnight, I could hear the storm brewing. I watched the green luminous dial on my alarm clock and clutched my own feet under the eiderdown.

I remember what Reuben told me once about the early years. About the hard, soot-smelling yard, the narrow linoleum-lined hallway where he used to play. About the long foreign-looking coat which hung there sometimes, and the strange man it belonged to, who came home late at night, grim-faced and filthy-handed, and fell asleep with his head on the kitchen table.

My brother told me: I was afraid of him.

The man was sullen and distant. He smelt of sawdust and glue. He roared anger at the slightest provocation. Sitting beside him, the boy would perform reading tasks and write out sums with a short awkward pencil. The man loomed over him like a malicious shadow, ready to condemn the smallest fault.

The boy was timid and dark, small-boned and light; he had a narrow face and dark steady eyes which gazed unblinkingly in fear like an animal's. He sat very still while his father shouted and when his father raised his hand he cringed in readiness.

(The dial read one o'clock, the rain poured down. I heard it crackling like firewood against my bedroom window.)

His father was always a great polisher of shoes, and sometimes Reuben would wake to find him hunched over his school brogues in the small hours, polishing them with brushes and cherry wax. Every morning the shoes were laid out gleaming on newspaper, shell-hard with lacquer, the scuff-marks painted with a new layer of tan. It never occurred to him to thank his father, whose fierce perfectionism only inspired him to greater idleness. A visitant had done this, like the elves in the story. When his teacher praised his diligence he did not disagree.

At school he was quiet and nervous, a model pupil at first, prone only to sudden lava-rushes of fury, fits of violence when the teacher would pull him collarwise from under a punching scrum of boys. She never troubled to discover why. The teachers turned a blind eye to the playground taunts, a deaf ear to the chanting at the school gates:

Reu-ben!
Reu-ben!
Reu-ben!

but for the first six years of school he was silent and diligent, polite and eager to please, a boy you would have said showed promise even if he was lacking in confidence; and no rebel. He preferred to sit on his own indoors, drawing pictures in a corner of the classroom. His foreign father never showed his face, but his mother when she came to collect him enfolded him in a suffocating hug which was sure to bring fresh taunts the following morning.

She fed him on cocoa and crumpets, pancakes and sweet porridge, but nothing she could do would fatten this spiderlike boy who seemed to bear no resemblance to his father or to her. She took him to doctors and specialists who diagnosed nothing the matter, and dosed him with dubious remedies his grandmother recommended. She drowned him in kisses and smothered him with love, and never allowed him to stray from her pitiless protection.

When he was seven years old they moved from the grey street to the suburbs, to a semi with a patch of lawn where my mother grew red peonies and begonias and attended bring-and-buy sales at the local church hall. Week after week he rode his bicycle back to Harris Grove, to moon over the windows of the old house he now missed and where, he was convinced, he had once been happy.

(A slight tap at the window: I turned back the curtain and there my brother was, his face pale in the darkness, dripping with rain, his shoulders hunched up against the downpour. He looked at me and said nothing. I had never seen him so vulnerable as at that moment.)

When he was twelve years old they performed their parental duty and sent him to the rabbi, to learn the letters of the Hebrew alphabet, to memorise his portion and chant the blessings for the holy Law. He played truant, sat stock-still and resistant, pocketed his bribes and yet refused to learn. After three months the rabbi came to them and said: "I'm sorry to tell you the boy is unteachable."

The boy grew sullen and silent; he turned sour and remote; he hid his shoes so his father couldn't polish them. Nightly at the supper table father and son confronted each other with the same angry eyes, muttered the same laconic sentences. The house became filled with secrets and accusations, taciturn mealtimes and clock-ticking tension. Sudden explosions of anger and rebuke.

(I opened the door and he stood there, swaying slightly. I could smell on his breath the beer he had been drinking.)

When he was fifteen my brother had a girlfriend. She was blonde and pretty and she had a lisp. Her name was Annabel. My parents didn't approve and put an end to it.

And when he was seventeen my brother grew his hair long and stayed out late and drank beer, he wore jeans and a Nehru jacket and chased girls, girls my parents didn't approve of, he got busted and taken down to the police station, he failed his exams, he listened to loud music and had bad friends, he wanted a car and my mother got him a car and he drove it too fast and crashed it into a ditch, he was moody and foul-mouthed, light-minded and irresponsible, he didn't know where he had come from, he didn't know where he was going, he would never amount to anything, my father said. My father said he couldn't understand him, that he would regret it later, that no parent deserved this amount of suffering.

They faced each other across the supper table and spat poison, and my brother wore murder and suicide in his eyes.

Sitting on my bed in the half-darkness, he laughed about his exploits in the lounge bar of the Cavendish Hotel, but underneath the laughter I could feel the trembling sadness of my brother, like a halo of deeper darkness round his tousled head. I touched his hand and felt the chill of it which told me how long he had been out, walking in the rain. I sensed the vertigo of our family disaster.

Perched on its edge I clung to the straight and narrow: a good student and a dutiful daughter. I passed my examinations, learned the liturgy by rote, sang on demand, memorised my declensions. Allowed my brain to absorb the whole archaic blackness of the Bible. As if by doing so I could make my father happy, solve his disappointment; answer his emptiness, satisfy his love.

But when my brother was seventeen-and-a-half years old he climbed on a Wallace Arnold bus, with a guitar in one hand and a battered suitcase in the other. He had a ham sandwich and twenty pounds in his pocket. And he rode away for ever out of my father's life.

Chapter nineteen

I am travelling by train to see Daniel. He is living in a small rural community near the coast.

I got the telephone number through the friend of a friend. I was not surprised to hear a woman answer. I kept my own voice steady as I spoke to her. Daniel was out, she said. He would call me back later if I liked. Instead I found myself planning a visit to their house.

I look out of the window of this new, glossy train, three-quarters empty and still smelling of fresh carpet, gleaming and quiet, gliding past reed beds and orange groves and rough fields, past cement houses and makeshift pergolas and abandoned cars. At one point we pass a heap of broken toilet bowls. A couple of armed soldiers and a businessman sit near me. One of the windows has been smashed: a web of cracks like veins radiates through the toughened glass.

After so long away I am tired of being in strange places, tired of struggling with foreign language and foreign money. My need for escape has been sated. I am almost ready to return home.

My visit to Daniel is unfinished business.

I sit in the nearly empty carriage and watch the landscape pass, compelling in its mixture of strangeness and familiarity, flat-roofed houses, acacia trees, green signposts, heaps of red earth. It is a landscape printed in my earliest memory: vines and cement, dusty orange trees, spoil-heaps and half-finished buildings. A country which was once beautiful lies buried somewhere underneath.

Locked in my sealed carriage I look out at a land which is meaningless without its smells: petrol and hot tar, overripe fruit, sea salt and dried asses' dung.

Someone asks me the time and I answer in my flat accent, my father's language pale and eviscerated in my English mouth.

Chapter twenty

I remember the day we visited Surprise View.

He was already confused then, unwell, not entirely steady on his feet. There was a tousled look about him as though he had forgotten to brush his hair. I remember his jacket was crookedly buttoned up. He stood like a small boy, patiently, while I redid the buttons.

I was fourteen years old.

In his last years he had returned to the occupations of his youth. For some time he had been following gentle pursuits: a little wood-carving, a little gardening, some embroidery even, though his fingers were almost too clumsy to hold the needle. He himself had grown slow and gentle. He worked in the rose bed from morning until dusk. He planted radishes; he built an arbor.

Sometimes of an evening I would watch him from the window, a distant shadowy figure in the falling dark, bending and lifting: something pastoral, a rustic scene. And when he came indoors, tired and silent, I would observe the lines around his mouth and eyes, the sad shape of his face, and he would smile at me then, as though at this late stage he accepted everything he had been and was.

Every week I went with him to the city market. We trailed

past shouting vendors, glittering heaps of ice, stacks of green apples and meat and gleaming fish. We bought sweets by the sackful and cut price potatoes. I carried the old shopping bag with the splitting plastic handles which hung heavier and heavier by my ankles.

Sometimes the odd item would land unnoticed in the bottom of the bag: a stray apple, a broken lollipop. Even at this late stage, the skill of his light-fingered impulse had not left him.

We walked out in the rain, in the slicing wind, between the rough stalls of wood and flapping canvas. He looked tousled and tired, the collar of his long overcoat twisted, water dripping down his face and neck. He was lost in memory, in the vanished past, he was searching for the smell of Machane Yehuda: roast corn and sesame, garlic and green zatar, cumin and coriander. We filled the bag with cabbages, bruised apples, a sack of carrots. He was looking for salt herring, heaps of melons, macadamia nuts.

Towards the end of his life his native language grew stronger, as though like a strong root it was growing through everything he had subsequently learned. Deep below the layers of sedimentary knowledge his first words were engraved forever, so that as the years progressed and his memory failed, the words of the English language fell away, leaving him more and more reliant on his mother tongue.

He was becoming a stranger, becoming himself again: none other than the young man who had reached England with his half-formed sentences and brief vocabulary, and an accent so thick he could barely be understood.

Now we were going on a visit to Surprise View. But he had forgotten the way. The old roads were unfamiliar to him. Turnings had vanished; landmarks had disappeared. The world no longer agreed with the map in his head.

For nearly an hour we drove round in circles. He began to lose his temper. His face was covered with a sheen of sweat. The gears jammed; once he stalled the engine. I noticed that his hands were shaking, his eyes covered with a network of broken veins.

I didn't know he was ill. It seemed unaccountable. At the age of fifty-seven he had become, quite suddenly, an old man. Everything he had once known had turned strange to him.

I spoke softly and calmly. I tried to soothe his fear. We stopped and asked a woman for directions to Surprise View.

We parked there at last, leaving the car askew, and stumbled out onto the windy hill. It was bright and clear: a cold summer's day. We climbed the brief slope before the view.

The valley opened out beneath us and he took my hand in his. I remember the feel of his hand, the short thick fingers; the nails yellowed and worn by years of manual work.

He grew old in a fortnight, all at once. He no longer remembered the streets of his own city. He was looking for Rothschild Boulevard, Pinsker Avenue, Dizengoff Square, Ben Yehuda Street.

Chapter twenty-one

Daniel's house is a long low bungalow, a white block with one wall of glass in the heart of a green garden.

His wife Rachael greets me at the gate.

Rachael is small and slim, with long wild hair, little white shorts and a striped T-shirt spattered with cooking stains. Her feet are bare. She carries a two-year-old on the shelf of her hip. Other children are running somewhere in the garden.

We introduce ourselves. She has a strong accent. She shifts the heavy two-year-old, who sucks his thumb and gazes at me in a bored, appraising way. Somehow this chills the warmth of her welcome.

I step into the garden. The path winds between lemon and guava trees. I duck beneath sprays of jasmine and bougainvillea. On a wide tangled lawn a tawny-haired boy and girl are chasing and laughing. Rachael shouts to them in guttural Hebrew.

She apologises for something, I'm not sure what. I can smell cooking smells: garlic and aubergine. She says that Daniel is in the workshop and will be here soon.

The house opens almost imperceptibly from the garden. We enter a glass loggia crammed with plants. Leaves and flowers press against its walls from the outside. I remark on its beauty. "It's hell to keep clean," Rachael says. "Daniel does it with a long brush twice a year."

Apparently Daniel designed the loggia himself. "This is where I work," Rachael continues. A clean room with a computer. She is a graphic artist.

One step up takes us into a white open space with a kitchen at one end, a dining table at the other, a quadrangle of grey sofas in the corner. Greenery presses at every window. I sink down into a sofa. Rachael asks, "What will you have to drink?"

They have lived here seven years. It is a small town in the middle of nowhere: large plots, dirt roads, white houses, fields of vegetables and baby's breath. A school with murals on its outer walls and a bus which turns round three or four times a day. A dead, peaceful place with a voluntary crèche. Some of the fields are derelict; people commute to the city in three quarters of an hour.

"And what do you do for a living?" Rachael asks.

Screams come from the garden. The children are fighting with a watering-can. The sofa is too soft, it offers no support. I slip down, pull myself up. My clothes stretch uncomfortably across my chest and thighs.

Rachael stands at the counter and chops salad. The knife moves like lightning. Before she was a graphic artist she was a trained chef. I sip my drink. Daniel enters the room.

Almost before he sees me he picks up the little boy and swings him to the ceiling in a fulsome display of fatherly affection. He too greets me with the child on his arm. The boy has inherited his looks, the same brown eyes, a headful of the dark glossy curls which were once his. When he grows up he will be another Daniel.

One can never imagine quite how people will age. They always surprise. The lines of the face blur and become looser. Or they sharpen anxiously and pull in. Odd features grow in prominence: nostrils, eyebrows, ears.

In front of me are a Daniel younger than I ever knew and a Daniel older than I have ever seen. The Daniel I loved fifteen years ago has vanished.

We sit down at a table filled with colourful plates of salad, dishes of tabbouleh and sweet rice, heaps of roughly cut bread; a big glass jug of homemade lemonade. "Fresh from the tree," Daniel says. He is proud of his garden. This year he is growing star fruits and mangoes. Fifteen years ago he couldn't tell a trowel from a toasting fork.

Rachael catches me watching her and handles the moment adroitly, smiling and offering me more bread. She expects me to be curious. Daniel makes himself busy with the children.

"And where are you living now?"

I explain briefly. "But I'm thinking of moving," I add.

We discuss the property market. Rachael still has half a flat in London. She can't decide whether to sell up. Daniel would like to modernise his workshop. The thought of Daniel in any kind of workshop strikes me as bizarre.

Suddenly he asks: "Do you still sing at all?"

I explain that I have long ago stopped singing. I am stung by the question and suddenly distressed. How could he imagine I would keep on singing? He had taken the music with him when he left. "And what about you?" I counter. "Do you still play saxophone?"

"Oh! No," he exclaims, wriggling, strangely awkward. "You know how it is. Kids—house—work. Never have time to practise nowadays."

Rachael gets up to make coffee and the children scatter.

"They're lovely," I say.

Rachael touches her stomach. "We tend to have plenty here, you know. Just in case."

I think about it. "In England we're having fewer. Just in case."

Rachael says: "Why don't you show Shulamit round the garden?"

Daniel leads me out. He takes me past the rabbit hutches and the chicken coop, and the tree where an empty and very dirty birdcage hangs. "That was Joey. We had him for nine years." There are tangled areas of the garden where the children have dragged planks and built dens. There is a hammock with a sediment of dead leaves.

I examine him carefully as he moves ahead of me: the shadow

of stubble on his cheek, the grey in his hair, the gleam of his scalp among the thinning curls. He wears a shirt with a narrow stripe and a gold watch; his hand as he points is well-veined and tanned. I am touched by a furtive grief: not for him so much as for the passage of time.

Deep among the foliage a wind chime sounds; patches of sunlight move across our arms and faces. The leaves are a dark, glossy green. I can smell citrus. He shows me the star fruit and the kumquat tree.

"She's lovely," I say.

"Rachael? She's a gem."

"Your place is lovely too."

"It's paradise. What are you smiling at?"

"I was wondering what happened to Palael."

He shrugs in embarrassment. "Oh, well, you know—I outgrew that kind of nonsense long ago."

"A pity," I say.

He turns back the branch of a tree I do not recognise, and shows me the fruit hanging, smooth and beautiful.

"Avocado."

Chapter twenty-two

I will never marry now, I will never have children. I do not know when this feeling, which for many years was only a vague intimation, resolved itself into a certainty. Perhaps it was the last time I went to see my brother.

He is living in a faraway place now, Reuben Michael who was reborn as Mike. A small anonymous English country village, full of information technologists and commuter-workers, a small anthill on the west edge of London where every day the lines go busily to and fro. After long struggles he has done well for himself at last. He lives in a big sunny house with his wife and daughter, a house without a history, newly built on a green field just for him.

It is a strange place to me, this home my brother has made, full of brand spanking new carpets and designer tiles, without a memento or an old photograph: nothing worn at the edges, nothing with associations, nothing, in short, belonging to the past. My brother himself is an all-new man, in soft white chinos and a grey silk shirt, a sheen of stubble peppering his jaw: older, and still handsome, and more sure of himself than he ever was before. He has a blonde-haired blue-eyed wife whom I like, who cooks gammon for us on a

Friday night; we sit round the maplewood table, drink wine and talk of serious things. He says: "I don't know how you can work in that ridiculous job." He says: "How are you doing up there in your ivory tower?" He gets defensive when I mention the family. "So far as I am concerned," he says, "I am the first generation. There's nothing to draw on. It begins with me."

Later I glance in at their blonde-haired, blue-eyed daughter as she lies sleeping in her darkened room. She has the face of an angel, the strange, otherworldly quality of children when they are asleep. I wonder who she is, this niece of mine, her head void of history and her house without candlesticks; I wonder if she wonders who she is. But she is happy and privileged, her room is full of toys: she eats well, she sleeps soundly; she is not like me.

It was then that I realised I would never have children. For to have children you must have something to hand on. Either that or the fervour of beginning. I possessed no such fervour; and how could you hand on something when you were floating in a void? All I could give would be memories and longing, a sense of dislocation, a source of pain.

I understood, then, something of the difference between Reuben and myself. I would rather give pain than hand on nothing. Reuben would rather give nothing than hand on pain. My brother thought of himself as the first generation. I saw myself as belonging to the last.

Chapter twenty-three

My father went alone to Jerusalem in the winter of 1968. His mother was dying in the hospital. Her death had been expected for a long time.

All day and night the family kept vigil at her bedside, but she never moved. She lay like a small bird in the white bed, a woman who had once been large and vigorous, who had borne many children, reduced almost to nothing, her skin like parchment, her bones as light as ash.

Sometimes they thought they could see her eyes flicker. Her glazed eyes gleamed from behind lids which were not completely closed.

My father took the midday and the midnight shift. He slept in the mornings. He walked through Jerusalem in the afternoons.

Sometimes it rained, sometimes the sun shone. The rain fell in sudden squalls, forming huge puddles at the street corners which were difficult to cross. Then the sun would come out again, a thin warmth grew.

Jerusalem suited his mood: a city which is in mourning no matter what the circumstances. This winter, after the war, it was at its saddest: heaps of rubble around the Old City, the Mamillah District in ruins. Jerusalem stood on the ashes of her seventeen destructions. The only city whose heart lies outside of itself.

He wandered up and down Ben Yehuda Street. He walked through the Sacher Park. In Beit HaKerem he came across a group of young boys playing football. He stood and watched them in his long coat. One kicked the ball out of play; he caught it and threw it back. Their eyes met.

He decided to walk back to Kiriat Shoshan, and arrived damp and exhausted, trembling all over because he hadn't eaten. Batsheva sat him down in the kitchen and gave him soup. The house felt unnaturally quiet.

He noticed that the window frames were rotting. The house was more dilapidated than ever. There were cracks in the floor tiles; the walls had turned a uniform shade of grey. All the doors squeaked. "It could do with a lick of paint," he remarked. Batsheva shrugged her shoulders.

Somewhere in one of the back rooms Saul was moving ponderously about. Sometimes when he came into the salon Amnon found his brother lying on his back on the divan with one arm across his eyes, listening to the radio. Meanwhile Shoshanah bustled purposefully in and out, convinced that she of all of them was doing the most for Mother, though as the doctors had repeatedly told her, there was nothing that could be done. She rushed through the kitchen, too busy to eat soup; she wore a tight green suit, as though she were going to a business conference. She hurried out of the warped back door, leaving it open, struggling with hat and gloves.

That night when he arrived at the hospital he found them washing his mother. He caught a brief glimpse of her naked body before withdrawing confusedly into the corridor. There he sat for half an hour with the image of his naked mother indelibly imprinted on his mind's eye. He was clutched by the fear and certainty of his own death.

Later he took up the vigil at her bedside and, filled with loneliness, wrote a long letter, the contrite frightened letter of an orphaned boy. "This parting has shown me," he wrote, "that if ever we were called upon to live without one another it would be a terrible struggle. I don't know whether I would make it. It seems to me not only a matter of love but of *life* itself."

Day came and still there was no change. A nurse entered, checked a few things. "She has a strong heart," she told him.

He left the hospital at dawn and stepped out into the freshness of a Jerusalem morning, in the company of street sweepers and vendors and the odd mule; a few Jews hurrying to early prayers. A cold breeze blew; the sky was pale. There were the usual sounds of Jerusalem: the chip of stone, nasal voices, bells. He bought a hot bagel from a bakery on the Jaffa Road and ate it as he walked to catch the bus.

All the years of his life seemed to fall down, in gossamer layers, one into another. The sun on his cheek was the sun of his earliest boyhood.

Chapter twenty-four

I am not sure if there are things I would like to say to Daniel. I am not sure if there are things Daniel wants to say to me.

It seems like a long silence, the time we stand under the avocado tree (it has long wandering branches, and a number of fruits in various stages of ripeness). Maybe he did say something which I didn't hear. Maybe he was just muttering to himself.

"Sorry?"

"I was just saying that this tree could do with cutting back."

So the moment passes and we move on, as moments do pass with their unstoppable inevitability, and thank God for that, I tell myself, thank God for that. Terrible to misjudge the moment and confess something, something which will do no good at all but only serve to open up new vistas of regret.

But more than that, I realise I have nothing to confess. I look on him with calm, this man I always thought was the love of my life. I look on him with a painless benevolence. My heart is elsewhere. And I remember that my life is but half over.

So we move on through the green shade of the trees, bending our heads under the drooping blossom, emerging at last onto the open lawn where the children are throwing water and chasing each other and little Daniel sits banging the ground with a spoon. We run around a bit, like awkward adults; and coffee is ready in the loggia.

The low table is spread with soft cakes and cinnamon biscuits, white china and a dish of sweets. The children dart in and out; we sit back in the warm breeze which stirs the banana leaves and talk of England.

Rachael came out here when she was very young. She says it is best that way: the more ignorant the better. The younger you are the less you have to lose. When Rachael and Daniel met he was on the point of leaving. It was she who persuaded him to stay.

"I told him it was me or England," she says, "and he chose me." I watch a smile pass between them. "Why didn't you ever move here, Shulamit?"

I think of Mr. Cantor from my childhood: a pupil of my father's who dutifully learned his numbers and his declensions and sold up his pharmacy business and went out with his wife to live in a small flat in Netanya overlooking the beach. Before they left they had a farewell party and all the way home in the car my parents argued bitterly about why we couldn't be like them. Nine months later they were back, disillusioned and exhausted, ground down by a malevolent bureaucracy.

"I swear," Mr. Cantor told my father, "they don't want us in that country."

My eyes meet Daniel's for a split second. "I suppose," I reply, "I was too much in love with England." We look away.

The sun travels from behind the line of acacias to the back of the walnut tree. The lawn changes colour from dark green to black gold. Rachael's bare foot swings back and forth, back and forth on the arm of her wicker chair as she says she will never go back, never through all eternity move from this position.

It is getting late and I will miss my train.

We say goodbye and they ask me to come again, to come and stay, they say I am always welcome. I accept their niceties with a smile: Rachael kisses me continental fashion and when he takes my hand I feel almost nothing.

Chapter twenty-five

For two hours he trailed back and forth on Allenby Street before making up his mind to head for Trumpeldor. He read the newspaper. He looked in shop windows lined with orange cellophane. He bought gifts for the children; he ate a bag of nuts. Finally he went back to the building he had identified soon after his arrival and stood below it, gazing up in a vain attempt to guess her window.

This is the image I see of him, which I never saw: dressed in his best clothes he stands on the pavement underneath the window of the woman he loves.

But maybe he didn't wear his best clothes. Maybe he wore his second-best trousers and an open shirt. That was how he generally dressed in Jerusalem, in Tel Aviv. Maybe he wore his second-best trousers, his new shirt bought for the journey and a tie. The blue tie I got him for his last birthday. He always wore a tie to more formal occasions.

I realise I do not know how my father would have dressed, I do not know how any man would dress to pay a visit, after thirty years' absence, to the woman he loves.

Nor do I know how long he stood there in the street, being

passed by incurious pedestrians, peered down at, maybe, by a suspicious Viennese with a duster in her hand, in the middle of cleaning the slats on her verandah. Nor whether, after some time, he entered the building, or whether, head bent, he walked disconsolately on.

What is he thinking as he stands there, a bunch of wilting roses in his hand? (but sprinkled with water by the vendor for a look of freshness). Is he remembering, is he filled with doubt? There are some places where curiosity should not be permitted to take us. But for him this is more than curiosity: it is an impulse which drags him beyond an awareness of his own baldness and decrepitude, beyond the fear of what she might look like now, thirty years after he last saw her. It is a need for comfort, or perhaps passion, for some part of himself he has long since lost.

He doesn't know why he stands there, like a man in a dream, or what his hopes and intentions are as he moves forward, dreamlike, up the path.

And supposing he did enter the building, supposing he was about to press the buzzer that would admit him (her name beside the number of the flat) when someone emerged and he managed to slip in unregarded, into the cool darkness of the entrance hall, slightly damp-smelling and dank, with an old bicycle propped against one wall below the fuse-box, and the pale red glow of the light switch shining out of the gloom, and the beginning of a concrete stairway leading up—what did he think he would do next, what could he say, when she finally opened the door, that would surprise her in the mundanity of that moment?

It was as though his entire life had telescoped, and from the time he last saw her to this was no time at all.

So perhaps it didn't matter, one should just act as though no time had passed. One should just be oneself: except that his self seemed scattered to the four winds, his mind filled with confusion as he mounted the stairs and the automatic light clicked out.

There in the darkness he could have been anyone, he might even have been young. He lingered for a few moments to indulge that feeling. He floated in the weightless darkness of the stairwell.

Then his eyes adjusted, he fumbled for the switch, the light popped on, there was a gilt mirror on the landing.

His own face appeared in it: an old man's.

I imagine, then, that he saw the number on her door. And the name next to it, written in the small window of the doorbell. But how long he stood there I cannot calculate. Nor can I say for certain if he ever rang the bell.

Was there a moment in which the door opened, in which they came face to face? Did his heart wince when he saw her? Had she changed beyond all recognition?

And supposing the door did open, supposing he stepped inside, (the roses forgotten in his hand) into the small neat flat in which she still practised her music and gave violin lessons, a dim sitting-room smelling of polish and lavender with dark paintings on the walls: what did they say to each other, what did they talk about?

There is no way of knowing whether he ever said those things which in repeated dreams had come flooding out of him, words which on waking he could not remember.

I will never begin to imagine what she said to him.

He waits on the landing and the light clicks out. The door closes behind him and he disappears.

I don't know if he ever went to see her. It was all a long time in the past then, a long time in the past.

My father lingers on Trumpeldor Street and looks up at the windows of a certain building. A shutter closes. He lays a bunch of roses on the ground. He walks on, turns the corner and is lost from view.

Chapter twenty-six

I am alone again, on the train back, but not discontented. I even feel a strange comfort in the empty seat beside me, the smooth movement of the train, the darkening country outside against which my own reflection grows gradually clearer. At each station people enter and leave, struggling with luggage, bearing newspapers and briefcases, in an odd companionable quiet. The train carries me into a night territory, warm sea-drenched darkness, glittering distances, lozenges of yellow light.

I am glad to be alone.

I think I have reached the warm heart of my life, the one place of safety, here on this train which might travel indefinitely so far as I am concerned and never reach its destination. I think I am lingering at the midpoint, without regret for the past or fear of the future: only a floating calm, a clear wisdom.

I have travelled a long journey, away from the old uncertainties, the old confusion, to a new, floating, undiscovered place.

If only this calm would last, this wisdom remain clear, and

knowing myself free, judged and condemned by no-one, I could embrace life like a lover. If only I could always travel, purposeful and independent, knowing the name of my station as the train flies on forever into the night.

Chapter twenty-seven

I don't know if she ever found them. If my mother found the letters he never sent.

Years after Reuben had left home she still sent the boy presents, met him for long distance lunches in the West End, bought him handmade shirts from Savile Row. She sent him cash through the mail, wrote letters, made secret telephone calls. He told her to leave him alone and then came back for more, like a spoilt lover who can't resist the trinkets. She set up assignations, purchased holidays, cried when he hurt her feelings and made it up again.

She never told my father any of this. A woman who feels betrayed needs to act out her own secret infidelities.

Little by little she anchored herself with food, weighed her body down, filled herself as if against a coming famine. She wore wide dresses which spread like tents on the breeze. She acquired goods, speculated in antiques, collected jewellery and figurines. Her life had been lived wholly in the senses: flinching at the least impact, forever dizzy with anger, jealousy, love.

All through those final years they lay side by side in the big double bed he had built with his own hands, the marriage bed with the green buttoned headboard in which she grew larger and larger, he grew smaller and smaller day by day; until one day she woke to discover that she filled the bed, and that he had shrivelled, dwindled; disappeared.

After she died I burned all the letters, burned everything unread. His drawer was full of them. She could not have failed to have found them.

Hannah divorced early, so Miriam says. She became a violinist with the philharmonia; she had an apartment near the Trumpeldor Cemetery. She gave lessons. Miriam would run into her sometimes on Dizengoff Street. She was always well dressed, beautifully turned out, but she aged quickly, the way some Europeans do in this climate. She always had a smile and a word to offer. Exquisite manners. That was her upbringing. She never asked about Amnon. She wore a coat, even in the height of summer. She always had beautiful shoes.

Chapter twenty-eight

I am travelling back with my own reflection clear against the night's darkness, myself out there, myself warm and safe in here. I carry that floating image with me all the way back from Daniel's house.

Who is that woman who hangs out in the ether, lonely and childless, strong and self-contained, gazing impassively at me and always there, in the train, in the taxi, in the aeroplane? She isn't yet sure who she is but she hangs out there, high in the stratosphere above half of Europe.

You know who she is: your constant, your place of safety. The courageous orphan. The mother and father you carry inside yourself.

Chapter twenty-nine

A convocation of Shephers, descending on the bungalow at Kiriat Shoshan, gathers together to discuss the Codex, this bright still afternoon in spring. Cobby and Fania, faded and worn from their journey of ten minutes, head up the carnival and, as befits their status as patriarch and matriarch, take the best seats in the chaotic salon. Miriam arrives in her little green Suzuki, a brilliantly painted scarf tied around her head. She is kissing me on both cheeks as her grandson enters in full military uniform. This strident woman in the wig and brown stockings, directing a flotilla of relatives with the natural foghorn of her voice, can only be Sara Malkah, and—wonder of wonders—who is this ancient creature, wizened and mummified, a hundred and ten years old if he's a day, if not her elder brother Yossel, supported on a frame, no more than a cobweb strung between its metal rods, and his eyes clouded over with the milk of blindness. Following hard on his heels, a jetsam of Shephers I never knew existed: Shephers old and young and tall and small, Shephers male and female, orthodox and apostate, white-collar and labouring Shephers; Shephers with and without spectacles, lanky or squat, long-faced and golden-haired, angel-faced and dark. All of them, nevertheless, unmistakably

Shephers, whether lounging against packing-cases picking their ears, or arguing with gestures, or peering rodentlike to read the spines of the piled-up books; and presiding in the shadows, if one can preside from the shadows, our own King Saul, in a state of moody rebellion, wishing them all to hell and himself very far away.

Now, bringing up the rear, and unexpected by anyone but Uncle Cobby it seems, a small television crew, consisting of a porcelain-faced female journalist, a cameraman and a soundman, who are kept out on the verandah (where excess Shephers of the more distant branches, and late arrivals generally, have spilled over) for a bit of fisticuffs. Meanwhile I am attempting half-heartedly to distribute refreshments. Passing children snatch at my dish of biscuits; greybeards frown disapprovingly at my trousers. No-one knows or cares who I might be. Sara Malkah looks imperiously through me; I scan the assembly and think I identify, from the mists of memory, a couple of grown-up cousins with whom I used to play in the sandpit thirty years ago, but cousins, of all family ties, are probably the most slippery.

"Shulamit!" one cries, approaching me; I am at a desperate loss for a moment to remember who he is. He has bleached blond eyebrows, piercing blue eyes, a compelling smile; something about him is teasingly familiar. He has the look of a traveller in distant lands.

"It's your cousin Itai," he says. "Batsheva's son. Where have you been hiding yourself? Why didn't you phone—why didn't you come and stay with us?"

I cannot produce an adequate reply.

"Don't you remember me?" he insists. "How we used to play together on the square here? How we used to trespass in the Plotsky garden?"

I can hardly contain or comprehend my feelings. I am confused, pleased; emotional. "Yes," I say. "Yes, of course I do."

"You heard about what happened to poor Plotsky? The poor guy—what a tragedy. I tell you, that family is one hell of a saga. The house is gone now, the garden—but you know that. How long have you been camping here?"

I begin to tell him, but now Uncle Cobby is calling the meeting to order: he stands in the midst of the gathering and, with quavering authority and fragile self-possession, is shushing them all; by no means an easy task, since numerous arguments have already broken out, like political trouble-spots, among his audience.

"*Hevre, hevre*," he announces. "Friends, friends: thank you all for coming. Really, it's a pleasure to see you all. Who would have thought that such an unexpected crisis—let's not call it a crisis, let us call it an unexpected *occasion*—would have brought about such an unprecedented gathering of the clan!"

Someone, from the back, is already shouting at him to get on with it.

"*Hevre, hevre*. Your toleration, please. We are here to settle a very important question. Maybe the most important question our family, as a family, has ever faced. A remarkable treasure has fallen into our hands. A biblical Codex, of exceptional age and provenance, and who knows, also of considerable value" (more shouts and remarks from various parts of the room) "has, through a chain of events now hidden by the veils of time, come into our possession." (A chorus of dispute, and a salty acknowledgment of "We know that!") "The question we must ask ourselves—and I put it to you advisedly—is this: Do we, in this moment of extremity, this decisive moment, one might even say, for the honour and prestige of the family Shepher, embroil ourselves in argument and petty wrangling; do we seek only personal and material gain; and do we, in the final outcome, sell the Codex, bury the Codex, or, as I believe we should, give this treasure of mankind free and gratis to the nation (maybe even for a token sum) to be readily available to those scholars and experts who are most eager to study it?"

General hubbub; amongst the rabble of response, an imposing gentleman of rabbinic appearance, and his satellites, repeat with vehemence: "Bury the Codex! Bury the Codex!"

"There's only one question right now I want answered," someone pipes up. "What's the television doing here?"

A chorus of common outrage follows; and poor Cobby, trying in vain to suppress it with hand gestures, explains that a small camera crew will be filming the exterior of the house and seeking a few opinions. This, however, brings down a hailstorm of opinions on his unlucky head.

My uncle succumbs, while the opportunistic Sara Malkah, her face raddled with a thousand grudges, takes the floor. "Now is the time," she declares, "to hear the real questions!"

"I wonder," an elderly gentleman in a stained waistcoat and open-necked shirt tugs at my sleeve, "if you could find me another of those very tasty almond macaroons."

It would be a pleasure; though I am somewhat surprised when he follows me through to the kitchen, an oasis of quiet just now, and hangs on my elbow while I fetch the biscuit packet. He is half-bent, as though passing through a very low-ceilinged crypt, and I get the impression that he is more than a little hungry. Would he like some tea? He certainly would. A sandwich perhaps? I am soon slicing him a pita.

I look at him as he sits, weary with eighty-odd years, on one of the rickety green chairs; I examine his face and wonder what serpentine series of links connects him to me. There are no superficial resemblances, though the bulbousness of his nose is faintly familiar, and when I offer him pickles he turns them down with a sharp intake of breath, showing his palms as though I had offered him poison. Is he a great-uncle, or somebody's cousin, or the bachelor son of a great-aunt long since dead? He could be a tramp who has wandered into the house in the hope of passing unnoticed and getting some lunch, but for a moment I am struck by the miracle of the idea that he and I have sprung, so to speak, from the same wellhead.

While he eats with detached concentration, I can hear from the salon the foghorn voice of Sara Malkah, who has snatched the proceedings from under the nose of Cobby, and is running away with them as anybody might have guessed she would. I can glimpse her now through the doorway: hands on voluminous hips, head wagging under an iron wig, she declaims on behalf of what she calls the 'true family.' The Codex was stolen once before, she asserts: over her dead body will it be stolen again.

Cobby: "Are you saying my father was a thief?"

She: "I am most definitely saying your father was a thief!"

Now she is bringing forth her ancient brother Yossel, trophy-style, to provide the historical evidence. He shuffles forward, trembling, on his frame. "Tell them, Yossel. Tell them what you remember."

He mumbles inaudibly. His head is nodding dangerously on his thread of neck, and he looks pretty much as though he could drop dead at any moment, but Sara Malkah isn't to be put off. "What's that, Yossel? What do you remember?"

"How can we know," someone shouts, "if we can't hear him?"

By a superhuman effort the old man raises his voice. It resembles one of those early phonograph recordings: spooky and disembodied, like the voice of a past era. "He came to our house," he says.

"Who came to your house?"

"Joseph Shepher, may he rest in peace, came to my father's house when I was a child."

"Well, there's a surprise! Joseph Shepher visited his brother-in-law!"

Yossel looks as though he would like to take a nap, but at a nudge from his sister he continues: "He was there during the war."

"Which war?"

This question seems to floor the old man, who adopts a dreamy expression, as though lost in the recollection of a plethora of wars, all indistinguishable and without dates.

"Did he take the Codex?" one of the clan demands.

"The Codex?" He seems to think about it. "How would I know if he took the Codex? If I even knew there was a Codex, do you think I would be standing here now?"

A puff of laughter greets this honest statement, which is rather too direct for Sara Malkah. She ushers her brother hastily away. "He's tired," she mutters. "Obviously he's exhausted."

Discord among the crowd: Miriam is just rising to her feet, calling for calm, when I am distracted by a touch on my shoulder.

"Excuse me—*gveret*?" It is the journalist, who has slipped in unnoticed through the kitchen door. At the sight of her my heart starts racing. "I wonder if I might ask you a few questions."

"Sure." I shrug my shoulders. "I don't know how useful I can be to you."

"You are a member of the family?"

"A distant relative. From England. Here for a holiday. I don't really have much of a clue about all this."

"From England?" She looks surprised. Maybe she thought I was American. "Then, you don't know anything about the Codex?"

"I'm afraid I have nothing to do with it. I'm not even sure I know what a codex is."

We smile together. She jots a few notes, glances over my shoulder, while I struggle to contain my desire to dash away, hide somewhere, run to the other side of the building. Why is a journalist so much like a police officer?

"That lady there," I point in the direction of Miriam. "You will get sense out of her."

But Miriam has been shouldered aside by a giant: a colossus in sidelocks, surely no product of the clan of Shepher, except that he must be, since he bears the name: Rabbi Gershom Shepher of Mea Shearim, who is declaring, in accents which make the fabric of the house tremble, that the Codex is the work of an imposter, a fake and a forgery, a rogue book which must be hunted down and impounded, cast into oblivion and suppressed, and he displays in his hands a smudged bill to this effect (which he is already having posted throughout Mea Shearim): that this corrupt Scripture, and anyone who promotes its dissemination, deserve instant banishment from the House of Israel.

It's too good a thing to miss: my journalist is writing furiously on her notepad, and has lost all trace of interest in me.

"The text is *pasul*—invalid!" the Rabbi thunders. "It should be given a proper burial!"

"How do you know that for sure?" someone demands: a little fellow, an academic type, in tight jacket and a pair of spectacles. I admire his pugnacity.

"I myself have examined it. I have myself made several exploratory visits to the Institute. It's plain to anyone with knowledge that the text is strewn with errors."

"How do you know it isn't a variant version?"

"Variant version? We need no variant version!" Rabbi Shepher turns on him his furious and blood-filled face. "You think I want to expose my congregants to the existence of such things? What do you think they should do with that kind of information? The book they have, that God gave them, isn't enough?"

An uncharacteristic silence has fallen on the company: they are all gazing in astonishment, wonder, anger, awe or contempt at the rabbi, who looms over his feeble interlocutor, indeed, seems nearly ready to tear him limb from limb.

But I am looking beyond the overbearing figure of the rabbi, into the motley of faces on the far side of the room. I am, for my own reasons, suddenly transfixed. For as if in a dream (and isn't this whole scenario very like a dream?) a pale olive face has appeared among the rest, one I didn't notice there before, lurking calmly and unobtrusively at the rear. Whether he slipped in later, or was there all along, it is hard for me to say. For he is so like the others, it is perfectly possible that I had overlooked the presence of Gideon.

No sooner have I caught sight of him than our gazes collide, as though he had been looking the whole time to catch my eye, and he grins, and indicates the back corridor, where we meet a minute later, somewhere between the bathroom and the broom-cupboard, and before we have even had a chance to say anything I am up the ladder and he is after me, into the warm dusty quiet of the attic.

"He has a point," says Gideon, indicating the rabbi down below, whose voice is still vibrating through the attic floorboards. I can't tell if he is being serious or sarcastic. I watch him steadily: he is peering about him with all the interest of the archaeologist or the detective, turning back fabric here, lifting a document there; he straightens, and runs his fingers lightly over the roof tiles.

"So this is the famous attic," he says. "This is the genizah of the house of Shepher."

From below, the clash of voices raised in fresh argument.

"Do you think they know?" he asks.

"Not yet," I answer.

"Of course they don't. Even when they do, they'll go on arguing."

"But at least it won't go to court," I say.

"There is that."

"Which won't stop the wrangling, of course."

"No, of course not."

"It's a matter of principle."

"Ah. Naturally. It's always a matter of principle."

"The question being—whom does the Codex belong to?"

"The answer being—none of them, after all."

We smile at each other. About three yards of tumbled bric-à-brac lie between us. His expression is calm inside the dark frame of his sidelocks, and I think with all certainty at that moment: He is one of us.

"This is the box," I tell him, "where they found it."

I beckon him over and he is standing close, looking down at the box, which is small and splintered, quite ordinary and unprepossessing, a salt box, perhaps, or one for holding pickles or spices or tobacco, stained with what looks like ink or fingermarks; and as I prepare to open it, just for show, he is looking down into it with the radiance of discovery in his face, like Ali Baba in the robbers' cave.

Gideon echoes: "This is where it was found."

He is crouching as close to me, now, as it is possible to be: I feel his breath on my cheek, the touch of his coat on my arm; his breath smells of sweets, in fact, like that of a child, and he seems quite unconscious of how close he has come, or how electric the half-inch is between us. Together we lift the lid of the wooden box, and as we do so our bare fingers touch: my arm is brushing his arm, my breath mingles with his breath, and I'm thinking how fine it would be if this were the true moment of discovery, the moment when the Codex was first found; if the clock were turned back and we were finding it, Gideon and I together, just as we ought to have done in the first place. So that now, when we lift it out, delicately and respectfully, wrapped in its ancient cloth, and when we lay it down on the attic floor, my cheek touching his cheek, my hand his hand, no-one should know except us and no-one need ever know, that we have discovered the Truth, the Revelation.

"*In flagrante!*"

A creak on the ladder: we quickly close up the box, dust ourselves off, rise shamefacedly to confront the intruder; who is Saul, of course, creeping up quietly in order to catch us. His bristling head appears, as though disembodied, through the hatch, and he turns his gaze suspiciously, like the beam of a searchlight, across the full area of the attic. I am about to stammer an explanation, but then I see that I am, to all appearances, alone: Gideon has vanished, and the book has too; a single shaft of light pours through the roof where several tiles have been moved for illumination.

"Where has he gone?" demands Saul.

"Where has who gone?"

"I saw you both. I knew what you were up to."

"I've no idea what you are talking about."

He drags himself, with a grunt of effort, through the hole in the floor, and stands nonplussed, his radio in his hand, still scanning the attic with disappointment.

"Excuse me, please," I say without more ado, and pushing by, leave him standing there in stupefaction. I quickly descend. I have no time to lose; but before I can make my escape I am collared by Cobby, who has been talking in secret to the journalist, who has a mobile phone pinned against her ear. Cobby looks mortified, as though he has committed a terrible faux pas, and he grips my arm with the hand of a man shaking from bewilderment and disbelief. His eyes are bloodshot and his face grey, but in the clarity of the moment I ask myself if they weren't always so, and answer myself that they probably always were. Nevertheless, he seems very distressed about something.

"Ayala here," he murmurs, "has been talking to the Institute."

I smile at Ayala, who looks so fresh and manicured I would believe her capable of talking to the Taj Mahal.

"It's gone," Cobby says, flatly.

"The Codex?"

"They can't find it."

"Umm. That seems careless."

"It was still there that day," Cobby continues, "when you went to see it?"

"When I went to see it?" I think briefly. "I suppose it was."

Ayala is looking at me perplexedly. "I thought," she says, "that you didn't know anything about the Codex?"

"I don't," I reply smiling. "But I still wanted to see it."

"Someone has taken it." Cobby is wringing his hands.

"Maybe they just misplaced it. Maybe someone in the department borrowed it."

"You're sure it was still there?" Cobby is looking at me pleadingly. Ayala is frowning at me suspiciously.

"Of course I am," I say. And then I say again: "Excuse me, please." I push past them into the kitchen, where the old man is seated in a feast of biscuit packets, cake crumbs, cheese and broken pita; in the salon the shouting intensifies; bomblike, I burst out of the back door. Under the cypress trees a lone cameraman leans smoking. There is no sign of anyone in the deserted square.

I round the house, and on reaching the front, I see that the convocation is in disarray: a sort of scrum has developed out on the verandah, and right in the middle of it, Saul and Cobby are having a set-to. Cobby yells; Saul yells something back; Cobby lands Saul a swipe across the jaw. I don't stay to see the outcome. Like an escaped convict I run full tilt from the house, and keep on running down the empty street.

Chapter thirty

He stood on the hilltop and before him stretched the vista of Surprise View.

Before him lay the green flank of England. Fields and trees under a blue sky. Hedges and houses; a bend in a brown river. A horizon of vague hills, a silvery haze.

He had come here finally, to this high place. By what means and by what roundabout route he could not remember. Somehow, through years, he had stumbled on his way. His eyes fixed always on the same horizon.

It was not what he had expected. It was not where he had thought to find himself.

But it was the same horizon, nevertheless, the one he had been chasing all these years, and if it was different from the one intended, it was at least beautiful, it was at least green. There were worse horizons to be gazing at, on the edge of twilight, at the cusp of night, when one knew that time had run out and the destination was as far away as ever.

Now it seemed to him that he had bungled his way through life, that he had gone forward always in a mist and around blind corners, that he had fallen into things by accident and without purpose; driven by anxiety and misgiving, pulled by a current beyond his own control. And it seemed to him, too, that he had never lived in the moment, but only ever in some future moment, torn and distracted by the thousand and one things he might have done with his life, powerful but always undecided; and how can a man who does not know what he wants bewail his lack of choices?

Now here he was at the end, crushed at last by the Jerusalem in his head, my melancholy Amnon; my Titus.

So we gazed at the landscape while the sun went down, as the fields changed colour and the air turned cold. And we kept quiet, for we had nothing to say. We turned our backs at last on the horizon. And we drove home in silence on the darkening road.

Chapter thirty-one

When the time came for Moses to die, God took him up onto the summit of Mount Nebo, and he looked out across the valley of the River Jordan: and behold, there was a land goodly and fair, flowing with milk and honey.

And God said: This is the land I swore to your forefathers, to Abraham, to Isaac and to Jacob. You may look upon it with your eyes, but you may not enter there.

And Moses looked upon it with his eyes, and the land was beautiful. And Moses said: O Lord, let me not die. Let me cross over into the Promised Land. But God answered: Be silent, for such is My decree.

And Moses pleaded, saying: Let me not die. Let me live there as a beast of the field, as a bird of the air! But God answered, Be silent, for such is My decree.

Then God called to the Angel Gabriel, and said, Go forth, and take the soul of My servant Moses, because his hour is come. But Gabriel refused to do the deed.

So God then summoned the Angel Uriel, saying, Go forth,

and take the soul of My servant Moses, because his hour is come. But Uriel refused to do the deed.

Then God said: Is there none among My angels who will do this thing? And the Angel Samael said: I will go and take the soul of Moses. And he departed.

And the Angel Samael appeared to Moses, saying: Come, Moses. Render up your soul, because your hours are numbered. And Moses drove back the angel, saying: Can one like you command the soul of Moses? And the Angel Samael was driven back.

Then God said: I will go Myself to take his soul. And God appeared to Moses in a cave on Pisgah.

Now, Moses, He said, Lie down. And Moses lay down.

Close your eyes, Moses, He said, and Moses closed his eyes.

Fold your hands on your chest, He said, and Moses folded his hands.

Then God commanded the soul of Moses to come forth, but she refused, sobbing, Do not force me to abandon him!

All men must die, God said. Come forth, and I will give you a seat at My footstool.

But the soul of Moses still refused.

Then God bent down and kissed His servant Moses, and took his soul with a kiss upon the mouth.

And God wept, and the earth wept, and the heavens wept.

Chapter thirty-two

Saul says: "You know, of course, your father never really loved your mother."

We are alone in the quiet of the dim salon; the family is gone and the uproar past; we are left with the silence of the packing cases. All today I wandered the rooms of the house, seeking some souvenir to take home for my brother, but I could find nothing suitable. Down on the bare back lot, close to the former site of the Plotsky garden, a billboard announced the building of sixteen luxury condominiums. I stood there for a while in contemplation of it; then I wandered back up and, lingering in the shade at the side of the house, I gathered cypress seeds for my niece to plant.

I thought I would tell her, when I returned home, of where these seeds came from: of how her grandfather planted their ancestors. I would tell her about the house, about her many relatives. There were so many stories, now, that I could give her: stories of Metatron and Sandalfon, fables of Moses, myths of the ten lost tribes beyond the River Sambatyon; a tale which began: The week following his bar mitzvah, in the spring of 1853, your great-great-grandfather, Shalom

Shepher of Skidel, got married. He took up residence with his father-in-law, the Rabbi of Bielsk.... All these things I was ready to hand on now: to do so with pleasure and without too much pain.

Now it is nearly dark. The streets are swept by a light evening wind. The lanterns glimmer outside the synagogue. The square has a restlessness about it which is almost ominous: one might think something fateful was approaching. Saul stands on the verandah looking out, a local phantom in his white shirtsleeves: waiting for a visitor long expected.

"The Ballabessel is coming," he observes.

I have cleared the big table in the corner of the salon; I have rescued my grandmother's silver candlesticks. I have wine and candles, I have braided bread. I have what is needed to embrace the Sabbath.

Saul sits sceptically in his usual chair, watching without comment as I lay the table. He appears bemused, if not actually hostile. We have spoken little since the contretemps: he looks at but dares not accuse me; I look at but cannot accuse him. It is a fortunate stalemate.

Only now, as I prepare the benediction, as though determined to find the one vulnerable place—like a man with a bad tooth, even, who can't resist searching and searching it with his tongue—he repeats the old mantra, knowing he'll get a reaction, knowing that this time, finally, I won't let it pass.

"I found them too, you know," he tells me, "him and his girlfriend. *In flagrante*. Up there in the attic, just like you today. Disgusting! How could they do such a thing, and in this house? Tell me that if you can—with your grandfather underneath them?"

He wouldn't have cared, but the attic was his, *his* place, where he went to be quiet and to write his poems. There weren't so many places in this house where you could get a little solitude and privacy! Not that he went up there to poke around—there was nothing to poke around in then in any case, and even if there were, why would he be interested? He was a boy—a young man, and a poet. That was where he went to find his muse. And then they sullied it. He would never go there again, it was spoiled forever.

"And as for your mother," he says, "he never truly loved her. He was in love with Hannah—Hannah was the one he really loved!"

I catch the look in his eye, and gather a frisson then, of something subtextual, something yet to discover. Did Saul too have secrets, did he have jealousies? Disappointments I could only guess at?

I fetch him, then, an envelope from my bag: the one I have been carrying all this time. My one survivor, my one rescued fragment. I hand it to Saul and watch him as he reads: with deep satisfaction I follow his expression.

This parting has shown me that if ever we were called upon to live without one another it would be a terrible struggle and I don't know whether I would make it. It seems to me not only a matter of love but of life *itself.*

He looks up at me wordlessly. I snatch back the letter from his open palm.

"Never, ever, say that to me again," I conclude with sternness, folding it away; and I pick up the matches for the Sabbath lights.

Saul rises to his feet reluctantly. But he understands my purpose and is, I think, appreciative, as I prepare the last sanctification in the old house. Standing beside him, here in the decayed gloom of Kiriat Shoshan, I examine his grooved, gnarled and twisted face—like the faces you see sometimes in the boles of ancient trees—and I think he will not be unhappy in his high place, his crumbling apartment with its lake view where he sits alone reading the old poets, where on misty days the hills opposite are hidden and he can look out to a horizon concealed in all its undiscoverable possibilities. I don't believe he will be miserable. In many ways I think Saul is the true north, he is the essential Shepher: lonely, disheveled, full of dead dreams and aspirations; nourished by dry bread and succulent regrets; forever awaiting the outcome of a deferred destiny.

Now as the sun sets and the stars appear I perform the blessing in my father's melody, the one he used when we were still at home, he and my mother,. my brother Reuben and I, in the days when we stood together around the family table. The notes with their fragile weight of melancholy rise against the night, solemn with joy, freighted with memory. My own voice sounds stronger and more strange in my own hearing than I expected it to; and I realise how long it is since I have tried to sing.

Chapter thirty-three

In Jewish cemeteries it is customary to place not flowers but stones upon the graves. Not blooms but small rocks as a mark of visitation.

Here on the Hill of Rest there are many tombs, white dusty blocks with black metalled lettering: from a distance the hillside looks as though it is covered in white coffins. The tombs descend in terraces down the slope; there are low hedges of lavender and rosemary. White steps lead from one terrace to the next.

The graves lie side by side in the shade of a conifer; close enough to be companionable, though forever separate. They cling together here as they might have done in life, locked in their corner among many strangers. Detached and self-contained

He was lovely and pleasant in his life

undisturbed and peaceful

And in their death they were not divided.

In Jewish cemeteries it is customary to place not flowers but stones upon the graves, to symbolise the hardness of acceptance. As though the dark splash of the tear which fell upon the grave had hardened itself up into a stone, into a token of finality and acceptance. And because my heart is hard, because I do accept, I place two stones upon my father's and my mother's graves, one for myself, one on behalf of my brother.

I stand and look at the view. At the head of the hills the vanguard of the tower blocks encroaches. I crush and sniff a twig of rosemary against my thumb.

There are numerous old stones lying on my father's tomb, among the flotsam of leaf mould and dead pine needles. I wonder who placed them there and when: how long ago; what kind of mourner.

Chapter thirty-four

Here on the edge of Mea Shearim, I stand at the corner of the sodden street, close by a murky shop which sells embossed prayer books and religious texts and Sabbath cloths under orange cellophane, beneath the rusted and collapsing balcony which lets out from the third floor of this ancient tenement.

A long time ago my father brought me here, to show me where he fell once, according to the story, at the age of five: the spot where he lay with his lifeblood running away in the gutter. Standing, pointing, under the rusted rail, he bent and showed me again the deep S-shaped scar, the place where the bone knitted into a permanent groove, shiny and off-white and suggestive, even then, of terrific injury. I still remember, as a tiny child, running my finger over this strange tattoo, thinking it symbolic, magical even: a mark of secret power. S for Shepher.

Perhaps he wondered himself if there was any symbolism in his special rescue, if this was in fact the moment for which he had been saved: no greater miracle than to show his own child, one day, the spot where he had nearly died and been resurrected.

My father taught me to love the Hebrew language: the blueprint of the universe in its seven constructs, the touch of infinity in its numbers, the humour and poetry in its derivations: *dikduk* grammar, *ledakdek* to be particular, *dakdak* fine like manna in the wilderness, or like the still small voice speaking in the desert. I was a willing student, and if I did not ride away like my brother, flogging his desperate horse into the sunset, perhaps it was because I was weighed down with too much treasure: Yiddish lullabies, fragmentary anecdotes, bad jokes and household sayings: *Toirah ist die beste Schoirah*, Learning is the Best Merchandise, *Auf ein Goniff brennt der Hittel*, The Hat burns on a Thief's Head. A swagbag of offcuts and end-of-line traditions, bits and pieces which would never fit together: no whole cloth, no finished garment, but the remnants of exile, snatched up and handed on in a sort of desperation. *If you believe, it need be no dream.*

Now I am free to sift through these many fragments, whose colours don't fade but, on the contrary, grow more brilliant with time, as bright as the gleaming olives I select here in the covered market. Now I clothe myself in my coat of many colours. Alone and autonomous I pick and choose; I eat the meat and spit out the stones; I am well satisfied. Somewhere among these many faces and voices I can still hear the voice, I still catch glimpses of the face of my father.

Chapter thirty-five

The streets of the Old City are almost clinically clean. They smell of metal polish and carbolic. The steps of David Street are scrubbed, the stones dangerously slick; there is fresh paint and new awnings everywhere. An air of hygiene hangs over the Old City: a civilised and clenched modernity.

Once, long ago, the bazaar was magical. Clutching my father's hand I entered a tunnel of colour and light, bright threads and beads and shining objects, music and shouting, warm peppery smells, many strange faces. I was brushed by pungent bodies; strangers grabbed at my sleeve. All around was a tantalising, smiling danger. I was filled with acquisitiveness, my head spinning with wants, dragged from one desired item to another.

When I reach the Jewish Quarter I find it empty and quiet, its pavements smooth, its buildings blank and clean-cut, like a university campus.

The House of the Hand on Habad Street was blown to smithereens by the Jordanians, along with the Hurvah synagogue, the Tree of Life Yeshivah and the cellar where Shalom Shepher kept his coffee pot.

The village of Deir Yassin was destroyed, along with many others, after the war of '48. The path which once led there is a paved road. The fields where the goats grazed are covered with houses.

Chapter thirty-six

Saul declares the Codex is with Cobby; Cobby thinks they lent it to Miriam; Miriam says they gave it back to Saul. Shloime Goldfarb simply denies everything. No-one seems to know where the Codex is.

Alone in my bedroom I count off the suspects. Any one of us could be the thief. Sara Malkah, perhaps, keeps it buried in her trousseau; or her brother Yossel hides it among his holy books. Perhaps Miriam's grandson, pretending indifference, arranged a secret service operation. Or maybe Rabbi Gershom Shepher, guiltily concealed in his cramped study in Mea Shearim, seeks clues to the end of the universe in its forbidden text.

Any one of us could be guilty; except for me. I have answered their questions, I have given what help I could. I even allowed them to search through my belongings. Dubi's testimony can bear me out; though unfortunately for him, he has for a long time neglected to follow procedure: his record of visitors being non-existent, a number of cameras, scandalously, out of film; and security at the archive will have to be re-examined. They have released me from the inquiry:

I'm in the clear. For why should I steal something I could never get away with?

Miriam speculates that Saul has it. Maybe he'll never acknowledge that he has it now. He will return with it, she thinks, to his flat in Tiberias; put it down upon a table there; soon it will be covered by a drift of trash. He will lift the heap with the book hidden in its midst and put it down in a corner, on the floor; where it will remain for years, buried deeper and deeper, while the mystery of the Codex grows and grows, and Cobby, Miriam and Sara Malkah, the detectives, the scholars and the Neturei Karta, the whole vast clan of the family Shepher, search in vain to discover what became of it.

But Saul alone will suspect the truth.

Nor will the family dare to distress themselves, by looking back to that miraculous moment, that window of opportunity lasting perhaps no longer than a day, when they might have sold the Codex and saved the house.

And I think to myself, Let it go now, let it go. Let its secrets remain locked inside itself. What would we do with certainty in any case, with the deadness of an immaculate mandate? Which is why, when it comes down to it, I have both longed and dreaded to examine the Codex. I'd rather it stayed the unattainable idea: the pursued truth, the perfect revelation. The complete picture.

No-one will visit or think of Saul up there, in the distant tower of his loneliness. Only the laundry-woman who cooks his meals will come one day and clear out the squalor of his abandoned flat, remove wholesale the heaps of newspaper and rotting food, the old clothes and shoes, all the detritus of an extinguished life; and, good citizen that she is and out of the kindness of her heart, send it in black bags to the municipal rubbish heap.

Chapter thirty-seven

As I recall these things I am seated in an attic, a lumber room, in what you might call the genizah at the house of Shepher. I am alone, with only a five rung ladder between myself and the world.

The attic is dusty. I breathe dust. Dust hangs in the double shaft of sunlight where two roof tiles have been removed for illumination. It settles in my hair and clothes. It strikes me that this is no ordinary dust. The flakes are large, dark grey and feathery, like the fragments which fly up at a book-burning, and whenever I shift my feet against the sea of papers more fragments rise and float into the air.

I sit on an upturned packing-case marked with the insignia of the Jerusalem Beth Din, which stands like an island in the middle of this great sea. Around me are more packing-cases, cardboard boxes, heaps of documents, old canvas laundry bags, a wooden chest, all tipped over and spilled in an orgy of confusion. The chaos seems to stretch out on every side, into dim distances where the sunlight cannot reach; under the far rafters whose secrets will never now be uncovered.

Repositories of treasured manuscripts, whose guardians wish to protect them against the ravages of time, are kept these days in measured strongrooms, with delicate equipment to control moisture and dryness, heat and cold. The hoard at the house of Shepher has not been treated so. For seven decades it has been exposed to the fluctuations of Jerusalem summers, Jerusalem frosts. It has been dampened by October rains and baked by August suns. The thin shield of roof tiles, cardboard and canvas has not offered much protection, and as anyone knows, an attic is an environment of extremes. No wonder that, when I reach down to pluck a piece of manuscript, the edge crumbles like a wafer in my hand.

There are such fragments everywhere, disintegrating slowly into that large soft dust. The floor sits half an inch in it. I run it through my hands like flour.

My uncle said: If you want it, take it. Everything that is left will be for the fire.

So I pick up a single scrap of paper, its writing spidery, almost illegible: a recipe for pickled cucumbers perhaps, or an official memo, or one of my grandfather's many shopping lists. I keep one tiny scrap as a memento, heavy with the weight of all that has been lost.

Nor do I discover the other treasures of junk which lie here waiting to become dust and rubble: the six jars of soil from the Territories, the calculations which date the end of the world, the faded manuscript of an unfinished novel; a portrait of Theodor Herzl, half-obliterated by bloom and mould.

For a long time I linger in the attic. And I think of all the other manuscripts and all the other attics: of the vanished codices and vanished truths; of the synagogue at Bielsk which was burnt along with the members of its congregation; and of the hundreds and thousands of forgotten souls, the lost members of a vast and scattered clan: the Shephers, the Shaffers and the Shaeffers, the Shifrins and Shapiros and Shapiras, the Siffres and the Saffres of whom no shoe or glove remains, whose very bones are the dust now circling the earth; and of all those texts which because of their many errors could not be used, and which because they bear the name of God will never be destroyed.

Chapter thirty-eight

In November 1938 my father boarded the vessel 'Methusaleh' at the port of Jaffa and sailed for Southampton. He wore a white shirt and no tie. He was filled with a great spiritual longing. On the quayside below, the woman he loved was waving him goodbye.

For months he had vacillated over his departure. For weeks on end he had argued back and forth. Now he had reached the inevitable moment: the parting he had never thought would come.

And if there was a contradiction in this, that the parting he considered inevitable had also never seemed quite real to him, it was only a reflection of his life in general, which rushed on regardless and never seemed quite real.

Only this morning, when they had woken together in the white room on Gordon Street, the lines of light on the floor, the small suitcase, her breathing beside him had seemed unquestionably real.

They had talked until late, although it was already too late, and lay down at last exhausted side by side. She kissed his cheek; she stroked his blonded eyebrows; and as she ran her finger over the dent in his head that held his death, she said in a voice which was both weary and loving:

"At the end of the day it isn't what you want, it's what you think you ought to want that guides you."

He had no idea how to tell the difference. The grave face of his father was always in his mind's eye. He lay awake beside her while she slept, all that night, as though with a clear conscience.

Now it was morning and here she still was, too actual to doubt, too real to believe. He put his face to her hair and breathed the scent of it. That moment also sped away from him.

In all the years which followed he would return to that moment, recall that scent like a word on the tip of his tongue. She was the letter which was changed in the scroll of his life: the sum total shifted, it told a different story.

Now here I am at the airport, ready to fly home. I am wearing jeans and a grey sweatshirt. I have a packet of sandwiches in my shoulder-bag. Tucked in my luggage, the inventory runs as follows: item—one file of letters, item—one manuscript diary, item—one pair of Sabbath candlesticks. My aunt Miriam is wishing me bon voyage.

She looks vivid and immaculate in green flowered trousers, a girlish ribbon fastening her hair. But she looks small, too, in the vastness of the airport: failing and fragile, vulnerable and frail. I am suddenly filled with the questions I meant to ask her. Who knows if I will ever ask them now?

"Don't leave it so long again," she says as we hug each other. "I hope I might still see you another time."

Then she is gone; and I am as alone as one can be, in the mêlée of itinerants departing for so many destinations: Athens and London, Budapest and Rome. I take on the loneliness as well as the resilience of the traveller; already bored with the distances I must cover, the great deal of waiting I must undergo.

Resigned to my condition I seat myself on a hard chair and do what generations have done in similar circumstances: I open a book. It is dense and dreamlike, redolent of sea and English mist: something so far removed from this reality that I can dive in there and quite forget myself, forget, for a brief time, even my bright and clashing environment. To sit in an airport, reading a description of the seashore, seems to encapsulate just now my place in life.

I have barely read three sentences when I become aware of a presence at my shoulder, seated in the next chair, peering with bold curiosity at my book. Gideon, of course, with a rucksack over his shoulder, looking brisk and travel wise and ready to go; but by this stage in proceedings I don't even have the astonishment left in me to show surprise, though I am ruffled, secretly, by how pleased I am to see him, by my own relief at the mere sight of him.

"So," he says, "you're on your way again."

"So," I reply, "you're also on your way."

"Yes, I am."

"Where are you off to, then?"

Gideon chuckles. "East."

"Baku?"

He looks at me narrowly. "Yes. How did you know?"

"Oh," I reply, serene, "I have my sources."

He glances again at my book: sees I am using a photograph as a bookmark. "So," he continues, "did you get what you came for?"

I tuck the picture of Hannah between the pages. "Yes. In fact I did. And how about you?"

"Oh yes," says Gideon.

"Where is the Codex now?"

"It's safe for the present." His smile widens. "In a genizah." I cannot help smiling too.

"How will you get it home again?"

"How else? Page by page. Don't worry. We can rebind it. So," he looks about restlessly, "will you return, do you think?"

"Yes; soon, I hope. And you?"

"Soon, perhaps." He considers. "But not yet."

"Tell me something. Is the Codex really perfect?"

I look him in the eye.

"As perfect to us as your one is to you. Who knows? Perhaps one day you can find out for yourself." He reaches into his pocket. "I have something for you. It's only a piece of paper," he says, giving it to me. "A little piece of what you might call evidence."

It is in fact parchment: a letter, once sealed, now broken open, faded with age and folded many times.

"Evidence?" I feel its weight in my fingers. "If it's evidence, why didn't you give it to me before?"

"Sometimes it's nice to see if a person can have faith in you without needing evidence."

"And Cobby—?"

"—wouldn't have believed me however much evidence I gave him. There are some people who believe in nothing but their own scepticism." He nods toward the parchment. "A hundred and thirty years ago your great-grandfather presented it to my great-grandfather, and now I am returning it to you. But don't open it yet. Well," says Gideon. "Now I will take your hand."

To my surprise he does take it.

"Now I will say goodbye."

To my astonishment, he kisses my cheek.

"A cousinly salute. And a mark of thanks. My mother would not forgive me," he adds, "if I didn't extend a family invitation. See you in Baku."

He rises briskly then and walks away, his rucksack slung casually across his shoulder, leaving me with a light wave of the hand.

For a long time I watch the distant place in the crowd where Gideon's biblical figure has disappeared. A great weight of feeling seems to fill me; it seems absurd, impossible that I should ever fly. I get up at last, step into the Ladies', splash my face with a little tepid water. The face in the mirror is puffy and tired-looking. Not for the first time, but still newly, I acknowledge to myself that I am middle-aged.

Half anxious, half curious, I unfold the parchment:

With God's Help, The Holy City, Kislev 5, 5626

Honoured and beloved brethren, since it became clear to us that the days of dissolution are upon us, and that the days of the Messiah are at hand, we were filled with longing for our scattered brethren, whom the Lord has scattered to the farthest corners of the earth, and we desired much to see the face of our brethren, in whatever place the Lord had scattered them, until such time as he should bring them back, like streams in the Negev and upon the wings of eagles, to the Holy City of Jerusalem. And so did he take it upon himself, our beloved brother, REB SHALOM OF SKIDEL, *to undertake this perilous journey, to seek out our lost ones, to lament with them over the glory of Zion which is past, and to rejoice with them over the King Messiah who is coming.*

For the next hour and more I gaze at the turning pages of my book, but I don't read them, and when I am belted into my seat on the plane I stare blankly out of the meagre window. A shimmer of heat rises from the dead tarmac. Summer is on its way. I don't know when I'll return, or in what season. As the plane rises with its merciless lurch I crane to catch a glimpse of that brief land strip, before the expanding blue of the Mediterranean.

Now we are both travellers: myself to the West and Gideon to the East. We carry on the family tradition. Rising higher, we pass through a ridge of cloud. Like my father before me I turn to face the horizon.

Acknowledgments

I am indebted to the work of my late grandfather, Yitzhak Yaacov Yellin, whose memoirs, letters and journal have been an invaluable resource, and on whose account of Rabbi Samuel Salant the early life of Shalom Shepher is partly based. The following people read the novel in whole or in part at various stages of its development, and offered encouragement and advice: Zoran Živković, Jeff VanderMeer, Dawn Andrews; my editor, Deborah Meghnagi; Victoria Hobbs, Alexandra Pringle, Des Lewis and Neil Williamson. Thanks also to my sisters, Judy and Sharon, and to my other sister, Monica Deb, for unfailing friendship.

Above all my love and gratitude go to my husband, Bob, whose support of every kind has made it possible for me to complete this book.

About the Author

Tamar Yellin

Tamar Yellin was born in the north of England. Her mother was the daughter of a Polish immigrant and her father a third generation Jerusalemite. She studied Hebrew and Arabic at Oxford, where she received the Pusey and Ellerton Prize for Biblical Hebrew. She has since worked as a teacher and lecturer in Judaism, and as a Jewish Faith Visitor in schools across Yorkshire. She began writing fiction at an early age, and the creative tension between her Jewish heritage and her Yorkshire roots has informed much of her work. Her short stories, which have been described as "ironic, humane and highly accomplished," have appeared in a wide variety of journals and anthologies. *The Genizah at the House of Shepher* is her first published novel. Her website can be visited at www.tamaryellin.com.

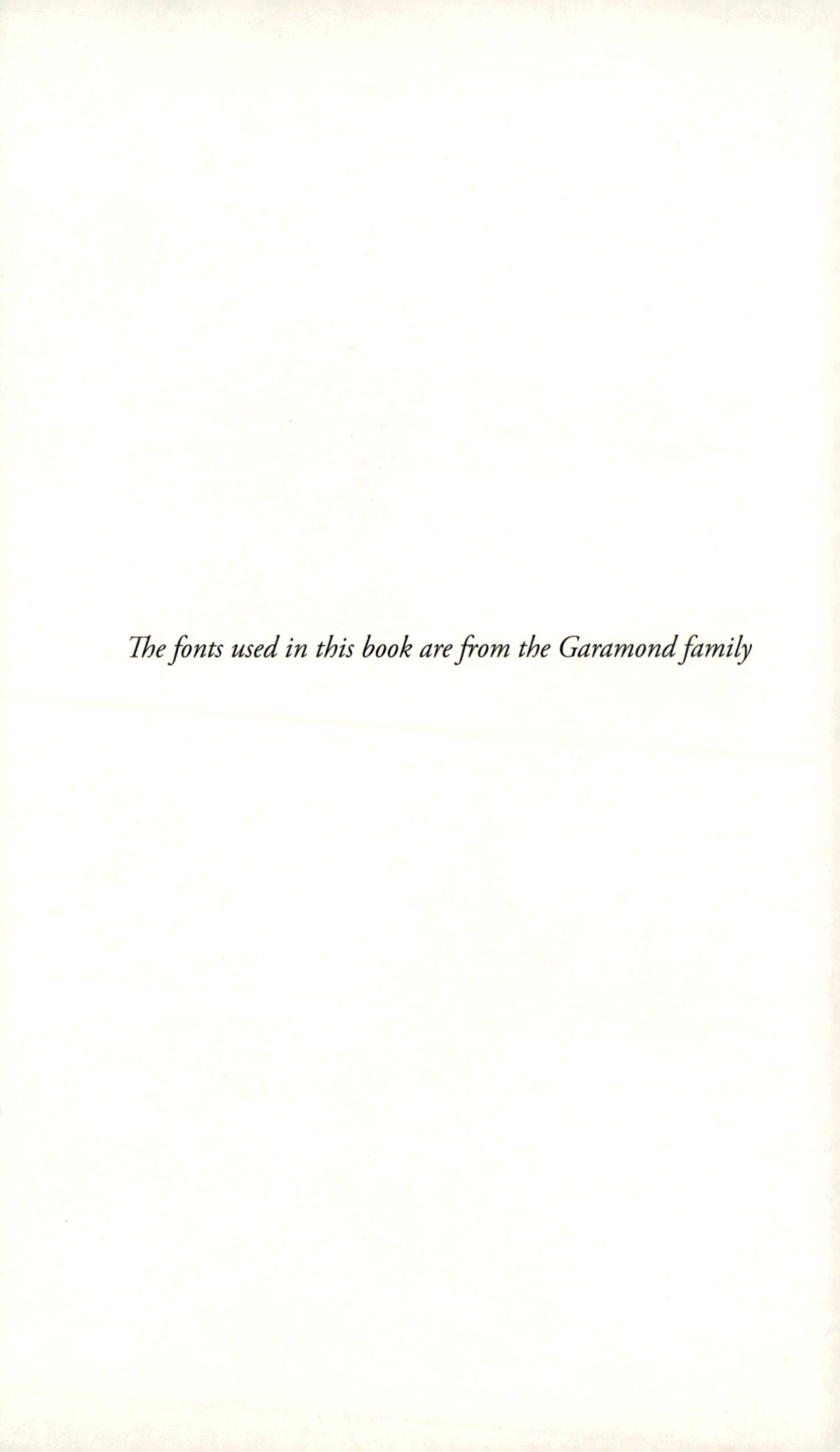

The fonts used in this book are from the Garamond family